BOCA KNIGHTS

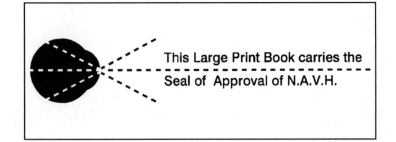

This Large Print Book carries the
Seal of Approval of N.A.V.H.

BOCA KNIGHTS

STEVEN M. FORMAN

THORNDIKE PRESS
A part of Gale, Cengage Learning

Detroit • New York • San Francisco • New Haven, Conn • Waterville, Maine • London

GALE
CENGAGE Learning

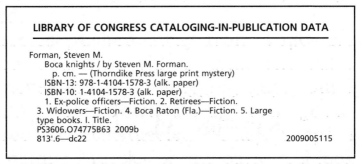

LIBRARY OF CONGRESS CATALOGING-IN-PUBLICATION DATA

Forman, Steven M.
  Boca knights / by Steven M. Forman.
    p. cm. — (Thorndike Press large print mystery)
  ISBN-13: 978-1-4104-1578-3 (alk. paper)
  ISBN-10: 1-4104-1578-3 (alk. paper)
    1. Ex-police officers—Fiction. 2. Retirees—Fiction.
  3. Widowers—Fiction. 4. Boca Raton (Fla.)—Fiction. 5. Large
  type books. I. Title.
  PS3606.O74775B63 2009b
  813'.6—dc22   2009005115

Published in 2009 by arrangement with Tom Doherty Associates, LLC.

Printed in the United States of America
1 2 3 4 5 6 7 13 12 11 10 09

This novel is lovingly dedicated
to my wife, Barbara.

ACKNOWLEDGMENTS

My heartfelt thanks to some of the many people who helped me complete *Boca Knights:* Fred Deluca, for sharing his business adventure with me and introducing me to his literary agent, Bob Diforio; Jim Frenkel, my editor, and Tom Doherty, my publisher, for believing in me; Dr. Jeff Silver, for medical advice; Dr. Glenn Kessler, for psychology research; attorneys Steven J. Brooks and Morris Golding, for legal input, and Anthony Salvucci, for physics lessons; author Douglas Preston, for his encouragement and help; Danielle Boudreaux, my personal consultant, my son, David, who helped me organize my thoughts, and my daughter, Jana, who always believed I could do anything; my brother-in-law Robert "Ted" Tomasone, who inspired the character "Togo" and taught me the secrets of the North End; Lenore Tomasone, for her encouragement and suggestions; my brother-in-law Matt Potash, for his opinions; and Carol J. Seminara, Deborah A. Hogan, and Lisa A. Davidson, who allowed me to share a little of Dominick with the world; and to all my friends in Boca Raton, for encouraging and inspiring me.

IN MEMORY

My dear friends Dominick Seminara, Joel Hirshfield, and Dick Sabul, three of the finest men I ever met. My parents, Rae and Harry Forman, who were my original readers, my sister, Frances, who told me I was her hero, and Bernie and Sylvia Wofsy, who were my biggest fans.

PROLOGUE

I must not fear. Fear is the mind-killer. Fear is the little-death that brings total obliteration. I will face my fear. I will permit it to pass over me and through me. And when it has gone past I will turn the inner eye to see its path. Where the fear has gone there will be nothing. Only I will remain.

— FRANK HERBERT, *DUNE*

THE UKRAINE PENINSULA — WINTER — 1896
THE VISHNOVET SHTETEL IN THE PALE

Fifteen-year-old Sirota stood alone in the center of the circle of villagers. He was covered in blood. He still clutched the kinjal — the short Cossack dagger in his hand. The village's feared enemy lay dead at his feet, throat slashed from ear to ear. Sirota stared silently at the villagers as he thrust the bloody dagger into the rope belt at his waist.

The inhabitants of the shtetel were familiar with the deadly, double-edged dagger in Sirota's hand. The Cossacks used the kinjal to kill dangerous enemies and defenseless Jews. But today the villagers had seen a fifteen-year-old boy wield the Devil's sword with an inhuman fury and fearlessness that frightened them.

Hesitantly, more timid villagers emerged from their huts and the circle around the boy grew larger. The people of the shtetel had never completely understood the one they called Sirota. They had found him when he was two years old in the smoldering remains of a neighboring shtetel thirteen years ago. The Cossacks had left no one else alive in the village. The suspicious Vishnovet peasants didn't know if the only survivor of the massacre was God's blessing or the Devil's curse, but they could not leave him there to die. They took the infant to Vishnovet where he lived among them but was never really one of them. Even the name they gave him made him different. He was called Sirota, Russian for *orphan*. They could have called him Yosell, the more familiar Yiddish word for *orphan* but they chose to identify him as an outsider. When he reached the age of reason Sirota knew he was unwanted. He was not shunned but neither was he included. The other children feared him after watching him beat a much larger boy unconscious in a fight over food. Sirota was never loved and he did not know how to love. As soon as he was able to fend for himself he built a hut of his own away from the others. He did his share of the work but shared nothing else. Everyone knew that Sirota would leave Vishnovet one day. It was not his home. It was a place where he survived.

Now that he had saved the villagers by killing a deadly enemy Sirota felt his debt to them had been paid and it was time for him to go. He had stayed long enough in a world where he did not belong.

Rabbi Kaminsky, holding the hand of his terrified twelve-year-old daughter, stepped inside the circle of villagers. Sirota glanced at the girl, who stared at him with large, brown eyes. They exchanged small smiles.

Sirota nodded to the villagers in a gesture of thanks for saving his life so many years ago. Some of the people returned his nod. Most did not. Still drenched in blood, Sirota covered himself in a heavy animal skin and walked alone toward the road that led to the frozen Ukraine wilderness. As he neared the forest he heard the rabbi's daughter weeping. She wailed, "Don't go, Sirota. Please don't go. Who will save us now?" No one answered.

In the last month of the last year of the nineteenth century, after many weeks of a desperate journey across the continent, Sirota departed from the port of Hamburg as a steerage passenger on a ship bound for Boston. He wore a dead man's clothes.

In 1903, deadly pogroms, incited by Czar Alexander the Third, descended on the Pale. No sensible reason was ever given for the carnage that turned the shtetels of the Ukraine into what became known as Cities of Slaughter. Jews of the Pale were either conscripted into the Russian army, murdered in cold blood, or forced to run for their lives.

THE RUSSIAN GHETTO
DORCHESTER, MASSACHUSETTS —
WINTER — 1900

Elijah Fleischman, a sixty-year-old butcher, discovered Sirota's half-dead body lying face down in the snow behind his tiny butcher shop. Elijah immediately brought the boy into the warmth of his shop and ultimately into the warmth of his heart.

Elijah had immigrated to America from Russia many years before. The journey that nearly took his life had devastated his soul. He trusted no one. He loved no one. For many years he chose to live alone. Eventually, Elijah's heart thawed, but by the time he was ready to rejoin the human race, it was too late for him to start a family of his own. So he lived a lonely, loveless existence in a ghetto of fellow immigrants, until the day this boy mysteriously appeared in his life.

Elijah never questioned the sullen Russian boy about the wrinkled, bloodstained immigration papers that identified him as Hans Perlmutter from Germany. Elijah simply accepted that one lost soul from Russia had made it to the new world, while one poor soul from Germany had been left behind.

When the boy and the old man had lived together for two years a bond of trust developed between them. Their trust slowly grew into the loving bond of father and son. Elijah taught Hans the hybrid language of the ghetto — a combination of Russian, Yiddish, and broken English, but the quiet young man rarely spoke to anyone. He kept to himself, even after he had lived among them for two years, and no one in the ghetto could claim to know him well. Then one day Hans Perlmutter stepped out of the shadows and ended his silence.

Victor Dragoff was a monster of a man who had extorted money from the merchants of his shtetel in the Pale for many years. After immigrating like so many other Russian Jews Dragoff renewed his reign of terror in Dorchester. He always carried a large club with him, which he used to crack the skull of anyone refusing to pay. Hans had watched Elijah pay Dragoff his "protection money" every Friday for two years. Then one Friday afternoon when the store was busy with Sabbath shoppers, Hans stepped between Victor and Elijah as the money was about to change hands, saying, "No more" with his eyes.

Dragoff, growling like an animal, raised his club above his head. Everyone in the shop cringed except Hans Perlmutter. The small young man withdrew the foot-long double-edge dagger from its sheath beneath his apron and drove the weapon into the bully's inner thigh by the groin. As a butcher, Perlmutter knew he was cutting into a non-vital but extremely painful area. Dragoff grunted and stared down in disbelief at the blood seeping through his filthy pants. The club toppled from high above Dragoff's head, crashing to the floor behind him. He clutched at the wound with both hands, leaned forward, and vomited. His head was now within striking distance, and with one violent slash of the blade Sirota severed Dragoff's right ear. A woman screamed. Dragoff collapsed to his knees, moving one hand to his ear and the other to his bleeding groin. He screamed in pain. Everyone in the shop averted their eyes from the bloody scene. Hans moved quickly behind Dragoff, grabbed a handful of his long, straggly hair, and pulled his head back. The kinjal was at Dragoff's throat. In a raspy whisper Hans Perlmutter hissed, "If I see you again after today, I will kill you. Do you understand?"

Dragoff nodded in terror.

"Go!" Hans ordered.

Victor Dragoff struggled to his feet and stumbled from the store. He was never seen in the ghetto again.

The store closed for the Sabbath, but on Sunday it was filled with the curious and the grateful. Elijah basked in the attention. Hans was uncomfortable but polite. Some in the ghetto were concerned that a new monster had simply replaced the old monster, but the young man quickly calmed their fears with his gentle manner. At the end of the day when the store was empty, the bell above the door rang once again. A young woman entered. She was short and sturdy with a plain, serious face. She walked directly to the counter and looked intently at Hans. She studied his face. Elijah watched the woman curiously, but Hans did not look up from his work.

"Sirota," she finally said to Hans, "I knew it would be you."

"He is no orphan," Elijah challenged the young woman. "He is my son."

She looked at Elijah kindly. "He is your son now. But once he was Sirota."

"How did you know?" Hans asked softly.

"I'm from Vishnovet," she said. "I'm Rabbi Kaminsky's daughter, Golda."

"You were a little girl when I last saw you," Hans said. "Is Rabbi Kaminsky well?"

"He's dead." She sighed. "They're all dead. There is only you and me."

Hans Perlmutter married Golda Kaminsky a year later and they settled in the Dorchester ghetto near Elijah. Golda gave birth to two stillborn daughters before she brought a healthy son into the world in November of 1912. They named their son Harry in memory of her father, Hyman. They gave Harry an *S* as a middle initial but no full name or explanation was ever provided. Harry S. Perlmutter, the son of Hans and Golda Perlmutter of the Pale, would work his way to middle-class respectability, never really knowing or caring about the desperation from which his parents came.

In 1936 Harry married Rachael Krantzman, the daughter of a tailor. For nine years they were unable to have a child. Finally, in March of 1945 Edward S. Perlmutter was born. He would be their only child. They named him after Elijah Fleischman, who had died peacefully in his sleep only a few years before "Eddie" was born. The S was passed on to Edward S. Perlmutter without explanation.

In 1950, Harry moved his family from Dorchester to a Jewish neighborhood in Brookline, an upscale suburb west of the city. Hans and Golda insisted on remaining in Dorchester despite the "white flight" that was taking place in the face of the black migration to their neighborhood.

Eddie Perlmutter was different from other boys his age. He could be polite and display a good sense of humor, but his behavior could be frighteningly erratic at times. With only the slightest provocation Eddie could explode into fits of rage and aggression. Before he was ten years old he became a fearsome fighter who showed no regard for his own safety. Eddie's parents were concerned and confused. There was no history of violence in the family, as far as they knew. Eddie's grandparents, who had kept the legend of Sirota from their son and his family, understood that the same fire burning in Sirota's blood had skipped a generation and was now their grandson's legacy.

Many years later, a senile Hans Perlmutter sat in a crowded boxing arena with his son, Harry, watching fifteen-year-old Eddie Perlmutter in an amateur boxing match, battling a much larger opponent. Eddie was his grandfather's favorite fighter. Hans compared his grandson's determination to ex-champion Barney Ross. Harry Perlmutter, however, didn't like his son's fighting style. Harry thought Eddie was too reckless in the ring and showed no respect for his opponent or for the science of boxing.

The fight was going badly for Eddie that night. He was overmatched and outclassed. He had been knocked down three times in three rounds. After the third knockdown in the final round, Sirota thought he saw his grandson rise from the canvas and stab his adversary in the heart with a double-edged kinjal. In the ravaged wasteland of Sirota's addled mind the other fighter had transformed into a monstrous brown bear and his grandson was chopping the beast down with repeated thrusts of the sword in his hand. The bear was falling.

Suddenly an explosion of light and the urgent clanging of a bell startled Sirota. A large crowd of cheering people reappeared around him. Sirota became dizzy and disoriented. He felt a sharp pain in his chest and put his right hand over his heart as if to protect it from further harm. But the damage was done, and the old man slumped slowly to the ground like a wilting blade of grass.

Sirota looked up from the floor at the faces spinning above him. His son, Harry, was kneeling next to him, holding his hand. His grandson's face appeared. There were tears of sadness in the boy's eyes, and his face was bruised. The old man motioned for Eddie to come closer. Harry saw his father whisper into his son's ear. He saw Eddie's lips move but could not hear the words. He saw his father wink at Eddie and saw Eddie wink back. Then the old man winced in pain and grabbed his chest. It was time to go.

In the twilight haze between life and death, there was no more pain. Sirota moved toward a bright light on the horizon that was slowly growing dimmer. A brown bear and a blond boy joined him at the end of the world. Then the light went out and there was only darkness.

CHAPTER 1

EDWARD S. PERLMUTTER — SIROTA'S GRANDSON

The *S* in Edward S. Perlmutter was never explained to me. I had no middle name and neither did my father, Harry S. Perlmutter. In 1952 when I was seven years old I asked my father about the unattached *S*. He told me that we were so poor we couldn't afford an entire middle name. His explanation satisfied me until I shared it with a kid at school two days later. "Middle names are free, dummy." He laughed at me, so I punched him in the nose and made him cry. He ran home and told his father. His father told my father. My father was upset.

"Why did you punch that boy?" my father asked.

"He was making fun of my middle name," I explained.

"You don't have a middle name."

"I told him we couldn't afford one."

"Jeez, Eddie, I was only kidding."

"I'm only seven. How should I know you

21

were kidding?"

"Well, you're always kidding," my father said.

"I never kidded about my middle name."

"Look, your grandmother and grandfather wouldn't tell me about the *S* when I asked them so I really don't know the reason."

"They didn't tell you they couldn't afford to buy all the letters?" I asked.

"Give it a rest," my father warned.

"You think Grandma and Grandpa would tell me about the *S?*"

"Why would they tell you when they wouldn't tell me?"

"Maybe they love me more than they love you."

"Your grandfather does. You're just like him," my father said.

"Is that a bad thing?" I asked.

"Sometimes," my father decided.

"Can I ask Grandpa about the *S?*"

"Sure you can. Right after you apologize to the kid you punched."

"Why don't you apologize? You started this."

I apologized the next morning, and that afternoon I asked my grandparents about the mysterious *S*. Both of them laughed and offered me a chocolate chip cookie instead of an explanation. I was only seven. I took the cookie.

In 1952 I already knew I wanted to be a cop. A lot of little boys had dreams of becoming a cop, a fireman, or a cowboy when they grew up. We even had a kid in the neighborhood who wanted to be Superman and didn't want to wait until he grew up. On his eighth birthday, he jumped off his front porch railing ten feet above the ground wearing a bedsheet for a cape. I remember the S on his tee shirt was written backward. He fell like a stone, landing face-first on the pavement below. He broke his nose, both arms, and left leg. I didn't even want to think about flying after that. I just wanted to be an earthbound cop.

Jewish boys, I learned later, were not supposed to grow up to be cops. Usually young Jews were awakened from their childish dreams by their "first generation upwardly mobile American parents" who only saw cops and robbers in their nightmares. These parents had dreams of their children growing up to become doctors, lawyers, dentists, and the occasional CPA, but never a cop.

My parents were nonpracticing Jews who never discouraged my dream of becoming a cop. They didn't encourage me to become anything else, either. This void set me apart from the other Jewish kids in my neighborhood. I just didn't fit the Semitic mold mentally, and physically I didn't look Jewish. I was undersized and scrawny with dirty blond hair, a small pug nose, a street tough attitude, and an open cynicism toward Judaism. I wasn't all that impressed with Christianity, either.

Christians and Jews made a whole lot of claims and counterclaims about their religion that I found highly suspect. For instance the Old Testament insisted that their superhero parted water. The New Testament proclaimed that their guy walked on water. Stalemate!

The Jews claimed that they had someone who was swallowed by a whale and lived to tell the story. The Christians had their own fish story. Stalemate!

The Jews had music for crazy-ass dancing like "Hava Nagila," but the Christians had classics you could sing to like "Ave Maria" and "Amazing Grace." I loved "Amazing Grace." Check, Christians.

The Old Testament said that the infant Moses could have died in the bullrushes but was miraculously saved and lived for 120 years. Then the Good Book claimed Moses talked to a burning bush and received Ten Commandments directly from God. That story is hard to top. The Christians, however, did just that. In the New Testament the Christians claimed that the baby Jesus was born to a virgin mother, died on a cross, rose from the dead, ascended to heaven, and was coming back when he felt like it. CHECKMATE, CHRISTIANS!

Nothing about organized religion made any sense to me but it always seemed to be in my face even when I turned the other cheek. When I was a kid the Jews secretly made fun of the Christians because they were afraid of them. Conversely the Christians overtly made fun of Jews because they weren't afraid of them. A typical Jew versus Christian confrontation in those days went something like this:

"You kikes killed Jesus," a Christian kid would say.

"Did you know that the word *kike* was actually invented by German Jews to describe Russian Jews?" a young Jew might respond.

"Who cares? You're a kike and you killed Christ."

"Who told you I was a kike and who told you I killed Christ?"

"My parents," the Christian kid would claim.

"Your parents are wrong. No offense intended," a Jewish diplomat would try.

"Says who?" the Christian kid would demand.

"My parents, with all due respect of course," the Jewish negotiator might respond.

"Oh yeah," the insulted Christian kid would challenge with a raised fist.

"Oh, shit," the intimidated Jewish kid would say with raised anxiety.

Mostly the Jews won the debates but lost the fights. In my case things were different. I never debated and I never lost a fight. When I heard the accusation, "You kikes killed Jesus," my immediate response was a punch to the nose, bringing an immediate flow of blood and a stunned reaction from my accuser.

"Jesus! You broke my fuckin' nose!"

"Eddie Perlmutter broke your fuckin' nose," I explained. "Jesus had nothing to do with it and I had nothing to do with Jesus."

A follow-up left hook drew more epithets and usually the question: "What happened to the Jews who always want to negotiate?"

"They're not here today."

I never planned any of this violence. It just happened. Whenever I felt threatened, bright red spots would explode in front of my eyes, and everything that followed was purely instinctive. My total lack of fear, the red spots only I could see, my natural ability to fight and my random offbeat sense of humor were as mysterious to me as my middle initial. The fact that my penis could talk in a voice only I could hear amazed me most of all.

Hey, check me out. I can stand, I heard one night in bed when I was about eleven years old.

Who is that?

Look. Down here under the covers.

I looked. *You can talk?* I couldn't believe it.

Of course I can talk but only you can hear me.

How come you never talked to me before?

You were too young. You wouldn't understand.

Do you have a name?

I have a lot of names. You can call me Prick, Cock, Dick, Schwants, Pecker, Schmuck, Mr. Happy, Sausage, Salami, Tool, Tube Steak, One-Eyed Snake, Willy, Weiner, Wang, Wanker, Putz, Pocket Rocket, Banana, Bone, Baloney, Big Ben, Big Ed, Bishop, Ding-A-Ling, Dink, Dip Stick, Dork, Drill, Goober, Hog, Shaft, Johnson, Mr. Johnson, Joy Stick, Knob, Longfellow, Pickle, Pud, Rod, Scmeckle, Schnitzel —

Enough already. What do you want me to

call you?

I like Mr. Johnson. It has class.

Okay, fine. Look, I'm tired, Mr. Johnson. Good night.

Don't go to sleep yet. Mr. Johnson sounded like he was on edge.

Why not?

I was wondering if you could lend me a hand so we can both get some sleep.

It was the beginning of a lifelong friendship with many ups and downs.

In 1956, the same year I first met Mr. Johnson, my father enrolled me in a boxing class hoping to channel my aggression into something more civilized. Unfortunately, the Marquis of Queensberry rules were no match for my street-brawler personality. I clubbed and clobbered my way to the head of the class without using much of the "sweet science" I was being taught. My frustrated boxing instructor told my father that he should take me either to the Franklin Park Zoo or to the West End House with the other wild animals in order to find more appropriate competition. So, when I was twelve my father enrolled me in the West End House Boxing program.

The West End House, opened in 1908, was dedicated to helping the poor children of Boston's hardscrabble, largely Italian

West End. The boxing program, the toughest in the city, was supervised by the Police Athletic League (P.A.L.) of Boston. My first day at the gym the cops were not very impressed with a puny Jewish kid from the upscale suburb of Brookline. They didn't pay attention to me until I won my first three fights by stops. A stop was what they called it when the referee would stop a fight before someone got knocked out or seriously hurt. I was stopping everyone. Suddenly, the cops loved me and I loved them back. I loved their uniforms, their camaraderie, and their dedication. My only goal was to become a supercop like them and do good things for good people and bad things to bad people.

I knew my limitations even when I was young. I was street-smart but I was never going to be a famous doctor or lawyer and certainly not a great scholar. But I wanted to make a difference in my small corner of the universe and I figured I could do that best as a cop.

I fought at the West End House in the Silver Gloves program for three years until the neighborhood was strangled to death by politics. Using the magic words *blighted area* and utilizing the federal funding made available to restore blighted areas, Boston politicians tore the West End down. The close-knit neighborhood was replaced with luxury, high-rise apartments and an expansion of the Massachusetts General Hospital. By 1960 an entire neighborhood of seven thousand people was gone. The year the West End House was torn down I won both the state and New England Golden Gloves championships at 126 pounds. Without the "Spirit of the House" in my corner though, my victories felt hollow and pointless.

My enthusiasm for boxing was flattened like the West End itself, until an irresistible challenge rekindled my enthusiasm. The scheduled Golden Gloves middleweight title fight was being cancelled because of an injury to the challenger. I was offered the fight, if I could gain enough weight to make the minimum of 135 pounds. My opponent would be the reigning Golden Gloves middleweight state champion, Gino "The Destroyer" Montoya, an undefeated, talented twenty-year-old boxer. I was a smallish, sixteen-year-old, unbeaten lightweight slugger with questionable skills. My father wasn't in favor of the fight. "That kid has too much size and talent for you," he warned me.

"I'm not afraid of him," I replied honestly.

"I know. You're not afraid of anything. But

maybe you should be," my father advised. "Montoya can really box. You still fight like a bum."

"A bum? I'm undefeated in twenty-one bouts, Dad."

"That's because you've been fighting other bums. This guy's no bum. He could hurt you."

"I'll take my chances."

While I was training for Montoya, my grandfather frequently came to my workouts. "You're looking good," he told me in his thick Russian-Yiddish accent one day while I was pounding the heavy bag.

"Thanks, Grandpa, but Dad thinks I fight like a bum."

"Don't let him discourage you. You're a good fighter. In fact, you remind me of that old *trumbenik* Barney Ross."

"What's a *trumbenik?*"

"A tough guy from the streets."

"Who's Barney Ross?"

"A street-tough Jewish boxer they called the Pride of the Ghetto. His real name was Beryl Rosofsky."

My grandfather's memory had been failing for the past couple of years, so I couldn't help but wonder if his recollection of the old-time fighter was accurate.

"Did he fight like a bum?" I asked.

31

"No, Eddie. He fought like the three-time world champion he was. He had over eighty fights and he won most of them."

"And I remind you of him?" I asked, satisfied with my grandfather's memory of the moment.

"Yes you do. Barney Ross wasn't afraid of anything."

"I'm not afraid of anything, either, Grandpa," I said honestly.

"Yes, I know," the old man agreed. "You're like me when I was your age. Anyway, I wanted you to know that you're my Barney Ross and my favorite fighter."

"Thanks, Grandpa."

We hugged. He felt frail.

"You feel okay, Grandpa?" I asked when the hug ended.

"Sometimes," he said, tapping his temple with his forefinger. He knew what was happening to his mind. "Listen, Eddie, your father has his own ideas about boxing, so let's just keep Barney Ross our little secret."

He winked at me, and I winked back.

"As long as we're sharing secrets, Grandpa, what about the *S*?"

He wagged his index finger at me like he had caught me being a naughty boy. We both laughed. Then I tried to unlock a different secret.

"Okay, Grandpa, forget the *S*," I conceded. "There's something else I want to ask you."

"Ask."

"Did you have anything to do with the murder of those two guys who hurt Grandma?" When I was about eight years old two black men, in their early twenties, had been found murdered in the Franklin Park Zoo. The murders took place shortly after my grandparents had been mugged by them in broad daylight on a bright summer afternoon in their Dorchester neighborhood. My grandmother had been pushed to the ground during the assault, and the back of her head hit the pavement. Afterward, she could not remember the mugging, and shortly after she began to drift off to a place where she could not remember anything. My grandfather had been knocked unconscious during the assault but he remembered the faces of his attackers. He went to the police. There were plenty of people who witnessed the attack, but no one stepped forward. No one seemed to care or have the courage to risk their own safety by speaking out against the thugs. No charges were ever filed. A few weeks later, the two muggers were found murdered near the bear cage at the Franklin Park Zoo. One had been stabbed directly in the heart, and the other had his throat slashed so deeply he was nearly decapitated. The murder, like the mugging, was never solved.

"It doesn't matter who killed those boys," my grandfather said. "What matters is that they won't be hurting anyone else anymore."

"I'm glad they're dead," I said to my grandfather.

"So am I," he told me.

"So, did you do it?"

"How could a little old man like me overpower two young giants like them?" He chuckled.

"You were younger then."

"I was still a little old man."

"Were you too old to kill those guys?" I asked.

"It would be almost impossible," he said.

"But not totally impossible."

"No, not totally impossible," he conceded.

"But how could the weaker guy win?" I persisted.

"Surprise and arrogance," my grandfather said. "The weaker man has to surprise the stronger enemy and the stronger enemy has to be arrogant enough to believe he can't lose."

"So, it could happen?"

"Yes. It could happen," my grandfather

said, and he jabbed my arm playfully.

I tapped his shoulder in return.

We understood each other perfectly.

The Montoya fight felt wrong from the start. When we met in the middle of the ring for the referee's instructions, it was the first time I had been up close to Montoya. He was bigger than I thought and even though I made the minimum weight, he made me look small. He was hairy as a bear, with no front teeth and breath that smelled like a garbage can. I held my breath until we touched gloves and separated. It was then that I noticed that Mr. Johnson was hiding somewhere in my stomach. He had never done that before.

What's the matter with you? I asked Mr. Johnson on the way back to my corner.

What's the matter with me? What the fuck is the matter with you? You see the size of that guy? One low blow, and me and the twins are history. I'm staying right here till this is over.

Where are the twins?

They're on their own.

So, I'm on my own tonight.

We'll see how it goes.

When the bell rang to start the first round I was still thinking about Gino's bad breath and Mr. Johnson's lack of confidence. By the time the bell rang to start the third and final round I had been knocked down twice, once in the first round and once in the second, and his breath had nothing to do with it. My face was puffy and I had a headache from Montoya's constant jabs between my eyes. Mr. Johnson was still hiding.

I told you so, he whispered to me after the first knockdown, but he had been silent ever since. The crowd was screaming for the fight to be stopped, but I kept punching enough to convince the referee that I wasn't seriously hurt and could still defend myself. I threw punches from a lot of crazy angles and actually hit Montoya on the ass with a left hook at the end of the second round when he turned to go to his corner. He looked back at me over his shoulder like I was crazy.

When we met in the center of the ring to start the third round, he smirked at me.

"Hey, little man," he said through his mouthpiece. "Take it easy. My ass is killing me."

"Wait till I stick your head up there," I told him as we touched gloves like gentlemen.

Thirty seconds later I was on the canvas again. I wasn't hurt. I was frustrated. I couldn't get near him. He kept swatting me away like a gnat with his longer reach. Although he wasn't hurting me physically, he was doing a good job of hurting my feelings and winning the fight. I got up from the third knockdown immediately and started to go after him again, but the referee stood in front of me.

"I think you've had enough, Eddie," he told me.

I pushed him aside. "I'm just getting started," I snarled through my bloody mouthpiece.

The referee knew me well enough to let the fight continue. Gino Montoya was standing across the ring with his arms raised in victory. He was smiling and bouncing on the balls of his feet arrogantly! That son of a bitch. With his mouthpiece covering his missing teeth and from a distance where I couldn't smell his breath, even I had to admit he looked like a champ. I looked like a chump. He put his arms down when he saw me standing in front of him again and shook his head like he couldn't believe I was back for more. He started toward me, with his hands still at his side, smiling — arrogantly! The prick! He was directly in front of me, and I was suddenly more alert than I had been before. I studied the Destroyer like I was looking at him through a

37

magnifying glass. Just below the left side of his chest I saw the almost imperceptible *bump, bump, bump* of the engine that was fueling the Montoya Express. If I was going to win this fight, I had to shut that engine down and I had to shut it down now. Instinctively I resumed my fighting stance, but as he got closer I dropped into a low crouch. My gloves almost touched the canvas when Gino threw a slow-motion, arrogant, roundhouse right at the top of my head. His glove passed harmlessly over my shoulder, just as angry red spots splashed in my mind's eye. *Surprise! You arrogant asshole!* I thought as I lunged forward and plunged my right glove into his chest, trying to drive his heart into his backbone. I heard him groan as if I had stabbed him with a knife. I pressed forward with both fists flying and continued stabbing that hairy bear in the heart until he collapsed over the top ring rope. When I couldn't hit him in the chest anymore, I tried stabbing him in the back and kidneys. Suddenly the referee was pulling me away. "Eddie, enough, enough," he was yelling in my face through the red spots. "Stop it."

I tried to get loose, but I couldn't break away. The red spots started to fade and I finally stopped fighting.

"You okay now?" the ref asked me. "Can I let you go?"

"Yeah, I'm okay," I told him.

The referee raised my hand in victory. The crowd cheered. The bright houselights came on, and the ring bell clanged repeatedly.

Hey, I knew we could do it, Mr. Johnson crowed as he came out of hiding. I ran to the ring ropes trying to locate my father and grandfather. I saw people standing in their section, but none of them were looking at the ring. They were all looking down at the floor. I did not see my father or grandfather standing among them, so I raced into the crowd. I saw Grandpa Hans lying on his back, holding my father's hand. They both turned to me when I arrived. I tore off my headgear and knelt beside them. Grandpa Hans touched my face with a cold hand. His face was chalky white, and I realized he was going to die right then and there. Tears came to my eyes. My grandfather beckoned to me to lean over. When my ear was next to his mouth he whispered, "You killed a bear, just like me, Eddie."

As far as I knew, my grandfather had never killed a bear and I didn't want to upset him by telling him there were no bears in Boston Arena — except maybe in his failing mind. So I comforted him with a lie.

"Yeah, Grandpa," I said. "I killed a bear. Just like you."

"Did you see red spots, Eddie?"

"How did you know about the red spots?" I was startled by his question.

Grandpa Hans didn't answer. Instead, he winked at me, and his meaning was clear. A part of Hans Perlmutter was a part of Eddie Perlmutter. I winked my understanding back at him. He grabbed his chest in pain and his eyes closed tightly. I knew he was leaving.

"Grandpa," I called to him. "Does this have something to do with the *S?*"

He was gone.

At my grandfather's funeral I couldn't help but wonder about the bear. I wish there had been time to ask him. But Hans Perlmutter had gone to his beloved Golda. I was a sixteen-year-old kid who still didn't have any answers and without Grandma and Grandpa there, I didn't even get a chocolate chip cookie.

I broke several bones in both my hands during that final round, and I learned many years later that I also broke Gino Montoya's heart in the process.

Thirty years after that fight, I saw Gino Montoya's name in the obituary column of *The Boston Globe.* I hadn't seen him once over those thirty years, even though we had both remained in the area. Gino Montoya had died suddenly, his obituary read, at the age of fifty from a massive coronary. I attended Gino's wake at Lombardi's Funeral Home in East Boston that same afternoon. I did not introduce myself to his family when I expressed my sympathy and found it extremely difficult to look at his young daughter and son. I overheard a conversation while I was waiting to view his body. I learned that Gino's heart attack was caused by an aneurysm that had ruptured without warning in the left ventricle of his heart. This kind of aneurysm, I heard, was usually the result of a previous chest trauma that went undetected until it was too late. I felt a chill as I stood by Gino's open casket and looked down at him. He looked like life had been good to him.

There were enlarged photos of Gino around his coffin. There was a picture of him at his confirmation and one of him on his wedding day. He was smiling in that second picture, and I noticed he had a full set of teeth. Then I saw the picture of him in his boxing trunks. There was a championship belt around his waist. He looked so vibrant and alive that it was hard to associate him with the dead body in the casket. His eyes stared proudly at the camera. I placed my right hand over my heart and lightly tapped it several times. I told Gino I was sorry and said good-bye.

CHAPTER 2

ME AND PATTY MCGEE

From 1958 to 1962, I wandered through Brookline High School without direction. The only person I felt close to was a blond, blue-eyed Irish girl named Patty McGee. I fell in love with her the first time I saw her on the front steps of the high school my freshman year. She wasn't perfect but she was perfect for me. Patty had a small hump on her back behind her right shoulder, the result of scoliosis as a child. The first time we met formally was when I beat the shit out of a sophomore football player who was making fun of her back.

"Thank you for coming to my rescue," she said after I had demolished the bully.

"No one makes fun of my girl," I told her.

She laughed. I had her attention, and she had Mr. Johnson's attention. In fact, Mr. Johnson and I thought about Patty McGee every night. I knew I would marry Patty someday, just like I knew I would be a cop.

The school population at BHS was comprised primarily of the descendants of Eastern European Jews, with the Irish Catholics a distant second. There was a smattering of Italians and Greeks, and one black kid named Houston Brown. There were identical twin Chinese girls in the class of '62; their last name was Chin. Naturally the kids called them the Double Chins. They seemed nice enough, but we never spoke to each other. Their intelligence intimidated me, and I must have scared the shit out of them with the bumps and bruises on my face after weekend boxing matches.

There was a three-strata structure in every class in just about every public high school in America, and Brookline High was no exception. In the top third were the serious students, who were destined to become doctors, scientists, and lawyers. At Brookline High, most of the top third were Jewish, except for the Double Chins, Houston, and some superstar Christians. I was strictly a middle-third guy. Kids in the middle third were average in just about everything. We didn't have long-term plans. We didn't have any plans, actually. We floated precariously above the bottom third, aware that the slightest misstep could plunge us headfirst into the abyss.

I didn't want any part of the lower third. They were in school only because the law said they had to be there. The boys in the lower third were destined to be the manual laborers of their generation. The girls in the lower third were destined to marry the guys in the lower third and have lower-third children. It all seemed predestined to me. Some losers did become winners, and some winners unexpectedly became losers. For the most part, however, kids didn't seem to change that much when they grew up. I did my best to stay right in the middle where I thought I belonged. Surprisingly, I had few fights at the high school because the ones I had early on were so one-sided that they discouraged further challenges. That was fine with me.

I graduated high school in 1962 when I was seventeen years old. My parents never talked to me about going to college, and it never entered my mind either, which was strange for a Jewish family. I worked odd jobs for a few years after high school, mostly in the wholesale meat business where my father had become well established. While the top third of my high school class matriculated into the halls of higher learning and the bottom third went directly to the bottom, I unloaded trucks and carried sides of beef in Haymarket Square, America's oldest wholesale meat market. The work was hard, the hours were long, and the pay was minimal, but I didn't care. I was just biding my time until I was twenty-one, old enough to enter the police academy. I kept myself in good physical condition by taking judo and karate lessons, and became pretty good at both.

In 1966 I entered the police academy. I asked Patty if she would marry me when I graduated. She said yes. I excelled at everything at the academy and finished in the top ten percent of my class. I was amazed. My parents were amazed. Patty was amazed. For the first time in my life I realized, if I was motivated, I had top-third potential. When I received my badge, I felt like I had everything. I had a woman I loved and the career I wanted. I was young and healthy, and all things seemed possible.

CHAPTER 3

LIGHT AT THE
END OF THE TUNNEL

My first assignment on the force was to Precinct One, located at the south entrance of the Sumner Tunnel in the North End. It was directly across the street from Haymarket Square where I had hauled sides of beef the year before. I loved the North End. I rented a one-bedroom apartment in a third-floor walk-up on Hanover Street for fifty-five dollars a month. There were apartments available for twenty-five bucks a month, but I wanted heat and my own bathroom. Patty and I married one year after I joined the force, and she moved into my apartment. We never moved again.

The first day on my beat I met a short, wiry guy standing in front of 98 Prince Street, where a sign identified the storefront as Huntington Realty. He smiled a crooked smile and held out his hand. He told me his name was Nunzio Nardelli.

"I wish you good luck, Officer Perlmutter," he said pleasantly. "But this neighborhood don't need guys like you."

"Why's that, Mr. Nardelli?"

"Because they got guys like me."

He was the local Mafia boss. He answered only to Raymond "Shady" Vali, of Providence, Rhode Island, the Boss of Bosses. The North End was safe because of violent men like Nardelli, just as he claimed. Many criminals lived in the North End, but they committed their crimes elsewhere. It was an amazing culture, and it worked.

Originally known as the Island of North Boston, the area was home to America's first grammar school, America's first playground, and Boston's first windmill. The North End was an Irish neighborhood before it was a Jewish neighborhood and was a Jewish neighborhood before it was an Italian neighborhood. The Irish left for the South End in the mid-1800s. Between 1870 and 1900, the Jews took over Salem Street with their pushcarts and traditions. By the time I started my beat in 1966, the North End was the Little Italy of Boston. It was a neighborhood of Madonna Della Cava and St. Agrippina di Mineo parades. It was a place where families and the Family coexisted in a wary truce. The Mafia had been in the North End since 1916 when Gaspare

Messina imported the Family to Boston from Sicily. The small neighborhood of narrow streets and Catholic churches was home to a lot of good guys and a lot of mobsters known as wiseguys.

I got my badge shortly after Albert De-Salvo, the Boston Strangler, was sentenced to life imprisonment in Walpole State Prison, but there were still plenty of crimes and criminals to keep me busy. Boston had it all. Murderers like Daddy Doe, Wimpy Bennett, and Chico Amico eventually became murder victims themselves. The Irish Mafia known as The Wayos — led by Walter "Whacko" Wallace, Red Ryder, and Steve "The Cannon" Carlino — terrorized South Boston for years and fought in the Irish gang wars of the 1960s. Only Red Ryder seemed to have survived.

In 1983 Nunzio Nardelli was arrested, tried, and sent away forever. He had been done in by a hidden microphone in his office and by his own big mouth. The North End changed after that. It became a more dangerous place. Red Ryder and Steve "The Cannon" Carlino tried to take over where Nardelli left off. Carlino's older brother, Vinnie "The Brute" Carlino, served as his brother's enforcer.

I got to know a lot of interesting characters

over the years and to appreciate the importance of the choices we make in life. There was a good-looking kid named Johnny "Handsome" Marcazi, who was a local high school football hero. Marcazi was a smart kid and received many scholarship offers to play college football. Instead he chose the higher education of the streets of Boston. Eventually, Marcazi would plead guilty to twenty murders committed in less than twenty years. Bad choice.

Angel DiNiro was a low-level thug from the area who I never got to meet but wish I had. Angel was not really cut out for a life of crime and fled the Boston crime scene for California in 1963. In Hollywood, Angel lost a lot of weight and got a part in the 1972 movie *The Godfather.* I saw the movie and thought Angel was pretty good. Usually, there was only one way out of the mob, but the wiseguys liked *The Godfather* movie so much they didn't go after Angel the Actor. Good choice.

Someone was always killing, maiming, robbing, raping, or defrauding someone else in the city, and Precinct One had all the business it could handle.

In those days if you were a kid growing up in the North End it was hard not to want to be one of the wiseguys. They had fancy cars, custom-made suits, flashy girls, and large bankrolls. Many of them were dangerous sociopaths, but they looked cool to the rest of us who didn't have their flash. A lot of kids in the North End talked, dressed, and walked like the wiseguys, but it was usually harmless play-acting. Every once in a while a good kid would cross over to the bad side, and the only way he would come back was dead.

There were a few kids in the neighborhood that kept their distance from the criminal element. They didn't imitate the wiseguys and had no ambitions to be wiseguys. Most of these kids hung out at the North End Association (NEA) located at the North Bennett Street Industrial School. A North End resident named Frankie Basilio was the antithesis of the wiseguys and was instrumental in the formation of the NEA to keep the neighborhood kids out of trouble. During my first year on the force Frankie convinced me to give boxing lessons to the boys at the NEA. I got to know some great kids during my years as a boxing instructor.

My favorite kid at the NEA was a gangly, seventeen-year-old boy named Togo Amato. His name was Robert Amato, but everyone called him Togo because of his love for Togo

Palazzi, the Italian, two-time all-American basketball player from Holy Cross College who was also a member of the Boston Celtics National Basketball Association championship team of 1957. His mother, Anna Maria, called him Robert. His father, Gianni, and his brother, Rocco, called him Bobby. To everyone else he was Togo. I called him "kid" sometimes even though he was only four years younger than me. I tried to teach Togo how to box, but he could care less. He was strictly a basketball player; he once apologized to me for his lack of interest in boxing. Togo was such a good kid that even the wiseguys liked him. He knew who they were, and they knew who he was, but they never bothered each other. Right after high school Togo got a civil-service job with the city. "I got no time for college, Eddie," he told me. "I gotta make money to help my family." I agreed with him. I hadn't gone to college, either. While I was chasing big- and small-time criminals, Togo was working his way up the civil-service ladder. He was a witness at the small wedding Patty and I had at city hall in front of a justice of the peace. Neither Patty's parents nor my parents attended the ceremony because of the Jewish–Catholic thing.

The wiseguys joked with Togo and me in

the streets of the North End, and I normally joked back. It was my nature. Togo was more reserved with the wiseguys, because he knew them better than I did.

"Hey, Togo, I got a parking ticket. Help me out."

"Sorry, no can do."

"Hey, Perlmutter, you got influence on the force. Gimme a break."

"I haven't arrested you in three weeks," I would joke.

I shared a few laughs with the wiseguys. I thought it helped keep the peace, but I was never sure. We got along fine, even though we didn't trust each other.

About the time that Red and Carlino killed Donnie Killeen of the Mullins Gang and took over their territory, I had worked my way up to detective. I was always in the thick of things, taking chances maybe I shouldn't have been taking. I shot some people, and some people shot me. I was wounded twice. I received four medals for valor, several merit awards, promotions, and a lot of public recognition. I was one of the most decorated cops in Boston from the late '60s to the late '80s. The local newspaper reporters who covered the police beat described me as fearless, and I guess I was. I don't know why but I never worried about myself. The first time I was shot, I remember lying on the street worrying about what would happen to Patty if I died.

I was a Boston cop for thirty-four years until I was forced to retire toward the end of 2000 for medical reasons. I was still in good physical shape but had developed traumatic arthritis in my hands and my knees. Twenty-one Golden Gloves bouts had made my hands brittle, and time had done the rest of the damage. My aching knees were the result of a small-time drug dealer hitting me with a Louisville Slugger in 1986. I had caught the son of a bitch in a sting operation in the snow-covered parking lot of Jimmy's Harborside Restaurant. He pulled the bat out of his trunk as soon as he realized I was a cop.

"What's with the bat, asshole?" I asked him. "You think you're Big League Lowenstein?"

"Who the fuck is Big League Lowenstein?"

Who the fuck is Big League Lowenstein? How could anyone not know him? Then I remembered that Big League had been serving a double life sentence since 1970 for a wiseguy-sanctioned double murder in 1968. This druggie with the bat was probably in diapers at the time. Big League was one of

Shady Vali's most deadly assassins in those days, and his trademark was killing people with a baseball bat to the forehead. He was called "Big League" for his hitting prowess in baseball. Lowenstein had a shot at the major leagues at one time. When he didn't make the grade, he hung up his spikes and glove forever but never really put down his bat. Big League was over six feet tall with a great head of black hair. He was a handsome, quiet, likeable guy with an athletic body. He also, allegedly, killed people for a living. I was glad I helped put him away, but I always had a problem with the contradictions in Big League Lowenstein's character.

"Just put the fuckin' bat down, numb nuts," I said to the druggie.

"Fuck you."

Bing! Exploding red spots were everywhere. Fuckin' drug-dealing, drug-using, useless son of a bitch! CHARGE! The idiot slipped on the snow trying to back away from me and went down on one knee. I hadn't expected that. I saw the guy swing the bat at my kneecaps from his kneeling position. Going, going, gone! He got up as I went down. He raised the bat over his head preparing to knock my head off. Instinctively I attacked. I launched a semiprofessional uppercut into his balls and did my best to drive them up into his mouth. I heard him scream in pain before he collapsed to his knees in front of me. We knelt there in the snow, staring at each other in mutual agony. Finally, I mustered the strength to push him onto his back and crawled onto his chest.

"You stupid bastard," I groaned, barely able to see through the red explosions.

In the process of knocking this senseless asshole more senseless, I rebroke two knuckles in each hand. I got a medal of merit for the arrest. My knees and my hands were rewarded with fractures and ruptures followed by crippling arthritis.

The Celtics captured their sixteenth NBA championship that same year, winning forty games at Boston Garden and losing only one. About a month before the kneecap thing, I attended one of those forty victories with a ticket that Togo gave me. I don't remember much about the game, but I do remember a middle-aged white guy slumped forlornly in the seat next to me in loge section eleven. He was a friendly drunk at first, but by the second quarter he seemed to be getting a little surly despite a large Celtic lead.

"Ain't like it used to be," he muttered

several times before passing gas. He was annoying everyone in the section, and I did my best to ignore him. Before halftime he made his third trip to the beer stand. When he returned to his seat with a beer in each hand, he observed loudly and proudly, "Look!!! The fuckin' Celtics are the only team in the NBA that can still play five white guys at the same time and win." He farted again for emphasis. I held my breath and checked out his theory. Sure enough Larry Bird, Kevin McHale, Bill Walton, Jerry Sichting, and Scott Wedman were all white and all on the court for the Celtics. "Take a good look, my friend." The drunk pointed at the court as he nudged me with his elbow. " 'Cause you ain't never gonna see a sight like this again." He sounded prophetic but another fart made him pathetic and then he messed himself.

Over the years the details of that game faded. But I'll never forget that sad little man who was so worried about his inability to stop the world from changing that he shit his pants and didn't even know it.

My physical condition and the physical condition of the Boston Celtics deteriorated badly after that championship season. We gradually went into a downward spiral that could not be stopped. With no more glory years on the horizon, Larry Bird and the other fading idols reluctantly retired. I retired at the same time but received far less fanfare.

I had become a limping liability to the Boston police department by the time I retired in 2000 on an annual pension of sixty-five thousand dollars. I was a fifty-five-year-old unemployed widower with the long-term prospects of a moth around a bright light.

My wife, Patty, had died of a brain aneurysm when we were both forty-two years old. She woke up in the middle of the night complaining of a headache. She turned on the lamp, got out of bed, put her hands on either side of her head, and with a look of surprise said, "Oh, Eddie." The doctors said she was dead before she hit the floor. One moment Patty was the light of my life. The next moment her light went out. I was devastated. The happiest days of my life were when I was with Patty. We couldn't have children, but having each other had been enough. We just didn't have enough time together.

My parents never accepted Patty because she was Catholic. Her parents never accepted me because I was Jewish. Her parents didn't like my parents, and my parents couldn't stand her parents. Neither family practiced organized religion. They practiced disorganized religious intolerance instead. Over endless beers and gin martinis, our parents wasted their time hating each other until they ran out of time.

I mourned for two years after Patty died and didn't see much of Mr. Johnson. One morning he popped up unexpectedly.

Hey, I loved her too, boss, but life goes on.

Patty was the only woman we ever knew.

It's time we moved on, buddy, he told me. But I can't do it without you.

Hey, it's not like we're attached at the hip, I said.

Close enough, he said.

All right, I'll give it a try but my heart's not in it.

We don't need your heart. Just get me in and we'll be fine, he promised. I gradually started dating other women. Patty and I had a good sex life together, but it was seldom spontaneous or experimental. I never thought anything was missing until I began seeing other women after she was gone. Making love with Patty had been warm and comforting. Fucking was different. Fucking was hot and exciting, and Mr. Johnson went crazy. For the first time in my life, I realized I could love someone besides Patty and something besides the police force. I loved sex, and I loved women. I loved reckless women. I loved reserved women. I loved black women. I loved white women. I loved the way women looked, and I loved the way they smelled. I loved the lustful impulses I felt when I was attracted to someone new. I even loved the mating games and the hunt. I was not tall, dark, and handsome, but there was no shortage of women who seemed to find me attractive. I was small in stature, but I was physically fit, and I knew I wasn't a bad-looking man. I had a certain degree of notoriety because of the way I did my job, and I think the danger of my profession was attractive to some women. I also had Mr. Johnson, who was a pretty big guy to be hanging out with a squirt like me, and he was always ready to stand up for me.

I had many women in my life after Patty died, but I never had one special woman. My affairs usually ended amicably enough when it became apparent that the relationship had run its course. I didn't "love 'em and leave 'em" like some guys. I loved 'em and let them leave me.

"Eddie, I'm thirty-two years old, and I need to plan for my future."

"Eddie, I'm forty-three years old, and I need to get serious. Everything is a joke with you."

"Eddie, I'm almost fifty. I need a long-term commitment."

Sometimes it was painful for me to let a woman go, but I knew it would be more painful to ask her to stay. After Patty's brain exploded in the middle of the night, I could no longer make long-range plans. When I was younger, I made a lot of plans. But when Patty was taken from me, I was painfully reminded of one of my Grandma Goldie's favorite Yiddish sayings. *"Mensch trach und Gott lacht."* — Man plans and God laughs. Well, God would just have to laugh at someone else for a change.

Through the good times and bad times, Togo Amato was always there for me. He was there when I started out as a twenty-one-year-old rookie cop. He was there when I married Patty and he was there when I buried her twenty years later. He was by my side for my unexpected early retirement. When I retired, Togo was the clerk magistrate of the Marblehead District Court. He was upset with my decision to accept early retirement.

"Why didn't you take the desk job they offered you?"

"I can't sit at a desk all day. You know that."

"Yeah, I know, tough guy," he said, shaking his head. "You're not happy unless you're beating the shit out of some bad guy in the street or getting shot in the ass."

"I've never been shot in the ass," I said in my own defense.

"That's because you never ran away from anything." Togo frowned. "So what are you going to do now?"

"Honestly, I don't know. I got nothing and no one."

"What about all your girlfriends?"

"Like I said, I got nothing and no one."

"You got me," he said, looking directly into my eyes and patting my hand.

And that's when I became the "official" boxing coach of the NEA boxing club. I had my policeman's pension and a job I enjoyed. It wasn't a terrible life, but I can't claim I was happy. I had lost too much along the way.

CHAPTER 4

FROZEN STONES

Winters were killing me. One Saturday morning in January of 2004, I was in so much pain walking to the North Bennett Street Industrial School to give boxing lessons that I almost collapsed on Hanover Street. I stumbled into the school's undersized, stifling gym, known as the "hot box," and limped to the radiator in the corner. I flopped onto a wooden chair and leaned as close to the old heater as possible. Togo arrived and saw me huddled next to the radiator. I looked up and saw him walking toward me. He wore a cashmere overcoat. Classy.

"Eddie. You look bad."

"My hands and knees are killing me. I can't stand this fuckin' weather anymore."

Togo nodded as he sat down next to me, like he was going to give me some advice. There was a clang of metal on metal before he got the chance to talk. The gym door opened, and two of Togo's buddies came in — Petey "Pants" Pantolioni was Togo's closest friend. He was a dark-skinned, brown-eyed Italian of medium height with short, jet black hair. Petey was followed by a kid they called Muscles, who was six foot six, movie star handsome, and weighed close to three hundred pounds. Bruno "Muscles" Marinara was a giant physically and the best athlete in the neighborhood. But mentally, Bruno Marinara wasn't all there, although he wasn't all gone, either. They waved to us from across the gym floor.

"We got a board meetin'," Togo told me.

"Muscles is on the board?"

Togo laughed, "Why not?"

The board members greeted us and "HOW you doin'? How YOU doin'? How you DOIN'?" echoed through the gym. The door clanged open again, and two more board members entered. Gangly Tommy "Rats" Ragusa was followed by a short, tough-looking Reggie "The Doctor" Infante. Reggie was called "The Doctor" because when he was a kid he once said he wanted to be a doctor. He never said it again but he got stuck with the name forever.

*How YOU doin'?*s filled the gym again. Hugs, back slaps, and noogies (those annoying little knuckle punches to the shoulder or ground into the head) were exchanged. I looked at them with envy. These guys belonged to an exclusive club I could never join.

They had grown up in the shadows of the Old North Church and Paul Revere's house. Their immigrant parents had learned to speak English together at the North End Union, and they had learned a trade at the North Bennett Industrial School, the oldest trade school in the country. The boys were raised in apartments that had no hot water or bathtubs. In the Forties and early Fifties they had gone once a week with their fathers to the North End Bath House, where they could get a bar of soap, a towel, and a hot shower for a penny. Their fathers had played cards together in storefronts like Club Torresi, where the favorite game was Boss and Underboss even though the players weren't necessarily Mafia.

The boys had played stickball together at the Saint Anthony Polcari Playground during the summer, spring, and fall. They played football in the Gino Capaletti League, named after the Boston Patriot's record-holding Italian-American placekicker and wide receiver. Then they played baseball in the Small Fry League, followed by Little

League, and finally the Yankee Clipper League (named after the New York Yankee's center fielder, Joe DiMaggio). The North End was a hotbed of Red Sox fans but Joe DiMaggio was the best player in the game and he was Italian. Blood was thicker than home-team loyalty for these guys. They played their games at the North End Park on Commercial Street by the Charles River and they met often at the Christopher Columbus Youth Center.

Streets, districts, and areas determined their neighborhood team. There was the Clinic team, the North Bennett Street team, the North Square District guys, and the Hanover Street boys. These areas competed with each other in local sporting events, but when it was time to represent the entire North End they became one community. These young men had smelled the same smells in their youth: Stella's Restaurant, Pizzeria Regina, Louis, La Cantina, and the European. They knew everyone who hung around Pat's Scratches, tough guys like Longy Zaza and Jackie Franko. Ralphie Santos they watched from a safe distance, because they knew he was a dangerous man, and they gave plenty of room to "Killer" Mike Fatone when he visited from East Boston. Togo's group had become a band of brothers, linked together by the common bond of their childhood on the streets of the North End. I knew I could be their friend, but I could never be one of them.

"Hey, Infante! Yo, stupid," Muscles shouted at Reggie Infante. "I dunked on you pretty good yesterday, didn't I? You couldn't do nothin'."

"You're ten feet tall, pinhead," Infante responded. "Big fuckin' deal. You was my size you couldn't do nothin'."

"Oh yeah. Oh yeah." Muscles sounded like an eight-year-old. "I could dunk on Wilt Chamberlain if I wanted to."

Infante got a pained look on his face. "Wilt Chamberlain is dead, you moron. 'Course you can dunk on him."

Muscles was confused. All he could say was, "Oh yeah? Oh yeah? So?"

"Why don't you stop picking on him?" Togo said without temper.

"It's too much fun."

"Havin' fun now?" Togo asked.

"Yeah, that's right. Havin' fun now?" Muscles said, making a fist and shaking it at Infante. Muscles turned to me. "Coach Eddie," he called me. "You look sick. Whatsa matter?"

I smiled as best I could. "It's my arthritis. It hurts a lot when it gets cold."

"You should go where it's warm then," Muscles said simply. "Like Mikey Scarfetti done."

"Mikey Tees?" Petey Pants asked.

"Yeah, yeah, Mikey Tees. 'Member him? I seen him Christmastime."

"That was just last week, numb nuts," the Doctor chimed in, placing a light noogie on the big man's shoulder.

"I know that." Muscles rubbed away the noogie with his palm. It was the tradition.

"If he was here how come he didn't come by to see us?" Petey asked.

"Why didn't he come to see us?" Togo laughed. "You know why, Petey. We all know why. We useta make fun of him all the time, 'cause all he wanted to do was hit golf balls."

"Yeah," Muscles agreed. "You guys was always makin' fun of Mikey Tees. Like when we was all playing baseball at the park and he'd be out in right field hittin' golf balls and getting in the way. He musta hit a million of those fuckin' things. I 'member he hit some so far they landed in the fuckin' Charles River."

"So where's he now, Muscles?" Togo seemed interested.

"He told me he's a golf teacher somewhere where it's warm all the time," Muscles announced proudly. He knew something the other guys didn't know. That didn't happen often.

"A golf pro," Petey said, shaking his head. "That figures. Fuckin' Mikey Tees teaching other assholes how to hit golf balls."

"Did he tell you where he is exactly?" Togo asked.

Muscles scratched his huge head. "Yeah, but I don't remember. I think he said Florida."

"That's a big fuckin' state, egghead," Infante teased.

"Oh yeah. Oh yeah," Muscles responded. "Well at least I know something. You don't know nuttin'."

"Will you guys stop it?" Togo held up a hand. They stopped. "Muscles, I want you to think real hard."

"He can't even think real soft," the Doctor started again.

Togo gave Infante an exasperated look. The Doctor held up his hands in surrender. Togo turned his attention to Muscles. "Try to remember exactly what Mikey told you."

Muscles squeezed his eyes shut. "Okay, okay." He clenched his fists and thought as hard as he could. He smiled and opened his eyes. "He teaches golf in South Florida. At a place that has two names."

"West Palm?" Petey tried.

"No, it has two Italian names," Muscles said.

"Italian names?" the Doctor moaned. "The Italians didn't settle Florida. What the fuck you talkin' about?"

"Spanish names maybe," Togo tried. "Could they have been Spanish names?"

"Sorry, Togo." Muscles looked sad. "I don't know the difference."

Togo patted him on the shoulder. "That's okay, Muscles. You done good."

"C'mon, guys," Reggie "The Doctor" said. "We got a meetin' to conduct here. Why you wastin' so much time on Mikey Tees anyway?"

"I was thinking," Togo explained. "If we could find Mikey Tees, maybe he could find some work for Eddie down there in the warm weather."

That caught me by surprise. "Hey, don't worry about me," I said. "I can take care of myself."

"Of course you can," Togo said. "But why should you be miserable six months a year? You're almost sixty, Eddie. You can't take much more of this shit."

"I'm happy here."

"Yeah, I can see that," Togo said sarcastically, pointing at my position close to the radiator.

"Besides I got this job and the kids I coach here. I don't know anyone in Florida."

"You'll meet people," Togo insisted, shaking his head. "I hate to see you in pain, Eddie."

The rest of them murmured their agreement.

Then, all of a sudden — "BOCA RATON! BOCA RATON!" Muscles shouted.

"Stop the yelling, Sasquatch," the Doctor shouted back. "And what's Boca Raton?"

"That's where Mikey Tees lives!" exclaimed excited Muscles.

"That's in South Florida." Togo nodded. "Between Palm Beach and Fort Lauderdale. My brother-in-law and sister-in-law have a winter place there."

"Yeah, Steve. The Jewish guy with the fake fish," Rats remembered.

I looked at Togo and said, "This is a nice thought, guys, but I'm staying right here. I love Boston."

"Boston don't love you no more," Petey said. "At least not in the winter. You're in pain, Eddie. The cold's no good for you."

"I'm okay," I insisted.

"Then why you rubbing your knees right now?" Petey pressed. "You're a fuckin' mess, Eddie. Face it. Your hands look like you got marbles in 'em."

"Hey, this is home," I said. "I'm not going to some strange place in Florida."

Togo wasn't happy with me. "You know," he began, "Muscles remembers almost nothing, but this he remembered for you. It's a sign."

Muscles lumbered to Togo and hugged him. Togo hugged him back.

"I done good remembering, didn't I, Togo?"

"You did very good, Muscles," Togo agreed.

Muscles pushed away from Togo. He walked toward me with his arms held out. I was never much for hugging guys, but I couldn't turn down a hug from good-natured Bruno Muscles. "Okay, okay," I said, patting Muscles on the back. "I'll look into it."

"Hey, Coach Eddie," Bruno said, "way to go."

"Good choice," Togo said.

Someone gave me a noogie.

CHAPTER 5

BEHOLD BOCA

The Lord parted the gates of his waiting
room and the elders of the Tribe of Israel
saw it was good. "This land is mine!" They
exulted and they wandered no more.

— FIRST BOOK OF ARVIDA,
CHAPTER 561, VERSE 33496

I felt like I had landed on another planet.
Everything at Palm Beach International
Airport looked strange to me when I got off
the plane from Boston. I hadn't been outside New England since my eighth-grade
class took an overnight train trip to Washington, D.C.

The people in the waiting area looked like
a council of tribal elders. They were mostly
little people with darkly tanned, wrinkled
skin, white hair, and capped, white teeth.
Many were wearing shorts, pullover short-
sleeved shirts, and sneakers. I saw Togo's
brother-in-law, Steve Coleman, waving to
me. He was easy to spot. He didn't have

white hair, he wasn't wearing shorts, nor was he short. He was a big man, over six feet tall; Steve was a successful businessman who had been wintering in Boca Raton for over ten years. We greeted each other with a North End–style hug, and since I had no luggage, we preceded directly to short-term parking. Steve was driving the Pebble Beach Special Edition Lexus SC430 retractable hard-top convertible. He kept the top up as we raced south on Interstate 95. In forty minutes, we were in Boca Raton, at the Two Course at Boca Heights. Steve walked me to the golf pro's office where he introduced me to Mikey Tees and told me he would wait for me outside.

Within fifteen minutes I was offered a job I didn't think I wanted by a man who was certain I wasn't qualified, in a place I wasn't sure I wanted to live. I accepted the offer.

"I don't know why I'm offering you this job," Mikey Tees Scarfetti told me honestly. "You know nothing about golf or country clubs." Mikey was a stocky, athletic-looking guy in his late forties with a full head of black hair. I could see him fitting right in on the streets of the North End, except he had never really fit in there at all.

"Nepotism," I said. "I'm part of Togo's

74

extended family."

"You and a thousand other guys," Mike said. "Togo was a pain in my ass when I lived in the North End. Him and his friends never let me alone."

"Well I appreciate you helping me out," I said, patting him on the shoulder. "I guess North End connections run pretty deep no matter what."

"Yeah, they do," Mike said. "Plus your reputation as a cop in the North End was pretty impressive. I figure I owe something to a guy like you."

"You don't owe me anything, Mike. I just did my job."

"You were outstanding," Mike said. He went to a bookcase in his office and selected a book entitled *Rules of Golf.* He handed it to me. "Try to learn something before you get back," he said, walking me out of the office toward Steve's car in the parking lot. "I'll use you mostly on security, but you might have to perform some golf-related services."

"Don't worry, Mike. I won't embarrass you."

"I know," was all he said.

I looked around at the course and the clubhouse. "Everything seems so new," I observed.

"It is new. This clubhouse just opened and this course has been totally redone. The One Club did the same thing a couple of years ago."

"There are two separate clubs?"

"That's another story," he laughed. "And we don't have time for that today."

"Who pays for all these improvements?"

"The members."

"They don't mind?"

"Of course they mind. You'll hear all about it when you get here permanently," he promised with a laugh. "It's a big topic of conversation. All you have to do is listen."

I looked around again. "Mike, I haven't seen this much green since Fenway Park. It's amazing."

"I hate to say it, Eddie, but you take it for granted after a while."

"That's sad."

We shook hands. "Thanks, Mike," I said. "By the way, where are the heights?"

"What heights?"

"The heights," I said. "You know, like in Boca Heights."

"There are no heights."

"Then why is it called Boca Heights?"

"Don't pay any attention to the community names around here," Mike said with a chuckle. "There's no point at Boca Pointe as far as I know and Boca West is east of Boca Isle, which isn't remotely an island. Broken Sound, just down Yamato Road, isn't broken as far as I know and I can't hear a sound. Can you? Boca Vista doesn't have a better view than Boca Green, which isn't any greener than St. Andrews, which isn't a church. You can't hunt at the Woodfield Hunt Club and I don't know what the story is with Boca Teeca. Le Lac has a lake but then again so does Boca Lago. I don't know, I come from a place where the North End is in the north end."

"No you don't," I disagreed.

"Why?"

"The North End is east of the West End and southwest of East Boston," I told him. "Remember, I know the neighborhoods and streets like the back of my hand. There's no school on School Street and no church on Church Street. There's no court on Court Street and no water on Water Street. And Back Bay was filled in years ago."

"Thanks for the tour." Mikey Scarfetti laughed.

"You're welcome," I said. "So, are all the gated communities similar here in Boca?" I asked.

"For the most part," Mike said. "Some are more expensive than others. Some have better facilities than others. But, yeah, I'd say they all offer about the same basic amenities. It's a nice way of life for a lot of people."

"Sounds perfect," I said.

"Perfect it ain't," Mike said, shaking his head. "These places have plenty of problems."

"Like what?"

"When the members of a club take over the management from the developer, the shit usually hits the fan," Mike explained.

"What happens?"

"Member-owners can't seem to agree on how anything should be run," Mike said. "We have major problems here at Boca Heights."

"What kind of problems?"

"First of all, like I told you, there are no heights." Mike poked my shoulder playfully. "Seriously, when the members took over the management of Boca Heights they inherited a nightmare. There were two classes of golf club membership sold here. If new property owners wanted a golf club membership they could join just the One Course, for one price, or they had the option to join both the One Course and the Two Course for more money. Now, the One Course members are fighting with the Two

Course members over who should pay for what."

"Sounds like a difficult situation," I said.

"It's a horror," Mike agreed. "And Boca Heights isn't the only club having this kind of problem. Our neighbors at Broken Sound have exactly the same problem with their East and West Courses. Boca Heights and Broken Sound are like mirror images of each other. They were both built by the same builder around the same time. Other clubs have other problems. There's one big dysfunctional family of gated communities here in Boca."

"Am I crazy to be moving here?" I asked.

"Not at all," Mike told me. "Boca is great. It's just not perfect."

"Like everyplace else," I said.

"No." Mike shook his head. "Boca is not like every place else. Boca is unique. You'll see."

Steve introduced me to a real estate broker he knew and the three of us looked at apartments in the area. With their help and advice I was able to find a nice, affordable one-bedroom apartment near Boca Heights. After I signed a one-year lease, Steve took me to the Boca Raton Historical Society to gather several pamphlets about the city and its history. I took some census information and a few environmental pamphlets as well. Driving back to Boca Heights with the top down and the sun warming my face, I saw a large, gold sign that read "Memories."

"What's that?" I asked Steve.

"It's a new concept in life after death," he said.

I asked him to stop the car. He pulled off the road and parked near the dusty construction site. The entrance was grand and gated, and a few hundred feet away two large, ornate buildings faced each other. The place looked like Rome, and it wasn't going to be built in a day. Steve said there were two facilities in Boca like Memories. One was called the Garden.

"A cemetery?" I pointed.

"You be the judge of that," Steve said. "But why are you interested?"

"My wife is dead."

"I know. For twenty years."

"I was thinking maybe I'd move her here."

"It's too hot here."

I opened the door and got out of the car. "Do you want to come with me?" I asked.

"I'm not ready for this place. I'll wait in the car."

I entered the gates of Memories alone.

I was on a plane back to Boston that

night. Mikey had given me two weeks to straighten out my affairs and return to Boca. I settled into the middle seat on the Delta Song plane, grateful I didn't need much legroom. There was a huge guy on either side of me, and they were cramped and grouchy. When the plane took off, I started to read the pamphlets I had gathered. After two hours of reading on the three-hour flight, I stuffed the material in the seat pocket in front of me, put my seat in the reclining position, closed my eyes, and tried to convert the Boca data into my own terms. I didn't bother with the ancient history of the Tequesta or the Seminole Indians but went directly to what was relevant today.

There were about ninety thousand people living in Boca Raton. Perhaps half of them were Jewish, which is about forty-eight percent above the national average. On Yamato Road, down the street from Boca Harbor, there were six impressive churches and one synagogue standing side by side. Steve referred to the area as the University of God campus.

Boca Raton translated literally from Spanish to English means "mouth of the rat," but it could have other meanings as well. I learned that the proper pronunciation of

Raton rhymes with *tone* and not *lawn.*

The big guy in the window seat next to me farted, shifted in his tight-fitting seat, and mumbled something that sounded like "fuckin' plane," then went back to sleep. I twisted open the fan nozzle above my head and continued to review the information.

In 1895, Henry Flagler's Florida East Coast Railroad arrived in Boca Raton from St. Augustine. The railway quickly moved on to Miami and Key West. The state of Florida gave Flagler one thousand acres of land for every mile of railroad tracks he laid from Jacksonville to Key West. Flagler's Model Land Company would then survey the real estate and sell it in parcels. In 1905, Japanese colonist Jo Sakai arrived in Boca Raton and purchased one thousand acres from Flagler for the purpose of forming an agricultural colony to grow pineapples. He named his community Yamato (*yah-mah-toe*), which meant "land of peace," among other things. A Japanese man named George Morikami joined Jo Sakai's colony in 1905 but soon went off on his own and made a fortune in real estate. Morikami never married and died without heirs. He donated two hundred acres of his land to the town. That land became the Morikami Museum on Ya-mato Road. Unfortunately, Jo Sakai's pineapple colony did not do as well as his land investments. In 1908, the pineapple crop, tended by only forty colonists, was destroyed by blight. By 1920 the colony was abandoned.

"Please be sure your tray table is stored and your seat is in an upright position," the flight attendant announced, and I complied, making both my row mates grouchier. Boca Raton 101 would have to wait.

CHAPTER 6
I HATE GOOD-BYES

"I'm moving to Florida, sweetheart," I said looking down at Patty's tombstone.

Patty McGee Perlmutter — 1945–1987
Loved by all who knew her.

In the summer I would sit by her grave and talk to her for an hour or more. But there would not be a long visit today. It was a blustery, bitter cold New England January afternoon and I would have literally frozen my little Jewish ass off if I tried staying in that Catholic cemetery for more than a few minutes.

"Can you imagine me living in fancy-shmancy Boca Raton, Florida?" I asked her while blowing on my aching hands. I pictured her smile. "Me neither. But that's where I'm going." I paused, out of habit, as if she were going to respond. "You wouldn't believe that place, Patty," I continued. "I never saw anything like it in my life." I was being honest. "They're building everywhere. Expensive houses, stores, malls, you name it. They're even building a cemetery that's fancier than where some people live."

I thought back to my visit to Memories. It had caught me by surprise when I saw it from the road while riding in Steve Coleman's car. I had never seen a cemetery so opulent and cheerful anywhere else, but Steve told me there were already two of them in Boca Raton.

I was walking around the dusty lot trying to get a feel for the project when I was approached by a pleasant-looking middle-aged man wearing a New York Yankees baseball cap. I didn't hold that against him. Gray hair poked out from the edges of the hat. I guessed he was my age. He was taller than me, but so was just about everyone else.

"Can I help you?" He smiled.

"Just looking."

"Would you like some information about Memories?"

"Sure. You work here?"

"I'm one of the developers." He held out his hand. "I'm Jackson Lehman."

"Hi, Jackson. I'm Eddie." I shook his hand. "What's the deal here? This place doesn't look like a cemetery to me."

"It's not supposed to look like a cemetery,

85

Eddie." Jackson went into action. "It's a new concept in how to deal with death."

"You learn something new every day."

"Are you interested in your own interment here, Eddie?"

"It's not on my agenda right now."

"I see. Are you considering interring a loved one?"

"Yes. My wife."

"I see. Is she terminally ill?"

"No. She's terminally dead."

"Oh, I'm sorry. For how long?"

"Forever."

"No. I mean how long has she been deceased?"

"Twenty years."

"And you're just getting around to burying her now?"

"I don't like to rush things."

"Be serious."

"Okay. My wife is buried in a Catholic cemetery in Boston. I'm thinking of moving her remains down here."

"I assume that's because you're moving to this area."

"Yes, while I'm alive."

"That's the best way to enjoy Boca."

"I'm sure. So, do you accept transfers?"

"Not after their junior year."

"Good one," I said. "Now it's your turn

to be serious."

"Fair enough. But to tell you the truth I don't have a special program for transfers. I'm sure we can work something out though."

"Can I get a preconstruction discount?"

"We don't offer discounts at Memories."

"Then I doubt I can afford this place."

"Don't be so sure. We have something for everyone here."

"Really? Then I'm dying to know more."

"That won't be necessary."

"We both have to get serious."

He nodded. We walked the area. There were two impressive mausoleums under construction. Jackson talked and pointed while I listened with my hands stuffed in my pockets, clutching my money. It wasn't long before I was swimming in numbers. Jackson told me the project would take several more years to complete and would cost around $125 million. Upon completion, the facility would be capable of accommodating over two hundred thousand members, making it the largest and quietest gated community in Boca. There would be up to 135,000 full bodies interred and somewhere around 100,000 cremains.

"Prices?" I asked.

"You can start as low as fifteen hundred

bucks for a single cremation niche."

"Too late for cremation. My wife was a full-body situation originally. But I'm not sure how full her body is at this point. Maybe it would fit in a niche."

"No. Her casket will still be full size, which will require a full-size crypt."

"What about just an everyday burial?"

"There will be no in-ground burials at Memories."

"Seems like a waste of a lot of good underground."

"We're building a mausoleum city here, Eddie, not a cemetery. The mausoleums will be spectacular; all in an air-conditioned, museum-style setting."

"No offense, Jackson, but do you think dead people really give a shit about climate control?"

"That's not the point, Eddie. Memories is going to be a place where people can celebrate life without the doom and gloom associated with old-fashioned cemeteries. We're going to have a biography library of those who are laid to rest here. We're going to offer support groups for the bereaved. Everything is being designed to help the living celebrate the dead."

"Sounds like my kind of party."

"You said we were going to be serious."

"I slipped. Any religious issues?"

"None at all. Jews and Christians will be able to visit their departed loved ones in an atmosphere devoid of bigotry, hatred, or contempt. We're building a Christian mausoleum right over there." Jackson pointed at some trees. "It will be made entirely of Siena marble mined from the Vatican quarry."

"You're kidding. The Vatican has its own quarry?"

"Absolutely. Other modern cemeteries are using Vatican marble as well. It's very trendy."

"Yeah, I heard this place was a knockoff of another cemetery in Boca," I offered.

"We are not alone but we are unique," Jackson said. "The Christian mausoleum will also have five-inch-thick cypress doors."

"From the Vatican cypress forest?"

"The Vatican doesn't have a cypress forest."

"So, why the cypress doors?"

"Cypress doors last forever."

"That should comfort dead Christians. But what about dead Jews?"

"Baruch — !"

"Bless you."

"Thank you. But I wasn't finished. *Baruch Chaim* means 'Blessing of Life'," Jackson tried. "It's the name we've chosen for the Jewish mausoleum, which will be an absolute masterpiece of architecture and inspiration. It will even include a replica of the Wailing Wall inside."

"Hey, what about a burning bush?"

"Uninsurable."

"So a parting of the Red Sea is probably out of the question, too?"

"Flood insurance in Florida? Be serious."

"Bummer. Can this place make money, Jackson?"

"Not in my lifetime, but many years from now Memories will be very profitable."

"So why are you doing this?"

"To make a difference. I want to change the way we all perceive death."

"You're serious?"

"Dead serious."

"That's appropriate. Is there anything else I should know?"

"Would you like to see one of our menus?"

"Menus?"

"Yes. We have different menus for catered receptions and concerts."

"Concerts? By who? The Grateful Dead?"

"I wish I had thought of that."

"Last question, Jackson. How much for a full-body transfer?"

"I can offer you a nice crypt for seven

thousand dollars."

"I'd rather have a plasma TV and a pool table."

"Life is all about choices, Eddie."

"And so is death, apparently," I observed. "So, what do dead rich people buy?"

"Supreme Crypts are very popular with our wealthier clients. We inter the deceased couple side by side on a platform in the crypt."

"I assume they're both dead at the time."

"Not necessarily. We'll start with one and add the other when the time comes. They can also include pets in their mausoleum."

"What about substitutions?"

"For instance?"

"Well, let's say the wife dies and the husband lives another few years and marries a Hard Rock Cafe showgirl. What then? Or, let's say the wife doesn't die and the guy is with a Hard Rock Cafe showgirl anyway. Can he substitute a mistress for a certain number of dogs or cats?"

"That's another interesting concept."

"I'm always thinking. So, what's the cost of a Super Crypt?"

"A Supreme Crypt," he corrected me. "Give or take a few amenities — four hundred thousand dollars."

"Does that include an in-ground pool?"

"Eddie, you should know better."

"That's right. I forgot. Nothing in-ground at Memories."

"Exactly. Shall I sign you up?"

"I'll have to ask my wife when I see her."

A burst of frigid air from the Montreal Express blew up my pant legs freezing my stones, bringing me back to the frigid present.

"Patty, I gotta go before I'm frozen into one of these statues." There were angel statues everywhere in the cemetery.

Next, I visited the grave sites of my parents and grandparents in the Jewish cemetery a few miles away. I placed a few pebbles on their headstones because I knew it was the Jewish thing to do. I read my grandfather's headstone, which was actually the second monument placed over his grave since he died. I had replaced the original headstone more than twenty years after he died because of a letter he had written over fifty years ago.

My mother died of leukemia in 1982 at the relatively young age of sixty-nine. My father died a few years later. He smoked himself to death. After my father's funeral, I went to their house in Brookline to clean it out. In the basement I found a small trunk covered with dust with an ancient-looking, rusted lock that I broke off easily with a hammer I found in my father's old toolbox. I opened the trunk, and the first thing I saw was a sealed envelope addressed to my father from my grandfather. The envelope was sealed with an old-world wax stamp, and the seal had never been broken. I wondered why Harry S. Perlmutter had decided not to read his father's message or if he had ever opened the trunk at all. Perhaps he didn't want to know any more about his origins as a first-generation American child of Russian refugees. He had worked hard to separate himself from those humble beginnings, and maybe he didn't want any reminders.

Without hesitation I broke the seal of the envelope and took out a thick stack of brittle pages. Unfortunately, the letter was written in Russian, Yiddish, Hebrew, and English, which is the way my grandfather talked. I couldn't understand what he was trying to tell my father in the letter, and I was frustrated. I returned the papers to the envelope and poked through the contents of the trunk. I found an elegant knife in a sheath about eleven inches long. I held the short sword in my hand. It felt comfortable and familiar in my grip. I could sense there was something important about this sword

and felt certain that the secret to its meaning could be found in the writings of my
grandfather. I put the sword back into the
rectangular box and placed the letter in my
pocket.

CHAPTER 7

THE *S* IN
EDWARD S. PERLMUTTER

I was excited about my message from the past. I drove to Temple Israel, the Orthodox Jewish synagogue in Brookline. I knew just where it was on Beacon Street, though I had never been inside the building. I found the rabbi in his sunny, cluttered office. He was a small man with a long, full, salt-and-pepper beard who appeared to be in his sixties. Dressed in black he looked to be a very serious person. I introduced myself to Rabbi Horowitz and explained my reason for my visiting him. I put the letter and knife on his desk. First the rabbi looked at the dagger. He did not remove it from the sheath. "This is a kinjal," the rabbi said with displeasure. "It was a weapon used by the Cossacks at the turn of the last century. Kinjals killed many Jews. Why would your grandfather have such a weapon in his possession?" I told the rabbi that I had no idea why this Russian dagger had been in my grandfather's possession and I suggested that the letter might offer an explanation. Rabbi Horowitz opened the envelope and removed the papers carefully and respectfully. He put on reading glasses and studied the writing as he turned the pages. Then he looked at me and shook his head. "I'm embarrassed," he said, "but I can't read this. Your grandfather uses Russian, Hebrew, Yiddish, and English like they were all the same language. I can understand a lot of the words, but the actual meaning is lost on me."

"Can you try?" I asked hopefully.

"I can do better than that," the rabbi said, and got up from his large leather chair. "Follow me, please."

We went down into the basement of the temple. The rabbi knocked on a heavy wooden door, and I heard a guttural voice respond. The rabbi opened the door, and we entered. I felt like I had stepped back in time. Everything in the dim room was ancient, including a little old man who sat behind a desk with open books strewn in front of him. His glasses were very thick, and he had to squint to see me. "Rabbi Rudolfsky, this young man would like you to translate a letter for him."

Without asking a question the white-bearded old man motioned for me to come forward and held out his hand. I gave him the letter. He spread it on the desk in front of him and leaned over so his face was very close to the paper. He turned a knob on the desk lamp to brighten the light without taking his eyes from the letter. After a few moments he looked up at us with surprise. *"Ani yodea may-ish hazeh."* The old man's voice was barely audible.

I looked to Rabbi Horowitz for a translation.

"Rabbi Rudolfsky says he knows this man."

"That's impossible," I told him. "The man who wrote this letter was born before the turn of the century and died in 1960."

"Rabbi Rudolfsky is very old," the younger rabbi explained. "He is ninety-eight years old and was born in Russia."

I did some quick calculations. Rabbi Rudolfsky could have known my grandfather but it was highly unlikely. "Ask him why he thinks he knows this man." I listened to their exchange and saw that the older rabbi was agitated.

"Ani yodea MAY-ish hazeh!" Rabbi Rudolfsky scolded Rabbi Horowitz.

Rabbi Horowitz held up his hands in front of his chest, palms out. *"Sha, sha,"* he said to the older man, trying to calm him in a polite way. Rabbi Horowitz turned to me. "I'm sorry," he apologized. "I misinterpreted his words. Rabbi Rudolfsky actually said, 'I know *of* this man.' He didn't say he actually knew him."

"Why would he know of my grandfather?" I asked.

"Hu haya mefoorsam," the old man responded.

"The rabbi says this man was very well known," the younger rabbi explained; he listened to the old man again. "He says this man was famous."

"Famous," I repeated. "My grandfather was famous?"

The old rabbi spoke again so rapidly I couldn't make out one word. Rabbi Horowitz translated.

"The rabbi says he was never sure if this man really existed. He thought it might just be a bedtime story his mother told."

The old rabbi interrupted, still agitated and talking excitedly. The younger rabbi struggled to keep pace.

"Rabbi Rudolfsky says your grandfather was a legend."

"Is he sure?" I asked. "My grandfather's name was Hans Perlmutter. Is that who the rabbi is talking about?"

A quick exchange followed. "The rabbi says your grandfather's real name was not Hans Perlmutter. He says he had a Russian name. It's right in his letter."

My heart was racing now. "What was his Russian name?"

The old rabbi ended a brief sentence with a word that sounded to me like *Zee-rota*.

"The rabbi said your grandfather was called Sirota. It means 'the orphan'."

"Hav harog dov ke-shehaya rak yeled."

The younger rabbi looked at me with respect. "He says your grandfather killed a bear in Russia with this sword when he was fifteen years old."

I sat in the chair in front of the rabbi's desk. I was sweating and dizzy from receiving too much information too fast. My grandfather had killed a bear with a Russian dagger when he was a teenager. It was hard for me to accept, although I was reminded of the two murdered men near the zoo years ago.

"Rabbi Rudolfsky asked if you would like him to translate your grandfather's entire letter?"

All I could do was nod and listen.

My grandfather wrote of a loveless childhood where he lived among people who never accepted him. He wrote of physical and mental abuse at the hands of several of the elders in the village of Vishnovet and of one bully in particular who called Sirota a curse and the cause of all their misfortunes. Sirota became isolated and bitter. One day, my grandfather wrote, out of frustration, he finally fought back against the bully. He retaliated with such ferocity that he nearly killed the man. His savagery alarmed the people of Vishnovet and they shunned him after that. Sirota became an outcast in the village. He moved to a hut separate from the others and made no attempt to enter the inner circle. He convinced himself that he didn't care about any of them. He decided he would leave the village one day, when the time was right. Then the bear came.

One winter day a starving bear roared in the streets of our village in search of food. The villagers ran screaming from the beast but the rabbi's young daughter fell in the bear's path. Her father was in temple and no one else stopped to help the girl. I watched from my hut as the hungry bear approached the girl on his four legs. When he was close to her he opened his enormous mouth, bared his teeth, and roared. The girl fainted and fell to the ground. The bear reared up on its hind legs and stood like a giant over his prey. He roared again and no one dared challenge him. The villagers were all hiding and praying in their flimsy shelters. I had no use for prayer and I was angered and ashamed by the common cowardice of Vishnovet. What was there to fear? Pain was fleeting and death was final. I decided that death was preferable to a life lived in fear. While the others prayed, I prepared. I rushed to my bag of meager possessions and withdrew the Russian soldier's dagger I had found in the woods over a year ago after a Cossack raid. I had sharpened and polished the kinjal's blade every night since it came into my possession. I ran from my hut with my weapon. I approached the towering, five hundred pound animal from behind. I remember not being afraid. As the bear prepared to swipe at the unconscious girl with a huge paw, I leaped on his back and with all my strength plunged the blade into the bear's throat. I slashed, and slashed and slashed. I heard the beast roar in pain and I felt it thrash beneath me but I could see only red explosions in front of my eyes. I held on to the bear's neck and stabbed until I could no longer lift my arm. The red bursts were replaced by a sheet of darkness. When I could sense light again I opened my eyes and found myself sprawled on the bear's back on the ground. The beast was dead. I was alive. The little girl was awake and standing. She was staring at me with large brown eyes. She didn't seem to be afraid of me. Her father had finally appeared and she was clutching his hand tightly. Other villagers encircled me in silence. I was covered in the bear's blood but I had shed no blood of my own. No one in the crowd spoke to me and I had nothing to say to them. I gathered my strength and skinned the bear while the others watched me. I put the bear's bloody hide on my back for warmth and left his carcass for the villagers to butcher and eat. It was the only way I knew how to thank them for saving my life thirteen years ago. As I turned and walked toward the road that would take me to the wilderness, I heard only one villager cry for me. It was the rabbi's daughter. I remembered her words. "I don't want him to go," she cried. "Who will save us now?" Years later the girl I rescued by killing the bear would become my wife.

"That was my grandmother," I said, thinking of her loving smile and chocolate chip cookies. Then I recalled my grandfather's reference to a bear the night I defeated Gino "The Destroyer" Montoya in my last boxing match. *"You killed a bear, Eddie. Just like me."* Now, after all these years, I understood what he meant.

Tears filled my eyes as the old rabbi continued reading my grandfather's words.

I survived in the wilderness by hunting and eating small animals. I knew how to make a fire. I drank melted snow. I learned from people I met along the way that ships set sail for America from the port of Hamburg in a country called Germany. I was told that the streets of America were lined with gold. I decided I would go to America but I had no idea where it was or how I would get there. In an alley in the port of Hamburg I saw two boys attack a young man who lay helplessly on the ground. I felt compelled to help him. Holding the kinjal above my head I ran screaming at the attackers. I must have been a fearsome sight because the two bullies took one look at me and ran away. When I knelt next to the young man I could tell immediately he was dying. The sunken eyes, the pale skin, the yellow mess coming from his nose and his hacking cough told me that he had consumption. I had seen the same look on children in Vishnovet. They never survived. The boy's hands were shaking and the papers he was holding made a rustling sound. I saw a ship ticket and immigration papers in his grasp that I knew he would never live long enough to use. The look in his eyes told me he knew what I was thinking. He knew he was going to die slowly and painfully in that alley. He forced a weak smile to thank me for saving him from a meaningless beating and he held out the papers to me. I shook my head "no" but he shoved them into my hand anyway. Then the boy took the wrist of my other hand which still held the kinjal and pulled the blade to his throat. He pressed the sharp tip of the sword against his pasty skin and tried to impale himself. His eyes were pleading with me to take his papers and put him out of his misery. I took the papers. I was crying. He was crying. I put his papers aside and took off the bear skin I was wearing. I covered the boy from his feet to his neck in the heavy hide. He looked at me until I placed my free hand over his eyes. With great sadness but no remorse I pushed the blade swiftly into the young man's throat. Blood spurted from the wound and splattered on me and the bear skin. The boy gasped and was gone. I continued crying as I removed the bloody bear skin from the boy and took off his clothes. I put them on, replacing the rags that had been clinging to me for months. I wrapped the boy's naked body in the bear skin and carried him to the end of a deserted pier. I dropped him in the bay and thanked him for his sacrifice as he disappeared into the murky water. The next morning I boarded a ship bound for America wearing a dead man's clothes and carrying papers that identified me as Hans Perlmutter.

The old rabbi read to me about my grandfather's excruciating ocean voyage. He read about Elijah Fleischman, Victor Dragoff, and my grandfather's struggles in the new world. Somewhere among all the words I heard the truth about the two men who had attacked him and my grandmother.

I killed the two men not because they had taken my wife from me. I killed them because I didn't want them to have the chance to take a loved one from anyone else. I killed to stop more killing.

The ancient rabbi stopped reading and set down the papers. He asked a question of the younger rabbi.

"Rabbi Rudolfsky cannot understand how such an old man could kill two much younger, stronger men," he explained to me.

"Surprise and arrogance," I said, understanding everything but explaining nothing.

We were all exhausted. The old rabbi handed me my grandfather's belongings and I noticed he had tears in his eyes. I stood, thanked them and turned to leave when a question occurred to me. "How do you spell *Zee-rota* in English?"

"S-i-r-o-t-a," the younger rabbi spelled slowly for me.

"Oh, it begins with an *S*. I thought it was a *Z*," I said "Thank you."

I was out the door and into the street before I realized I had uncovered the mystery of my middle initial. The *S* was for "Sirota." I was the grandson of a legend from the Ukraine, who had saved an entire village with his fearlessness. To honor my grandfather I changed his headstone to read:

Hans "Sirota" Perlmutter
Legend of the Pale
Beloved Husband — Father —
Grandfather

When my father's headstone was displayed

for the first time it read:

Harry "Sirota" Perlmutter
Loving Husband–Son–Father

Now that I knew my legacy I understood why I was never afraid.

A few days after my visit to the cemeteries I went to the North End and visited a few street corners to say good-bye to old friends. I saw Togo at Mike's Bakery, and he promised to see me when he came down to visit his brother-in-law, Steve. I exchanged noogies and hugs with Muscles, Doc, and Rats. I couldn't find Petey but I did come across Sal "The Momzer" and we hugged. I said good-bye to some kids playing basketball in the hot box.

When I returned to my apartment I found my landlord and the new tenants sizing up the space. "No problem renting this place, huh, Angelo." I patted the elderly owner on the shoulder.

"You kiddin', Eddie?" he said with an Italian accent. "These apartments are like gold now. Fifteen hundred a month."

I said hello to the nice yuppie couple who were taking my place, and I wished them luck. I did some final cleaning up while they measured things. I rechecked the bathroom one last time and looked in the mirror. I was fifty-nine years old. Everyone told me I looked ten years younger. Of course there was the matter of my ninety-year-old limp, but if you didn't see me moving in the winter, I suppose I could pass for a younger man. I was still lean at five foot six and 140 pounds. If you didn't focus on my twice-broken nose, I didn't look that bad. I had most of my hair, though it was flecked with gray. I thought I looked pretty good, considering how lousy I felt. I walked resolutely from the bathroom and said good-bye to my landlord and his new tenants. They were absorbed with inches and angles and waved good-bye without looking up from their work. I wasn't insulted. They were looking to the future. I was the past.

I carried some of my belongings down the stairs and packed them into the small, overloaded U-Haul I had rented and hooked up to the bumper of my 1997 Mini Cooper (*You don't need a big one to be happy* was their motto). The dull-gray Mini, with the dent on the front of the hood, had ninety thousand miles on it, but that was nothing for the new, twin-point injection engine Cooper started making in '97. The car was small, unimpressive to look at, and didn't perform well in the snowy north. But the

Mini was sturdy and dependable just like me, and just like me, it was going to be out of place in Boca.

CHAPTER 8

THE AREA CODE

The tribe of Tequesta Indians settled Boca Raton, Florida, one thousand years ago. The tribe of Israeli Jews settled in Boca Raton, Florida, 758 years later. Tequesta artifacts can be found in the Boca Raton Historical Society. Jewish artifacts can be found everywhere.

Within two weeks of moving to Boca Raton I knew the layout of the city. Interstate 95 ran north and south. There were several exits for Boca Raton off I-95 and these roads went east and west. To the east was the ocean. To the west was a kingdom of gated communities, which were common in South Florida. Aside from the self-contained communities, however, Boca was no different than many other cities. If you had money, life could be a bowl of cherries. If you didn't have money, life could be the pits. Some of the pits of Boca, however, looked like a bowl of cherries to me.

When I first arrived in the area I felt like a stranger in a strange land. I had no frame of reference for a place like Boca or the people who lived there. I wasn't prepared for all the different ways people spoke English. I knew the Boston accent was strange, but it felt like home to me. The harsh New York City accent made me homesick. The Chicago twang sounded like the Buffalo twang to me. Everyone with a Southern accent sounded like a televangelist. The Philly accent, like the city itself, didn't affect me one way or the other. I was able to understand the accents after a while, but understanding the people was harder.

After thirty-plus years as a policeman I thought I knew a little about a lot of people, and I did. But I knew nothing about retired people, and now I was surrounded by them. Power walkers were on the streets of Boca Heights at four-thirty in the morning or burning calories in the health club at six a.m. when it opened. By seven, "thick people" joined "stick people," and all shapes, sizes, and ages exercised at their own pace. The twenty-two tennis courts and two golf courses were filled by eight in the morning. I couldn't help wonder why retired people started their activities so early in the morning. Where were they going afterward?

A free breakfast was served directly outside the health club. To get to the fitness center in the morning members had to run a gauntlet of bagels, cream cheese, muffins, juice, and coffee. The breakfast had a loyal following that ate for free and complained about the food. They complained about a lot of things.

As an ex-cop I looked for crime everywhere. I spied Mrs. Sylvia Goldman, a slightly built seventy-nine-year-old lady, sneak four bagels into her handbag every morning along with a slew of Sweet'N Low packets. I didn't think it was a crime to steal free things, so I didn't bust her. When she stole the bagel toaster, however, I was compelled to do something. I followed her to her car in the parking lot of the health club and had a private conversation with her. I quickly realized that Mrs. Goldman had mental problems, probably Alzheimer's. She was carrying the toaster in her arms under a stolen health club towel, and she handed both items to me without protest. We made a quiet, out-of-court settlement standing by her car. Shortly after the incident, I bought Mrs. Goldman a toaster and we became friends. But that's another story.

A sumptuous buffet lunch was offered after the morning's exercise. After lunch, many of the men played cards and some napped. Many women played cards or mahjong; other women shopped. But after three o'clock the focus changed.

"Where are you eating tonight?"

"Home."

"You're kidding."

"Of course I'm kidding."

"So where are you going?"

"We're going to Renzo's."

"Fabulous. I love the chicken scarpariello there. Who's going?"

"The Rittels, the Antels, the Kurlanders, the Sabuls, the Ginsbergs, the Stones, the Shapiros, the Pinskys, the Cramers, the Adlers, the Bakers, and the Crisciones. We weren't in the mood for a lot of people. Besides, the Coopers, the Samuels, the Potashes, Curleys, and Greeburgs said no."

"I understand."

"And where are you going?"

"P. F. Changs."

"You'll never get in unless you eat at five o'clock."

"I'm sending Irving there at six to put our name in. We'll get there at seven-thirty. There should be an hour wait by then."

"Fabulous. Does Irving mind waiting all that time?"

"No. He enjoys it. He drinks at the bar

and watches the game."

"What game?"

"Any game."

"Excellent. And who are you going with?"

"The Cohens, the Friedens, the Finkelsteins, the Krozys, the Woolfs, the Levines, the Schoenbergers, the Mandells, the Grumets, the Freedlands, the Ablows, the Livingstons, the Tuckers, the Stillmans, the Kesslers, the Patricks, and the Starrs. The Bettingers and Cantors might join us with the Bines and Bergers."

"Fabulous. Do any of the men keep Irving company while he waits at the bar?

"Irving doesn't like any of the men."

"Does he like the wives?"

"No. He likes the wives less than the men."

"Then why does he go?"

"What else does he have to do? He likes to drink at the bar and look at the young waitresses."

"Aren't you worried he'll go after one of those young ones?"

"He doesn't like young girls, either."

"He doesn't? What does he like?"

"Irving doesn't like anything. Besides what's he going to do with a young waitress besides order cheesecake?"

I was having lunch at the tennis club with Togo's brother-in-law, Steve, on a beautiful

February afternoon at the end of my second week on the job. Steve had a cynical way of looking at things and a comical way of expressing himself.

"So what do you think of Camp Boca?" he asked.

"I guess this place is like summer camp for adults."

"Yeah, except it's in the winter. It's too hot here in the summer to do anything besides change your underwear three times a day."

"Some members told me they like it better here in the summer."

"Whoever told you that was pulling your pecker, Detective Perlmutter."

The name's Johnson, Mr. Johnson spoke up.

"There's nothing to like down here in the summer," Steve continued, "unless you're a fuckin' gecko. Wait till you get into your car on a July afternoon."

"Hot, huh?"

"Your balls will melt on the leather seats."

"And what if you're a woman?"

"Think of sitting on a soldering iron."

I winced.

"I'll bet the same schmucks who told you they like it better in the summer also told you there were no waiting lines at the good restaurants or the movies that time of year, and you can get in anywhere. Right?"

"How did you know?"

"Because it's a fuckin' recording."

"Well, is it true about the restaurants and movies?"

"Of course it's true."

"So they're telling it like it is."

"Yeah, but they're not telling you *why* it is, Dick Tracy."

"Okay, why is it?"

"You can get into any place in Boca in the summer because if there was a line out-side . . . people would drop dead from the heat. In fact, that's exactly what happened two summers ago."

"You're kidding."

"No, I'm not. A new deli opened on Glades and they had a grand opening with a big special on opening day. People here can't resist specials, even if it's for a casket. So the line at the deli was out the door and around the building. Some eighty-seven-year-old guy died of heatstroke waiting for a good deal on a corned beef sandwich."

"I don't believe you."

"Okay. Maybe it wasn't corned beef. But a guy did drop dead in line."

"That's terrible."

"It gets worse. His wife left him lying in

116

the sun while she had the special. They gave the guy an open casket funeral because he had such a good tan."

"Enough already. I get your point."

"Okay," he relented. "Let's talk about camp again. You ever go to summer camp?"

"No."

"Well I did, and all camps, including Camp Boca, have one thing in common."

"What's that?"

"Schedules! Everything is on a schedule except your bowels. Breakfast at seven, softball at eight, tetherball at ten, general swim at eleven, lunch at twelve, then a rest period from one to two, which is when most adolescent boys jerk off."

"I assume you're speaking from experience."

"Of course. I became ambidextrous at summer camp. Anyway, like I said, summer camp is all about having scheduled fun, and so is Camp Boca. But there are some notable differences."

"Like what?"

"First of all, speaking from personal experience again, the boys at Camp Boca don't jerk off as much during rest period as the boys at regular summer camp."

"I'd agree with that," I said, "based on my own personal experience."

Steve nodded.

"Another big difference is that when regular summer camp is over, the campers go back home to the real world and prepare for their futures. Camp Boca, on the other hand, is in session until the camper dies. At Camp Boca, campers only plan for the immediate future."

"Fun to the end. That doesn't sound bad."

"It's not bad. It's great. Look at this place. It's absolutely great and gorgeous. Everyone's laughing, running, jumping, riding, swinging, hitting, missing, schmoozing, bullshitting, complaining, ball busting. They're doing everything here except fucking, and no one seems to care about that anyway. There's only one problem."

"What's that?"

"The campers don't have to think anymore so everyone's brain slowly turns to puppy shit."

"I think you're exaggerating. I've met a lot of smart, successful people here."

"You're a hundred percent correct. There are a lot of very smart, very successful people here. Tons of them. They're great. You could write a book about them. But these former high-powered lawyers, doctors, and businessmen aren't mentally stimulated anymore. You can't just turn an active mind off for a long time and expect it to run on all twelve cylinders like a Boca Volkswagen."

"What's a Boca Volkswagen?"

"A Bentley Continental GT."

"I didn't know that," I laughed.

"If you didn't know that," Steve remarked, "I suppose you don't know about Boca midnight, either."

"No," I admitted. "What's Boca midnight?"

"Ten p.m.," he explained.

I laughed again.

"When I first got here," Steve went on, "I had trouble remembering everyone's name."

"Yeah, I'm having that trouble, too," I agreed.

"So, I'm at a cocktail party one night," Steve continued, "and I see a guy I'm sure I've met before but I can't remember his name. I figured I'd try the honest approach so I shook his hand and said, 'I'm sorry but I forgot your name' and he said, 'So did I.'"

Steve and I both burst out laughing.

"Seriously. You know what really happens to high-powered people when their brains aren't kept active enough?"

"Tell me."

"They make unimportant things important."

"Like what?"

"Like golf, or tennis, or where they're going for dinner every night."

"Aren't you being a little hard on these people?"

"Not really. I love most of them but they're pretty hard on me, too," Steve said. "These people nag the shit out of me. Do you know how many times a season I'm asked why I work so hard and don't play more golf? It's unbelievable. They make me feel like I broke a covenant."

"What covenant?"

"Hell, I don't know. How about 'Thou shall not find joy in thy work while we're fuckin' around on a golf course'?"

"Is that from the New or Old Testament?"

"The Koran," he decided. "But seriously, I don't work hard. A guy who digs ditches works hard. I go to a nice, air-conditioned office where I get to match wits with some of the best business minds in the world. It's fantastic. I love it. I'm good at it. I don't need anyone telling me how to turn my shoulders, move my hips, or stay behind the ball."

"I don't understand golf terms."

"Neither do I. I'm just making a point. I'm happy with what I'm doing, and I don't need golf. I don't need tennis. I have other

120

interests."

"That's easy to understand."

"Yeah? Well try explaining this to some big-swinging-dick former brain surgeon or CEO who's retired. He's traded his prestige and Armani suits for shorts, a golf shirt, and a baseball hat. Then take these former world beaters, cover them in sunblock until they look like Bozo the fuckin' Clown, and convince them that their new mission in life is to sink a two-foot putt to win a five-dollar Nassau."

"What's a five-dollar Nassau?"

"A five-dollar Nassau is a golf bet. It's nothing really. But it's everything if you have nothing better to do. Understand?"

"No."

"Just remember this," Steve advised. "A person can never be happy having someone else's fun."

"That's good. Did you think that up yourself?"

"I read it in a self-help book."

"Did it help?"

"No."

"What does your wife think of your philosophy?"

"Barbara thinks I work too hard and should play more golf. Speaking of golf, how's the job?"

"It's okay. I'm learning the ropes and meeting the members."

"What do you think of the members?"

"I have a lot to learn about these people. Some are real nice, some are not so nice, and some I just don't understand."

"Join the club."

"I can't afford to join the club."

A foursome of women passed our table and Steve waved casually. They all called him by name. I nodded, but Steve didn't introduce me. Mr. Johnson stirred and stretched for the first time in a while.

When they were gone I asked Steve, "Who was the one in the white shorts?"

"You have good taste. That's Alicia Fine."

"Oh that's right." I was having difficulty remembering all the names. "She's very nice."

"Nice tits, too."

Great tits, Mr. Johnson agreed. I crossed my legs and throttled him.

"I mean she has a nice way about her."

"Her husband didn't think so. He left her for a younger version two years ago."

"You're kidding."

"It happens. But you're right. She is very nice."

Mr. Johnson and I were enthralled watching Alicia Fine walk away. It was a pleasure for both of us.

"Oh, by the way," Steve interrupted us, "there is one thing that bothers me more than compulsive golfers."

"What could that be?" I asked.

"Country-club politics," he said without hesitation.

"I don't know much about country-club politics," I said.

"The trouble with country-club politics is that ninety-nine percent of the issues are inane, and ninety-nine percent of the people are totally incapable of agreeing on anything anyway. And last year the politics here got way out of hand, as I'm sure you heard."

"No. What happened last year?"

"No one told you about the murder at Boca Heights?"

"Oh, cut the shit, Steve."

"I'm serious."

"You expect me to believe someone was murdered at Boca Heights over country-club politics?"

Steve raised his right hand. "Honest to God."

"Bullshit."

"No, really. I can't believe no one told you. A guy named Robert Goldenblatt was murdered last year over country-club politics. He was found in his garage with a

Bazooka four iron imbedded in his fore-head."

I laughed out loud and pushed Steve on the shoulder playfully.

"C'mon, Steve, cut the crap. You're not serious."

"Oh yes I am." He looked at his watch. "Hey, I gotta go."

"Wait, you have to tell me what happened."

Steve was up and moving. "No time. But you can ask anyone here. Everyone knows the story. It was front-page news for a long time," he said as he walked away.

"Wait. You gotta tell me! Who killed Robert Goldenblatt?" I called after him.

"We'd all like to know that," said a man sitting at the table next to me.

CHAPTER 9

BOCA BABES AND USETABES
(YOU-STAH-BEES)

I forgot about the Goldenblatt murder and focused on learning the names and nuances of the Two Course members. I had no trouble remembering Mrs. Alicia Fine. She made frequent appearances in my daydreams, and one night she became a headliner. Mr. Johnson and I enjoyed the performance very much. I understood that Alicia Fine and I were from different worlds, and I had no expectation of ever actually being with her. The dreams were fun though, and I was grateful that I could still dream like that at my age.

The membership at Boca Heights was diverse but they had certain things in common. When the members were young they were all wannabes. Now that they were older they were all usetabes.

"I usetabe a heart surgeon, Eddie," said an octogenarian.

"That's awesome, Dr. Goober. Hey, let

me get that golf bag for you."

"Yeah, open heart surgery."

"Wow. You driving or riding, Doc?"

"Driving. Angioplasty was my specialty."

"Balloons, right?"

"I guess that sums it up."

"Sounds exciting."

"It was. Years ago I held life and death in my hands. Can you imagine that feeling, Eddie?"

"As a matter of fact I can, Dr. Goober."

"No, you can't. You're a bag boy."

"Actually, I'm the head of security here, Dr. Goober."

"Is my golf bag secure?"

"Looks that way to me," I said, rattling the bag for him to make sure.

"Good. So what does a security officer know about the power of life and death?"

"I usetabe a police detective, Dr. Goober. When I had my gun aimed at a suspect, I had the same power you did with your scalpel."

"I didn't know you usetabe a police detective."

"Everyone usetabe something before they got here, Dr. Goober."

"Yes, that's true," the former heart surgeon said reflectively. "Everyone usetabe something." He paused a moment. "I usetabe a heart surgeon, you know."

"I know, Dr. Goober. Well, hit 'em straight."

"It would be easier for me to open a chest cavity." He drove away, deep in thought.

"Where you from, Mr. Shankman?"

"Philly. I usetabe a lawyer."

"Do you know Dr. Shapiro? He's from Philly."

"Know him? I sued him."

"I usetabe in business back in Chicago," short, dapper Louie Lipshitz told me. His pure-white hair was slicked back and always in place. His golf clothes were coordinated, and his tan was perfect. He wore a big gold Jewish star around his neck.

"What kind of business, Mr. Lipshitz?"

"All kinds of business."

"Anything special?"

"You writin' a fuckin' book, Eddie?"

"No. Just curious."

"Don't be."

"No problem, Mr. Lipshitz."

Another man said, "I usetabe a dentist."

"Painless?"

"Not really. I hated every minute of it."

"I usetabe a proctologist. No stupid comments, please."

"Hey, what do you think I am? An asshole?"

127

And another man said, "I usetabe in ladies underwear."

"I'm sure you still are, Mr. Bellows."

"Yeah, but don't tell my wife, Eddie."

"You told me you were single."

Dr. Sloan said, "I usetabe an anesthesiologist."

"I thought so," I said, stifling a yawn.

And then there was an entirely different kind of usetabe.

"I usetabe married, but my sixty-five-year-old husband left me for his forty-year-old Cuban manicurist."

"I'm sorry about that, Mrs. Weintraub. Have a good round."

"He doesn't even speak Spanish, the idiot."

"You're on the tee, Mrs. Weintraub."

"Well, fuck him."

I'm sure she did, Mr. Johnson said to me.

Twenty minutes later a man told me, "I usetabe married but I left my wife for a hot, Cuban manicurist about half my age."

"Your nails look great, Mr. Weintraub."

I found most of the members likeable and interesting although some were more likeable and interesting than others. I had never been exposed to such a heavy concentration of highly successful people before and it took some getting used to for me. I did my best to get along with everyone and to avoid the difficult people I had come to refer to as the Killer B's: Boca Bullies and Boca Babes.

Boca Bullies were men who simply hadn't mellowed with age. They maintained an aggressive attitude and turned every situation into a confrontation. They were *gimme* guys:

"Gimme a cup of coffee."

"Gimme this."

"Gimme that."

Never *"May I have"* or *"Please."* Just *gimme*.

Whether the men were pleasant or not there was something about all of them I found unsettling. These former captains of industry and highly respected professionals appeared to have lost their individuality in this homogenized environment. They blended together in a leisure universe of white hair and tightly scheduled fun. They reminded me of thoroughbred race horses that had been put out to pasture as a reward for a winning career. They could still remember the thrill of the race, but their racing days were over. I don't know why this bothered me. It didn't seem to bother them. Most of the men were friendly and active and shared a camaraderie that reminded me of the tight-knit cliques in the North End. The big difference was that the North End groups developed their sameness growing up, while the Boca Harbor groups developed their sameness by growing old.

Boca Babes were a mystery to me. There were a lot of very nice, normal women in Boca Heights who were extremely likeable. But the local phenomenon known as the Boca Babe was totally foreign to me. The Boca Babe was an unmistakable combination of a bad attitude, chic clothing, beauty-parlor magic, and surgical surprises. Under the professionally applied makeup and carefully selected designer clothes were good nose jobs, bad nose jobs, good boob jobs, bad boob jobs, good lip jobs, bad lip jobs, and face-lifts that stretched the imagination.

Don't get me wrong. I have nothing against cosmetic surgery and Mr. Johnson doesn't care if a woman's breasts are real or not. He's a penis. But even Mr. Johnson found Boca Babes scary. It wasn't just the obvious surgery, either. Many of the women who had cosmetic enhancements were super ladies and if these repairs made them happy I thought that was great. But a true Boca Babe had the same effect on Mr. Johnson as a cold shower. Boca Babes didn't act as if they appreciated their pampered lifestyle. They acted as if they were entitled to the pampering. I don't know if this attitude was caused by overindulgent parents in childhood or by indifferent husbands later in life. There were no serious demands on the time of these Boca Babes, so they were free to indulge and entertain themselves. Less than perfect was not in their plans for the day.

For the most part, there was a pleasant working relationship between the male and female gophers at Boca Heights and the male and female golfers. There was little relationship or appreciation, however, between the staff and the Killer B's. If something wasn't perfect, someone had to pay. One day it was my turn.

Mike Scarfetti called me into his office.

"Did you read the rule book?" he asked me.

"Cover to cover, boss."

"You know what a ranger is supposed to do?"

I had studied the responsibilities of a ranger and committed the basic stuff to memory. "The ranger has the full authority to enforce all the rules, including the makeup of each group, the speed of play, the conduct of play, and the care of the golf course."

"Okay, great," Mikey said. "You're a ranger."

"Is there a swearing-in ceremony?"

"No, but I need a ranger on the course right now at the seventh hole, and there's a good chance you'll get sworn *at.* Consider that your ceremony."

"Will I need body armor?"

"No, but a thick skin would help."

"I have that on already. What's the problem out there?"

"There's a group on the seventh holding up the pace of play something awful. It's my fault. I put Mrs. Fine and Mrs. Freidman out there in the finals of a women's tournament against each other, and they're like oil and water. To make matters worse, I filled out their foursome with two friends of Mrs. Feinberg, Mrs. Frost and Mrs. First. You know them?"

I nodded. Three Boca Babes. Three face-lifts, two nose jobs, one failed tummy tuck, one successful stomach stapling, and enough dental work to fill a book entitled *The Bridges of Palm Beach County.*

"The three of them are probably ganging up on poor Mrs. Fine," Mike added.

I don't want anyone ganging up on Mrs. Fine except me, Mr. Johnson said.

"Hey, boss, with all due respect, why don't you go out there and deal with these ladies?"

"Two reasons," Mike said. "One, I'm a

coward and you're not. Two, this is a job for a ranger and everyone else is busy."

"I'll bet everyone else is hiding."

"Right."

There were no white steeds available, so I drove to Mrs. Fine's rescue in a golf cart marked "Ranger." It was a beautiful February day. The sun was shining, and the temperature was a pleasant seventy-eight degrees. My hands and knees were at peace with the universe. The grass was a brilliant green, the water was dark blue, and the sand in the traps was a glistening white. Everything looked bright and cheery, except for the golfers. Every fairway was occupied by a miserable, grumpy group of frustrated players waiting impatiently to hit their next shot. Some of the golfers shouted at me, but I just kept moving.

When I reached the seventh tee, I saw the problem. The foursome in front of the F troop was already leaving the eighth green, and the F troop hadn't even hit their drives off the seventh tee. They were either oblivious to the chaos they had created behind them or they just didn't care. Mrs. Frost was on her cell phone, which by itself was a violation of the rules. I saw Mrs. Mildred Feinberg shaking a finger at and lecturing a subdued Alicia Fine. Mrs. Feinberg stopped her lecture when she saw me approaching. She teed up her ball, took a practice swing, and prepared to hit the ball. My cart screeched to a stop, and Mrs. Feinberg stepped away from her ball to glare at me. Anne First glared at me. Michelle Frost glared at me and whispered into her cell phone, "I'll call you back." Mrs. Alicia Fine glanced at me. She seemed upset.

"Yessss?" Mrs. Feinberg said theatrically. I noticed her outfit was an elegant blend of bright pastels. Perfect.

She's a scary one, Mr. Johnson said. *Don't get me anywhere close to her. Even I have a limit.*

No you don't but you got nothing to worry about, I assured my friend.

"Sorry for interrupting you, Mrs. Feinberg, but I have to ask you to please pick up your pace of play. Your foursome is holding up the course."

"They're playing an important match," Mrs. First told me as if I should have known.

"I understand, but you're still going to have to play faster," I told her.

Mrs. Feinberg left the tee area and sauntered toward me. "You know why we're playing so slow?" she asked me. "It's because of her." She pointed at Alicia Fine.

"She doesn't know the rules, and she doesn't know how to count."

"That's not true," Alicia Fine protested. "You're challenging everything I do out here. You've called the clubhouse three times already for rulings. It's ridiculous."

"We're playing for a championship," Mrs. Feinberg reminded everyone.

"People told me you would try to distract me during the match, and they were right." Mrs. Fine was livid.

"I'm not distracting you. You're distracting me."

I raised my voice. "LADIES! Either pick up the pace of play or let the next group play through."

"Who are you?" Mrs. Feinberg challenged me.

"I'm the ranger."

"I know that. But who are you? What's your name?"

I pointed to my name tag. She read it carefully. "Well, Eddie Perlmutter, no one is playing through us. This is a championship match."

"You're backing up the whole course."

"I told you it's because of her," she said, pointing at Mrs. Fine with contempt. Mrs. Fine looked away and bit her lip. I thought she might cry, and I wanted to give her a big hug and promise everything was going to be all right. Mr. Johnson had other ideas, but I didn't give him any space. I noticed the other two women were nodding their heads in approval of what Mrs. Feinberg was saying about Mrs. Fine. I was watching a three-on-one gang bang. I hated mismatches, and I was fascinated by Mrs. Fine, so I decided to even things out. "Who's winning this match?" I asked.

"What difference does that make?" Mrs. Feinberg snapped.

"I'm winning," Mrs. Fine said. Her eyes were wet, and her lower lip was quivering. She was losing it completely, and I was getting angry.

"That's what I thought," I answered.

"What do you mean by that?" Mrs. Feinberg snapped again.

"It's usually the losers who complain the most," I snapped back.

"Who do you think you are?" Mrs. Feinberg's voice was louder. "You can't talk to me that way."

A foursome of men playing behind the F troop had finished playing the sixth hole and had arrived at the seventh tee. Their body language clearly showed how irate they were with the slow pace of play.

"What's going on here?" one of them

asked. They all looked exasperated.

"We're playing a match. Mind your own business," Mildred Feinberg scolded them as if they were annoying children.

A big red spot exploded in front of my eyes. DANGER ZONE! Oh, shit, this was going to be close. I got out of my cart and walked to the foursome on the men's tee. I rubbed my eyes trying to get rid of the dangerous red flashes dancing in front of my eyes. The women watched me curiously. Mrs. Feinberg returned to the tee area and prepared to hit her ball.

"This slow play is ridiculous," one of the men said to me.

"Yes, it is ridiculous. I'm going to let you play through."

The four men looked at me with surprise. "You're kidding," one of them said.

At this point Mrs. Feinberg swung at her ball and popped it straight up in the air. It traveled only a few yards forward and rolled down a hill to the water's edge. She threw her club to the ground. "I'm taking another shot," she said like a seven-year-old. "You were talking." She pointed at me. She retrieved her errant ball, ran back to the tee, and hit again. This time she hit the ball long and straight down the fairway. She turned to face the men with a triumphant smile on her face. By then I was at the ladies' tee area. Mrs. Frost was getting ready to hit. I stepped in her way.

"I'm letting these men play through. Please leave the tee area."

"You can't do that," Mrs. Frost insisted, stepping toward me.

"Yes I can, Mrs. Frost." I took my rule book out of my back pocket and offered it to her. "As a golf course ranger I have that authority."

She ignored the rule book and glared at me defiantly. When I glared back through the haze of red spots I saw her face turn pale. It must have been one hell of a glare. "And speaking of rules, Mrs. Feinberg, I'm going to see to it that you're disqualified from this tournament for illegally moving your ball just now and teeing it up a second time."

"I was taking a second tee shot because you distracted me," she protested.

"There are no second shots in golf, Mrs. Feinberg."

"You can't disqualify me. You'll ruin this whole tournament."

"You've already ruined this tournament for me," Mrs. Fine interrupted. "You're a bitch, and I quit." Without another word, Alicia Fine drove away, leaving her cart mate, Mrs. First, without a ride.

"Well, I guess I win the championship by default," Mrs. Feinberg declared, unfazed by the turn of events.

"Not if I have anything to say about it you won't," I told her.

"Why you little pissant," she shouted after me, officially swearing me in as a ranger. "Give a little man a little authority and he thinks he's a big man. I'll see to it that you don't work here another day."

"I'll see to that myself," I said to her and drove away. I called into the clubhouse on my two-way radio. Mikey answered.

"Hey, Eddie, what's going on out there? Mrs. Fine just came in crying and ran to the ladies' room. What the hell did you do?"

"I did my job, Mike. And Mrs. Feinberg should be disqualified for cheating. Mrs. Fine should be declared the winner, or you should cancel the whole damn tournament." I put down the radio then picked it up again. "Mike?" I called him again.

"I was just calling you," he told me. "What's up?"

"I quit." I disconnected again. I felt good. I didn't belong in this place.

I returned to the golf-cart area where I parked the ranger's cart. I left my two-way radio on the seat and headed for the parking lot.

"Hey, Eddie," Mike called my name from the pro-shop door. "Get in here. We got a problem."

I saw the three F troop Boca Babes lurking behind him. Mrs. Feinberg looked like a vulture. Obviously they had gone directly to the clubhouse from the eighth tee box. "We haven't got a problem," I called to him. "You've got a problem."

"Hey, Eddie," he shouted, "us North End guys have to stick together."

"Not this far south," I said.

"I took a chance on you, Eddie," he reminded me. "You owe me."

"You're right," I said. "I'll paint your house."

"Come back here, please."

"I'm too dangerous right now," I told him honestly. "I need some time to cool off. Make an excuse for me and I'll get back to you."

"Hey, you were the toughest cop in Boston," Mike reminded me. "You can handle a little thing like this."

"Nothing I ever did before prepared me for this place," I said.

I drove west on Yamato, passing the Morikami Museum on my way to State Road 7 (aka 441). I wondered what Sakai and Morikami would think of their plantations now. My cell phone rang, but I didn't answer. I drove north on 441 for about twenty minutes before I realized I didn't know where I was or where I was going. I was operating a motor vehicle under the influence of red spots. I decided to stop the car before I found myself in southern Georgia.

I pulled to the side of the road and turned off the engine. I rubbed my eyes. The red spots were fading, but my hands were shaking. I got out of the car and walked in no particular direction. I put my hands on my knees, bent over, and took a few deep breaths. When I straightened up I noticed small, flimsy-looking shacks across the highway on the southbound side. I noticed a few dark-skinned people walking in and out of the dilapidated structures, which had incongruous television antennas on their roofs. Apparently people lived in these shanties, which could not have complied with any health or zoning laws. My guess was that these were illegal immigrants working for minimum wage at one of the various commercial enterprises located on this section of 441. There were construction companies, tree farms, and other agricultural enterprises on either side of what was also called State Road 7. Apparently neither the town nor the state cared about the living conditions of these people. I couldn't help but compare these squalid shacks to the palaces of Boca's kings and queens only a few miles east of the highway. Boca's history was probably filled with an endless supply of "shack people" who had helped build the palaces and the gated walls that surrounded them. The walls were built to keep out the people who built them.

I saw a small brown-skinned girl of about five or six emerge from one of the shacks, followed by a woman who appeared to be her mother. They were both laughing. The mother took the little girl in her arms, lifted her off the ground, spun her around, and kissed the child's face repeatedly. The girl giggled helplessly and feigned displeasure with her mother's affection, but they were both obviously delighted with their game. I envied them. They were happy living in squalor with nothing to save them from complete hopelessness except their love for each other.

I thought of Mildred Feinberg. She was a person who had everything, but who could only be happy when someone else was unhappy. She seemed to be a woman who would never be content with who she was or what she had. There are some people whom nothing can make happy and then there are some people who are happy with nothing.

The little girl and her mother noticed me watching them. They stopped playing and looked at me curiously. I waved to them. The little girl waved back at me as the cars whizzed by on 441. The mother hugged the girl tighter, and her eyes told me to leave them alone.

When I returned to the car, my cell phone was ringing again. The caller ID told me it was Mikey Tees. I also saw that I had a voice message, which I figured was from him, too. I didn't want to talk to him, but out of respect I flipped open the phone and said hello.

"Eddie, where are you?"

"I'm on 441 with the shack people."

"Shaquille O'Neal?" He was serious.

I laughed. "No. I'm talking about people living in shacks by the side of the road on 441."

"There are shacks on 441 in Boca?"

"I'm not sure where I am, to tell you the truth."

"Well, what are you doing there?"

"I'm applying for a job as a golf course ranger."

"Very funny. What the hell happened on the course today?"

"The F troop must have told you what happened."

"Yeah, according to three of them you physically and verbally intimidated them."

"I didn't touch anyone."

"They didn't say you touched them. Mrs. Frost said you stared at her like you wanted to kill her."

"Mrs. Frost is wrong. I stared at her like I intended to kill her."

"They're filing a grievance against you."

"To who?"

"The grievance committee."

"There's a complaint committee at Boca Heights?"

"Yes," Mike said. "That's the way it works around here."

"Can I file a grievance against having a grievance committee?"

"I'm sure you could," Mike said.

"How?"

"Put it in writing and submit it to the grievance committee." He laughed. "And, by the way, you have to appear before the committee next week to defend yourself against their grievance."

"I'm not appearing before any committee."

"Then they'll fire you."

"They can't fire me. I already quit."

"I know." Mikey was exasperated. "I wish you hadn't. Mrs. Fine said you did nothing wrong."

"Mrs. Fine is a nice woman," I said.

Mrs. Fine is a fox! said Mr. Johnson.

"Will you appear before the grievance committee or not?"

"I'm not grieving."

"You might be able to help Mrs. Fine. I'm sure she'd appreciate it if you did."

We'll be there. Mr. Johnson made the decision for me. He did that from time to time.

CHAPTER 10

BOCA CRIMES

I drove from State Road 7 to the Regency Shopping Center on Powerline Road. When I walked into the Publix supermarket I was still ruminating about the "haves and have-nots" in the area. I had a throbbing headache. I was hungry. I needed a nap. The supermarket was crowded, and the lines at the registers were long. After waiting patiently for fifteen minutes in line, it was my turn. I started unloading my groceries on the counter when a short, white-haired old lady darted in front of me and started placing her items on the counter.

"Excuse me, but I'm waiting here," I said politely.

The woman looked at me over bifocals. "So wait," she said, as if it was logical. This drew a few laughs from people behind me in line, but the woman didn't acknowledge the attention. She just unloaded her cart casually. The teenage boy at the register,

146

dressed in Goth black under his mandatory green Publix vest, smirked at me.

Bing! One red spot. *Stay calm,* I said to myself, knowing that mayhem was only a red spot away. I studied the old woman in front me. Why was she in such a hurry? How old was she? I guessed midseventies.

"Stop staring at me," she said, glaring.

"I'm not staring at you."

"Yes you are," she snapped. I noticed that there weren't any wrinkles around her eyes. I glanced at her hands holding a hundred-dollar bill toward the Goth. They didn't look like an old woman's hands. *Alarm. Distraction Action!* I watched as the cashier took the woman's money. He placed the hundred in the cash drawer on top of other hundreds.

I'll be damned, I said to myself.

The cashier gave the woman forty dollars in change, which she put in her pocketbook. She gave me a "get over it" look and walked across the aisle to the customer service counter. I watched her. She cut in front of two people in the customer service line, creating a minor disturbance. She cashed a check, producing two forms of identification while arguing with the two people she had cut off.

"I'll be damned," I said, out loud this time

When the cashier gave me my change, I pointed to the hundred-dollar bill the woman had just given him.

"I want that hundred," I told him. I took two fifties from my wallet and held them out to him.

He looked exasperated.

"Next, please," he said.

Bing! Bing! Two red spots.

"What didn't you understand?" I was losing my temper. "I told you I want that hundred-dollar bill for my two fifties."

"I heard you," he said. "Next."

Bing! Bing! Bing! Man overboard!

"If you don't give me that hundred, I'm gonna pull that ring right out of your nose and stick it in your ear."

"You don't scare me, you old geezer," the cashier said.

I had never been called a geezer. Under different circumstances I might have thought it was funny. But with this imbecile, I was seeing red. I made a move with my right hand for his left nostril. He jumped backward and held both hands over his nose. "Are you crazy?" he shouted.

I reached across the counter and removed the hundred-dollar bill I wanted from the register. I placed my two fifties in the drawer.

"Hey, you can't do that," he protested.

"I can't do what? Give you two good fifties for this phony C-note?" I held the bill up to the light to confirm my suspicion.

"What do you mean, phony?"

I looked out the window. The old lady had just reached her car, which happened to be near mine. I still had time. I held the hundred toward the Goth. "Take your hands off your nose, Pinocchio, and look. I'm not going to hurt you."

He ventured closer, but his hands remained on his nose.

"Whose picture do you see in the watermark?" I pointed.

"Lincoln's!" he said proudly.

"Good boy," I said. "Now whose picture is in the middle?"

"Franklin's," he said with equal pride.

"Right again."

"So what's the problem?"

"The problem, Einstein, is that Lincoln's picture isn't supposed to be there."

"Well, it's there," the kid said indignantly.

"That's because it's counterfeit money, numb nuts."

I put the hundred in my shirt pocket and hefted my shopping bag. The old lady was in a Honda and backing out of her parking space. I threw my groceries in the back seat of my car and jumped behind the steering wheel. I followed the Honda east on Yamato and then south on Second Avenue. I watched the car turn left into the potholed parking lot of a defunct auto-parts store. I turned left into the adjacent driveway and parked as close to the lot line as possible. Through the foliage I could see the empty Honda and another empty old car parked behind the building. The woman must have gone inside to meet someone.

I shut off my car engine and waited. About a half hour later, the back door of the building opened. A blond woman, who looked to be about thirty-five or forty, exited the building. She was followed by two large, balding white males with colorfully flowered short-sleeved shirts worn casually outside their jeans. The woman walked briskly to the Honda. *So much for a white-haired, old lady,* I thought. The three of them exchanged comments and checked their watches. She got in the Honda and drove away. The men followed in the other car.

I decided to wait a while before approaching the building in the event they made a quick return. I got out of my car and surveyed the small commercial area. There was an air-conditioning repair shop, a vacuum-cleaner repair shop, and a body-piercing store. I also saw the initials *P.A.L.* hand-painted above a metal door. In Boston, P.A.L. was an acronym for the Police Athletic League. I walked across the lot, opened the metal door . . . and stepped into my past.

The gym embraced me like an old friend. I heard the familiar rhythm of the speed bags mixed with the ponderous pounding of the heavy bags. I heard the whir of a jump rope. I smelled sweat. Across the room I saw an elevated boxing ring. Two black teenagers were sparring while an older white man stood on the ring apron coaching them. To my left I saw a weight-lifting area where six teenage boys in workout clothes looked me over stoically. I walked toward the elevated boxing ring and read the signs along the way:

FATIGUE IS THE ENEMY!
TRAIN HARD OR GO HOME!
DO NOT SIT IN THIS AREA!
FIGHTERS ONLY!

There were flags hanging from the high ceiling advertising Title King boxing equipment and Contender gloves. Posters announced coming events and events that had come and gone.

"Can I help you?" a man in a gray sweat-suit asked. I looked up and saw that the two sparring partners were resting in their corners.

"No, not really. I just sort of wandered in," I explained. "I'm a retired cop from Boston, and when I saw the P.A.L. sign on the door, I had to check it out."

"Welcome." He smiled. "We've been getting a lot of visitors lately."

"Why's that?"

"One of our kids just won a national Silver Gloves championship. The local papers have been playing it up big."

"Hey, that's great."

"Take a break, kids," he called to the resting sparring partners, who left the ring immediately. The coach descended the wooden ringside steps carefully. He was over six feet tall with a middle-aged body.

"I'm Barry Anson," he told me, holding out his hand.

"Eddie Perlmutter." We shook hands.

"Are you with the Boca police?" I asked.

"Me? No. I'm just a volunteer trainer. I love the kids, and I love boxing."

"Were you a boxer?"

"I tried, but I wasn't much good," he said frankly. "I just didn't have what it takes. That's why I respect these kids. They're do-

152

ing something very few people can do."

"You got that right."

"Were you a boxer?"

"I was more of a brawler."

"Brawlers are tough to teach."

"I know," I laughed. "Do your brawlers ever beat your boxers?"

"Not often," Anson said. "Golden Gloves' rules favor boxers. Three unanswered punches, and there's a mandatory standing eight count. If there's a knockdown, there's a standing eight count. Big soft gloves and head gear do the rest. Not many knockouts, and only a handful of stops. Brawlers usually lose on points."

He looked at his watch. It was almost four in the afternoon. "I better do some coaching," he said. "Matt McGrady should be here any minute, and you can talk to him about the program. He's with the Boca police department and really runs the show."

The metal front door creaked open, and we both turned in that direction. A small entourage appeared, led by a slight Asian boy who looked like he was eleven or twelve years old. The boy was followed by a middle-aged Asian man, who I guessed was his father. A young man carrying a professional-looking camera and another young man

153

holding a pad of paper and a pen followed them. The last one in the procession was a small, cream-colored boy of about eight. The photographer had begun taking random pictures in rapid succession upon entering the gym. The *click, whir, click* of the camera seemed to slow the frenetic pace of the boxers. Barry Anson and I had our picture taken. *Click, whir, click.* The Asian boy was talking to the reporter, who was busy taking notes.

"What's that about?" I asked.

"Very interesting," Barry said. "The photographer and the reporter are from the *Boca News,* a small local paper. They're doing a story on that kid, Han Zhang. He's called 'The Pugilist Professor.' "

"Why?"

"Because he knows more about the subject of boxing than just about anyone I ever met," Barry explained. "I think he has a photographic memory."

"No kidding."

"He's amazing," Barry continued. "What he doesn't already know about boxing he researches on the Internet. We let him use our computer when he's here at the gym, so he's never far away from his information. He's a computer genius, too. He set up his own Web site."

"Impressive. Is that his father with him?"

"Yeah. Nice guy."

"And the little kid?"

"That's Tommy Bigelow. He idolizes Han and follows him around all the time."

"They seem far apart in age."

"They are. Han's twelve, and Tommy's only about eight, I think. I wouldn't call them friends. Han is more like a role model for Tommy."

"Isn't that Tommy's father's job?"

"No one really knows who Tommy's father is," Anson sighed. "His mother was single, and when Tommy was born, both the mother and the boyfriend were addicted to crack cocaine."

"Oh shit."

"That's the right word." Anson shook his head. "The State of Florida took Tommy away from his mother and put him in a foster home. A few years later she got him back after she went straight. Now he's back in foster care."

"Did his mother go back on drugs?"

"No, she never did," Anson told me. "She tried to straighten out, but she had this new live-in, shithead boyfriend who beat the two of them and molested the boy."

"What happened to the boyfriend?"

"Tommy's mother killed him. Shot him in

the head with his own gun while he was sleeping."

"What happened to her?"

"She killed herself with the same gun after she called the police and told them to rush over and get Tommy. The cops found the two bodies in one room and Tommy in his bed asleep. He's been in foster care ever since."

"How old was he when all this happened?"

"I think he was about four."

"How come no one has adopted him in all this time? He's a cute kid."

"Yeah, he's a cute kid," Barry agreed. "But he's half black and half white, which makes him hard to place. He can also be very difficult. People don't want to bring his attitude into their homes no matter how bad they want a kid."

"He probably doesn't trust anyone."

"Can you blame him? Although, I think he trusts me," Barry said. "And I know he trusts Matt McGrady. Those two should be father and son."

"Why aren't they?"

"Matt's a cop on a cop's salary and has two kids of his own to worry about."

I nodded my understanding.

Matt McGrady arrived just as the interview with the Pugilist Professor ended. Matt was a good-looking, friendly guy about the size of a light heavyweight, six feet one, 180 pounds. Barry introduced us, and we talked about boxing and police work for a while. The Pugilist Professor and his protégé were nearby, and Matt called them over.

"How was the interview, Han?" Matt asked.

"Same old thing," the Professor said.

"Were you with him, Tommy?"

"Yeah," was all Tommy said.

"Well, boys," Matt said, "I want you to meet Eddie Perlmutter. He's an ex-cop from Boston, and he used to fight in the Golden Gloves. You ever heard of him?"

"They couldn't have heard of me," I said. "That was over forty years ago."

"I know about fighters from eighty years ago," the Professor said.

"Yeah, so do I," Tommy said.

"Okay." I directed my question to Tommy. "Who was Barney Ross?"

The four of them looked surprised and exchanged glances.

"You told him!" Tommy said to Matt and Barry.

"Tommy, we didn't say a word," Matt promised.

"Something wrong?" I asked.

"Why did you ask about Barney Ross?" Tommy challenged me. "He's not famous anymore."

"It sounds to me like I picked a guy you don't know about."

The kid rolled his eyes. "Barney Ross was called 'The Pride of the Ghetto.' He was a champion in three different weight divisions," Tommy recited. "He fought Jimmy McClaren three times —"

"Okay, okay," I stopped him. "You know all about Barney Ross. So why did you make such a big deal out of it?"

The boy didn't smile. "Everyone here knows Barney Ross is my favorite fighter. Someone must have told you."

"No one told me anything, Tommy."

"I don't believe you." The kid was getting aggressive.

"Tommy," Matt interrupted. "Watch your manners."

"There are a million fighters, Officer Matt. Why did he pick Barney Ross?" The boy glared at me.

"Barney Ross was my grandfather's favorite fighter," I explained. "And he told me I fought like Ross."

"Were you any good?" Another challenge.

"Not as good as Barney Ross," I said honestly.

" 'Course not," the boy said. "Did you win any championships?"

"A couple."

"I can look you up on the Internet, you know." He was testing me.

"You probably won't find anything. It was a long time ago."

"If you're telling the truth, I'll find you."

"Tommy," Matt said sharply. "Stop it."

"It's okay," I said to Matt.

"No, it's not." Matt was annoyed. "Tommy, apologize to Mr. Perlmutter."

The boy stared at Matt, then at me. "Did you know Barney Ross was a war hero?" he asked unapologetically.

"Yes," I replied. "He won a Silver Star at Guadalcanal."

"Did you win a Silver Star?"

"I wasn't in the war."

"Did you win any awards for anything?"

"A few," I replied honestly.

"Like what?" the boy raised his voice.

"Tommy, I didn't say I was Barney Ross." I tried to calm him down. "My grandfather just compared me to him."

"You can't compare to Barney Ross," Tommy shouted. He turned abruptly and ran toward a small office at the front of the gym.

"Tommy! Get back here," Matt called

after him, but the boy darted into the office and slammed the door behind him.

"Barry." Matt turned to his assistant. "What's with him today?"

Barry shrugged. "He's probably on the computer checking Eddie out."

"Don't be too hard on him," I said. "He doesn't know me."

"That kid's a handful," Matt said. "You know much about kids?"

"I know I like them," I said. "I coached a youth boxing program in Boston for a while."

"You did?" Matt said. "Well how about doing some volunteer work for us? We could use you."

"Let me think about it," I hedged.

We walked around the gym and talked about the Boca P.A.L. program. It sounded a lot like the Boston version, with emphasis on creating a bond between the youth of the community and the police in their neighborhood. He gave me a brochure. "We do good work, Eddie," he said earnestly.

I nodded and glanced at my watch. Forty-five minutes had passed since I entered the gym. "I have to get going, Matt," I apologized. "I've got an important appointment nearby." I shook hands with Matt and Barry. I was about to leave when Tommy Bigelow returned on the run. Tommy's face was red, and he was wide-eyed. He held up a stack of printed paper.

"Is that all about me?" I laughed nervously.

He nodded his head. "Me and the Professor found it," he said proudly and started to read slowly, like an eight-year-old.

" 'Eddie Perlmutter, Massachusetts and New England Featherweight Golden Gloves Champion in 1959 and 1960, Massachusetts Middleweight Champ in 1961.' "

He looked up at me. "You moved up two weight divisions at sixteen years old. That's unbelievable."

" 'Held your own,' you said," Barry Anson chuckled and poked my shoulder.

"Get this, Matt," Tommy said. "He had twenty-two wins, no losses, with nineteen stops. That's incredible. Even Barney Ross lost four fights."

"Barney Ross fought over eighty times as a professional," I said. "I was an amateur. You can't compare me to him, like you said."

"I'm sorry I said that," he apologized.

"It's okay," I said.

"I'm impressed," Matt McGrady said, patting my back. "That's quite a record."

"I got more impressive stuff here," Tommy said.

"More impressive than an undefeated record?" Matt asked.

"Way more impressive, right, Professor?" Tommy said.

"Right," the Professor answered. He took some of the papers from Tommy. "Listen to this," the Professor began. "Eddie Perlmutter received two police department Medals of Honor, two medals for valor, three medals for merit, and a Mayor's Commendation."

"You were a super cop," Matt said.

"It was a long time ago," I said.

"Officer Matt, can I tell the other kids in the gym about Mr. Perlmutter?" Tommy asked.

"Call me Eddie," I told him.

"Sure," Matt said, and the kids were off and running.

"This is embarrassing," I said.

"You should be very proud of your record, Eddie."

"I can barely remember the things I did as a kid," I said, checking my watch. "Hey, I gotta go."

"Here's my card, Eddie. Call me anytime."

I thanked him and put his card in my shirt pocket. I started for the door.

"Hey Eddie," Tommy called after me. "Wait up. The guys want to meet you."

"I'll be back," I said, but I had no idea if I would keep that promise.

The lot next door was still empty when I returned to my car. The late afternoon light was dim, and soon it would be dark. I took a flashlight from my glove compartment and stumbled through the bushes into the adjacent lot. I couldn't find a door on the back wall. It didn't make sense. I had seen the three people come from the back of the building. I walked the perimeter looking for another point of entry. I found nothing until I got to the front. The lock on the front door facing Second Avenue was standard, and it was easy pickings for me. I opened the door slowly. No alarm. I stepped inside and locked the door behind me.

I was in a large open room with only a front counter separating me from what appeared to be the back wall of the building. A small bathroom was to my left, but the toilet and sink were gone. Trash and old mechanical parts littered the floor. I smelled mold in the damp air. I walked to the rear wall, turned my back to it, and surveyed the room. The building appeared smaller from the inside than it did from the outside. Why? I reviewed the facts.

A woman of about thirty-five or forty had disguised herself as a woman of seventy-five and passed a counterfeit hundred-dollar bill at a local supermarket. She got forty dollars change and a free bag of groceries. A small-time crime. The woman then went to the courtesy counter and cashed two checks. I assumed they were phony and made out for significant amounts. In each instance the old-young woman had created a disturbance preceding her transactions. The distraction action was performed to call attention to her but not to her transaction.

Conclusion: She was a professional.

More facts: The woman had then driven a few miles to this building, entered, and exited it from the rear where there was no exit or entrance I could find. I broke into the building from the front and was now standing at the rear. The building looked smaller from the inside than it looked from the outside.

Second conclusion: There was more to this place than met the eye. There was definitely a back entrance that I would eventually find, and there was another room behind the rear wall I was leaning on.

I thumped the painted wall with the flat of my hand. It didn't take me long to figure out that the entire back wall was made of flimsy plasterboard. I stood away from the wall and kicked it hard with the toe of my right sneaker. My foot passed through the plaster easily. I continued kicking holes in the wall until I was able to remove the entire panel of plasterboard. There was a cinderblock wall on the other side of the plasterboard facade.

Conclusion: The plasterboard wall had been built to create the optical illusion that the entire building was one big room from the front door to the rear wall. The cinderblock wall had been built for security reasons.

I removed my Swiss army knife from my pocket, extracted the largest, strongest blade, and poked at the cement that joined the blocks together. It had the consistency of dry oatmeal. God bless mold, water leaks, and unqualified workmen. I chipped away at the four edges of one block. In only a few minutes I was able to remove the entire block from the wall. I stuck my flashlight in the opening. I couldn't see very much. I had to remove more blocks. Forty-five minutes later I was looking through a large hole into a room that looked like a medical lab.

My flashlight illuminated stainless-steel cooking pots, plastic beakers, and pipe neck tubing. I saw a hot plate and other heating devices on a table in the middle of the room. I worked the light around the room and saw computers, printers, metal cans, and stacked boxes. I aimed the beam at the various boxes and read the stenciled lettering: acetone, benzene, carbon tetrachloride, chloromice T, and high-performance erasers often used by counterfeiters. I stepped through the hole in the wall and entered the room.

I was familiar with the chemicals. They were used to produce ecstasy, the designer drug also known as the disco biscuit, hug drug, clarity, and white dove. Ecstasy was a derivative of MDMA (methylenedioxymethamphetamine). One ecstasy pill cost about fifty cents to produce and commanded a forty-dollar price on the streets. The exact same chemicals used to make ecstasy could also be used with high-tech erasers to make ink disappear, as in counterfeiting.

Suddenly the invisible back door burst open and two handguns, designed to make me disappear, were pointed in my direction. Behind the guns were the men I had seen in the parking lot. Behind them was the "not so old" lady shopper. She didn't have a gun pointed at me. The daggers from her eyes were enough to kill me.

Silent alarm, schmuck. I cursed myself. I was angry for being so careless, but I wasn't afraid. I had been at the wrong end of a gun before. I noticed an open pack of cigarettes and a Zippo lighter on the table to my left, next to a can of acetone and a can of benzene. I had all the elements for fire.

"Who ze fahk are you?" the bigger of the two men growled at me in a strong Russian accent.

What could I possibly say that would make any difference? I said nothing.

"I said, who ze fahk are you?"

"I heard you the first time, Boris," I said.

"How do you know my name?"

Under different circumstances I would have thought that was very funny.

"Wait a minute," the woman said, moving closer to me. "I know you." She had a slight Russian accent I hadn't noticed in the market.

"No you don't. A lot of people think I look like P. Diddy. That's probably it."

"No." She studied my face. "No P. Diddy." Then she remembered. "You're the guy from Publix."

"What guy from Publix?" the smaller man asked.

"He was behind me in the checkout

167

line, Yuri."

"Actually, I was in front of you first," I said.

"What are you doing here?" she asked, ignoring my stupid banter.

"You dropped your All-Bran. I was trying to return it."

"What do we do wiz theze guy?" Boris asked. "He's seen everything."

"Hey, no problem. All I saw was some counterfeiting stuff and the ecstasy lab." I tried to make him feel better.

Boris pointed his gun at my head and cocked the hammer. "I keel you, asshole."

I picked up the can of acetone from the table and held it in front of me. "If you shoot a bullet into this can you're gonna keel everyone in this room, Khrushchev."

"I'm not Khrushchev," he said defensively.

The woman put a hand on Boris's arm and had him lower the gun.

"What do you want, meester?"

"Call me Eddie," I said.

"Okay, Eddie, what do you want?"

"Right now I'd settle for getting out of here alive."

"You a cop?"

"No." I wasn't actually lying.

"What are you?"

"I'm an unemployed golf course ranger."

Boris had heard enough. "Yuri, go take the fahkin' can from zees idjut and knock heem on heez ass. Then we'll take heem for a nice long ride to nowhere."

Yuri stuck his gun in his pants and lumbered toward me. He looked at me like I was his next meal. But I had the acetone and the Zippo lighter on my side. I quickly unscrewed the cap of the acetone, and I doused Yuri with the highly flammable liquid. He stopped.

"What zee fahk?" Yuri pawed at his face. "Zat burns."

I held up the Zippo lighter.

"No, don't do zat!" Boris exclaimed.

I smiled at him and flicked the flint. Nothing! *Flick! Flick!* Nothing. *Flick! Flick! Flick!* "Fahk," I said.

Yuri laughed and lumbered closer to me. "Now I'm gonna fahk you up," he forecasted.

Faster and faster, I kept trying. *Flick! Flick! Flick . . . YOU FAHK! FLICK! FLICK!* FLAME! FINALLY!

Yuri stopped laughing and lumbering. "Fahk," he said, understating his problem.

I tossed the Zippo into the puddle of acetone at Yuri's feet. Poof! Whoosh! LIFT-OFF! The world's largest Molotov cocktail was running in circles. "Boris! I'm on fire!

Help me!" He ran toward his two comrades, who backed away from him.

"Get the fahk away from me," Boris shouted at Yuri, avoiding the human torch. "Lay on the fahking floor." Yuri went down. Boris went for a fire extinguisher in the corner. He wasn't pointing his gun at me anymore, so I rushed past the woman. I wasn't worried about her. She was small and skinny.

I had made a bad decision. The small-caliber bullet hit me on the top of my right shoulder. The gun blast hurt my ears more than the bullet hurt my shoulder.

A fahking twenty-two, I said to myself and looked toward the woman, who continued to point her Saturday night special at me. She was astonished I was still standing, and when I started to move toward her, she panicked and fired a shot above my head. I was on her before she could get off another shot. I grabbed the wrist of her gun hand and twisted sharply. She screamed and dropped the gun to the floor.

"You bastard," she shouted into my face. I smelled cigarettes and vodka. I used a short, sharp, backhanded karate punch to the left side of her jaw to knock her out. She slumped, and I caught her under the arms before she could fall to the floor.

I wasn't being chivalrous. I needed a shield. I turned in the direction of the borscht brothers, placing Natasha, or whatever the fahk her name was, in the line of fire.

Is Yuri burning? I asked myself.

Actually Yuri was only smoldering, and Boris was able to turn his attention to me. He dropped the extinguisher and picked up his Glock nine millimeter. If he shot me with that gun I was going down for the count. Boris was confused when he saw me hiding behind my female shield. "Natasha, wake up," he called to her. I shuffled toward Boris, keeping Natasha in front of me at all times. When he leaned one way to get a shot at me, I turned with him, keeping Natasha in the bull's-eye position.

"You coward," he tried. "Hiding behind a woman."

"Yeah, and you're hiding behind a Glock. You put down your gun, and we'll go at it man to man."

"I don't believe you."

"I don't give a shit what you believe. That's my best offer."

He squatted on his haunches and put the Glock on the floor. "There, I put it down. Now let her go."

I was sure he had a backup piece tucked

in his belt behind his back, but I really didn't care.

"Okay tough guy, now back away from the gun."

Boris took a couple of steps back with his hands on his hips. He was making his move for the backup piece. I shoved the unconscious Natasha toward him forcefully. He didn't move to catch her, and she fell hard on her face. I figured her nose broke in the process.

Boris didn't even give her a look. Russian chivalry was apparently dead. Boris was reaching behind his back when he noticed that I was holding Natasha's twenty-two in my hand.

"Now where did this come from?" I asked.

"Fahk your twenty-two," he laughed, making me wonder what cannon he had hidden behind his back.

I decided not to wait to find out. I fired three shots into his right knee. His laughter changed to screams. Personally I found his laughing more annoying. He went down on his back then rolled onto his side clutching his wounded knee. While he was writhing in pain, I picked up the Glock he had placed on the floor in front of him, and I pulled the other nine millimeter from its hiding place in the back of his pants. "You're lucky you didn't shoot yourself in the ass, Yuri."

"I'm Boris." He grimaced in pain.

"I'm Eddie. How you doin'?"

I felt dizzy and leaned against the wall for balance. I looked at my wounded shoulder. It didn't hurt much, but blood was pouring out of the wound. I put a hand over the hole in my shoulder. I knew I couldn't last long bleeding this fast. I removed my cell phone from my pants pocket and the business card from my shirt pocket. I punched in one of the phone numbers on the card.

"Officer McGrady," he answered.

"Matt," I said weakly. "Eddie Perlmutter."

"Hey, Eddie, I didn't expect to hear from you so soon. What's up?"

"My number."

"What's the matter?"

"I just got shot, and I think I'm bleeding to death."

"Holy shit, where are you?"

"Next door."

"In the vacuum cleaner place?"

"No," I gasped. I was having trouble staying awake. "Listen, Matt, walk outside the gym. Okay."

"Okay." I heard him running. "I'm outside, Eddie."

"See the building in the next lot?"

"Through the trees?"

"Yeah. Go through the bushes to the back of that building. The back door is open, but I don't want you to come in. I'll come out." I could hear him running again.

"Why can't I come in?"

"I made a citizen's arrest," I said. "We don't want to give them an illegal search and seizure claim. Call for backup, Matt. Tell them to come with a warrant for this place."

"But they shot you." Matt was breathing hard. "I can enter."

"Probably," I said. "Just don't take the chance."

Moments later Matt was at the back door.

"Oh, man," he exclaimed as he surveyed the scene.

Yuri was groaning from his burns, Boris was rocking back and forth holding his shattered knee. Natasha was still unconscious.

"Don't come in," I told him. "Make the call, Matt." I slumped against the wall.

Matt called for backup and warrants. Then he called the gym and Barry arrived in a couple of minutes carrying towels. Matt pressed a towel hard against my wound.

"Who are these people?" Barry asked.

"The guy I set on fire is Yuri. The guy I shot in the knee over there is Boris. The woman I knocked out is Natasha."

"What's going on here?" Matt asked.

"It's a regular party house," I said. "They print their own money then cook up some ecstacy to celebrate hitting the counterfeit lottery."

"You're kidding," Barry said.

"Do I look like I'm kidding?" I asked, and then I passed out.

Chapter 11

YOU PAY! YOU DIE!

I floated on the edge of consciousness. I had no idea what time it was, what day it was, or where I was. I remembered being shot by a woman named Natasha. I had intravenous tubes in my arms, an oxygen tube in my nose, and a catheter in Mr. Johnson. I guessed I was in a hospital. Nurses were constantly taking my vital signs. A gorgeous brown-skinned nurse, who reminded me of Halle Berry, floated above me, and I told her I loved her. When I had to pee, I peed but I didn't know how I did it or where it went. Mr. Johnson didn't say a word. I think he was in shock.

The next time I opened my eyes I was able to keep them open, but my vision was blurred. Through eyeballs that seemed like they were coated with Vaseline I noticed a window and thought I could see the darkness of night outside. I saw the foggy image of two men at the foot of my bed looking down at me. One of them was talking in a deep voice, but I was having trouble hearing him. I thought I heard, "You pay. You die." This got my attention, but I wasn't sure if he was saying "You buy" or "You die." Maybe he was saying both. The man next to the talking head smiled and said nothing. The words "You die!" became clearer and more insistent. Who were these men who kept promising me I was going to pay and die? Plenty of criminals wanted to kill me when I was in my prime in Boston. But I was in Boca, and I was retired. Who would want me dead in Boca? Maybe Yuri, Boris, or Natasha would like to kill me, but they couldn't be in my room. Yuri was a smoldering ember, and Boris had three bullets in his right knee. There was no way either could be standing at the foot of my bed now, unless I had been in a coma for months.

"You pay! You die!" There it was again.

Well fuck you, I said to myself, because I still couldn't speak. *I'm not going to lie here and wait for you two assholes to kill me!*

With all the strength I could muster I sat upright, threw my legs over the side of the bed, and lunged for the two guys. The intravenous tubes were torn from my arms, and the oxygen tube flew out of my nose. I felt the catheter rip out of Mr. Johnson.

What the fuck? I heard Mr. Johnson scream.

I felt something hard and sharp against my head. I stumbled and fell forward. I heard that deep voice tell me again, "You die," and this time I agreed with him. At least I had gone down fighting like Barney Ross. Tommy Bigelow and the Pugilist Professor would be proud of me. *Good-bye, everyone,* I thought. *Good-bye Mr. Johnson,* I said to my best friend. Everything went black.

I opened my eyes and felt so much pain I knew I wasn't dead. Dead doesn't hurt. My arms ached, and my nose felt broken. I didn't even want to think about peeing. The sun told me it was daytime. But I still didn't have a clue what day it was. My bed was surrounded by concerned people. The two nurses looked concerned. The doctor holding the stethoscope to my chest looked concerned. Barry Anson and Matt McGrady looked concerned, and so did Tommy Bigelow. Mikey Tees was there as well.

"Welcome back," Mikey said. "You had us worried."

"Did you catch those bastards?" I asked.

"What bastards?" Matt McGrady asked.

"The two bastards in my room last night."

"Mr. Perlmutter," the chubby nurse said, smiling, "I was the first one in your room last night after you fell. I didn't see anyone. I just saw you on the floor."

"You didn't hear those two men?"

"No," the nurse said.

"There were two guys right there." I pointed to the end of the bed. "One was telling me I was going to pay, and I was going to die."

"You must have been dreaming," Mike tried to convince me.

"Dreaming, my ass," I snapped. "I could see and hear them, just like I'm seeing and hearing you now. I jumped out of bed and went after them."

The doctor was wrapping a blood pressure cuff around my bicep. "Well, you're not going to pay, and you're not going to die," the doctor announced.

"How do you know that?" I asked.

"Your insurance will cover everything, so you don't have to pay. And you're not going to die because you're in surprisingly good health for a man who was shot last night and then fell out of bed."

"I've only been here overnight?" I was surprised.

"That's it," the doctor confirmed. "The officer and his friend brought you in an

179

ambulance last night. If they weren't so fast getting you here, after some pretty decent first aid, you could have bled to death."

I smiled gratefully at Barry and Matt.

"As soon as we refilled your tank, you were out of danger," the young doctor continued. "How old are you, Mr. Perlmutter?" I told him I was sixty. "You're in remarkable shape for your age; probably helped save your life."

"How old are you, Doctor?"

"Thirty-four," he told me.

I laughed.

"What's so funny?"

"The first time I got shot, you were in diapers."

"Pampers," he corrected me. He removed the blood pressure cuff. "Anyway, you're going to be very sore. You tore all the tubes out of your body when you fell out of bed. I can't imagine how your penis must be feeling right now."

You got that right, Mr. Johnson groaned.

"And I didn't fall out of bed," I insisted. "I got out of bed to go after those two guys."

"If you say so." He patted my shoulder. "Anyway, you're a famous man now."

"Famous for what?"

"I'll let your friends tell you all about it." He shook my hand. "Nice job last night," he congratulated me, and left.

I looked at my new friends. "Okay, famous for what?" I asked.

Mikey Tees said, "Well, I can guarantee you it's not for falling out of bed and nearly tearing your pecker off." He snickered, and everyone joined him, including the kid.

Mikey handed me a copy of the local *Palm Beach County News.* An old picture of me with the complete story of the bust on Second Avenue was front-page news.

"How did they get the story and that picture of me?" I was numb.

"Modern technology. This was a pretty big bust, Eddie," Matt interjected.

"It was? I thought we just caught a momski-and-popski operation."

"Nope." Matt shook his head. "These guys were part of Russian organized crime."

"Oh shit," I blurted out.

"What's the problem?" Matt wanted to know.

"I'm supposed to be retired."

"Well, you're a retired hero now," Matt said.

"It's just a local story isn't it?" I asked.

"I'm afraid not," Matt said. "The Associated Press has the story. By tomorrow afternoon you'll be in newspapers all around the country."

"Goddamn," I said.

"It's starting already," Mike said. "Togo called me this morning and said you had made the front page of the *Globe*."

"Goddamn." I couldn't think of anything else to say.

CHAPTER 12

BUSTED IN BOCA

EX-COP BUSTS ECSTASY & CONTERFEIT RING

RETIRED BOSTON POLICE OFFICER WOUNDED IN SHOOT-OUT

The *Palm Beach County News* headline sensationalized the events on Second Avenue using terms like "brilliant police work" and "decisive and fearless action." A legend had been born in Boca. The article also contained a summary of my career on the Boston police force, including a list of the medals and awards I had received.

The article told how I saved a baby girl who had been accidentally locked in a car by her mother on a hot summer day in the North End. I couldn't pick the door lock, and I was afraid to smash a window, fearing flying glass might hurt the baby. I knew I had to act fast. Pacing around the car, I remembered that I had seen a windshield removed from a police car at the department's repair shop not too long ago. I pictured what the mechanic did, proceeded to remove the windshield, and removed the baby in a matter of minutes. I won a medal for merit. That was twenty-five years ago, and the baby I saved was now an unwed mother living on welfare in East Boston. Her sad, old story, however, would be a new "feel good" story for *Palm Beach County News* readers today.

"They got everything about me in here," I said to the group.

"It's the information age," Matt said.

My visitors departed within an hour and the gorgeous, brown-skinned nurse arrived to take my vital signs.

"Would you do me a favor?" I asked her.

"If I can."

"Would you make sure I don't get any more calls today?" I knew that a barrage of unwanted phone calls from favorite friends, rabid reporters, annoying agents, and crass cranks would be coming soon. I had been the center of sensational situations before and I wasn't feeling well enough to face that level of frenzied attention.

"I'll see what I can do," she said. "Now let's get you moving."

She helped me out of bed and guided me carefully to a comfortable chair. It felt good to move. I looked at her name tag: Claudette Premice — Haiti.

"Thank you, Claudette." I looked out the window at the lake eight floors below. "How long ago did you leave Haiti?" I was making conversation.

"Twenty-five years ago," she told me.

"You were only a kid."

"I'm not as young as I look," Claudette said. "I'm forty-five years old."

"You're kidding?"

"What woman would lie about her age by telling you she's older than she is?"

"Especially in Boca," I conceded. "Well, you look much younger."

"Thank you," she said.

"Do you have any family here?"

"Just my grandmother."

"No siblings?"

"I had a younger sister," she said. "But she died four years ago."

"I'm sorry," I said. "Was she ill?"

"In a manner of speaking," Claudette said. "She was a drug addict and she OD'd."

"What about your parents?"

"They never got out of Haiti."

"Are they still alive?"

"They were murdered a long time ago."

"That's terrible," I said. "How did it happen?"

"My father was a white diplomat from London. My mother was a black Haitian schoolteacher. They were political people. They were killed for political reasons."

"Who was in power in Haiti at the time?"

"I'd rather not talk about it."

"Okay," I said. "How did you get off the island?"

"I'd rather not talk about that, either."

"Okay, no problem," I said. "How old is your grandmother?"

"She claims to be ninety-three," she said. "But no one knows for sure. All her papers were left behind."

"Is she well?"

"Very well," Claudette said. "She just started using a walker, but aside from that she's fine. She lives in Delray near me. Her name's Queen. She claims to be a descendant of Henri Christophe, the one and only king of Haiti."

"Is she?"

"Maybe. Who knows?" We smiled at each other. "That little boy who visited you today thinks you're a hero."

"Actually I remind him of someone who was a hero of his," I said.

"I read about you in the paper, Eddie Perlmutter," Claudette said. "A boy could choose a worse hero."

"Thanks." I changed the subject. "Did anyone ever tell you that you look just like —"

"Halle Berry," she interrupted me.

"I guess you've heard that before."

"Only from patients on painkillers."

"That's not fair," I protested. "You do look like her."

"I guess," she said. "We're both half black and half English."

"Obviously a good combination," I commented.

"Barack Obama is half Kenyan and half European-American."

"I think you're much prettier than him."

She laughed. "Booker T. Washington was half African and half white."

"He's not my type."

"How about Vin Diesel?" she tried. "He's Italian, Scottish, Irish, and African-American."

"You're still my favorite formula."

"What about all-white Germans?" she asked.

"Actually, my ancestors were white Russians . . . without the alcohol."

"Perlmutter is a German name."

"Yes. It means 'white pearl' in German. But we're Russians. I'm sure of that."

"Can you trace your heritage back to Russia?"

"I knew my paternal grandparents," I said. "My mother's mother died from cancer. Her father was murdered in the old country."

"Why was he murdered?"

"For religious reasons," I said.

"How sad," she said.

"Sad and pointless," I agreed.

I saw two pretty young women peeking into my room. They waved to me shyly. I waved back. Claudette Premice turned to the door.

"Hello, ladies," Claudette greeted them pleasantly.

"You're Eddie Perlmutter, aren't you?" the taller brunette asked me as she ventured a few steps into the room.

"Guilty," I said with a smile. She had a dazzling smile of her own. "What can I do for you?"

Claudette rolled her eyes and left the room.

"Bye, Claudette," I called after her, and she waved without looking back.

"A nurse told us you were here. We thought we'd just take a peek. We're here to visit our father in the room next door."

I relaxed. "Nothing serious I hope."

"Very serious," she answered sadly. "He has leukemia."

"Oh, I'm sorry to hear that. What kind?"

"A very bad kind, I'm afraid. Do you know much about leukemia?" she asked.

"I know a little," I said. "My mother died of leukemia a long time ago. She had multiple myeloma."

"My father has myeloid leukemia," she told me.

"I've never heard of that," I said. "It sounds nasty."

"Nasty is the right word for it," she said, advancing into the room until she was standing next to me. She held out her hand. "I'm Debbie Aiello," she introduced herself, "and this is my sister Lisa Becker." Their handshakes were confident.

"Eddie Perlmutter," I introduced myself. "What's your father's name?"

"Dominick Amici," Debbie told me.

"Well someone thought a lot of him," I commented.

"Why do you say that?"

"The name Dominick means a 'child of God'."

"We know." Lisa spoke for the first time. "Do you speak Italian?"

"No. Just a few words and sentences," I

said. "I was a cop in an Italian neighbor-hood."

"His middle name is Manfredi," Debbie told me. "Do you know what that means?"

"Sure. Manfredi means 'peace and friendship.' What a great name. Dominick Manfredi Amici: child of God, man of peace, and good friend."

"He's all of those things," Lisa said proudly and sadly. "It's just not fair for him to be so sick."

"Life's not fair," I agreed.

They both nodded.

"So, Officer Perlmutter." Debbie changed the subject. "Tell us what happened to you yesterday."

"I'd rather talk about your father."

A pleasant-looking middle-aged woman appeared at my door. She was holding a copy of the *Palm Beach County News* under her arm. She knew who I was, and I didn't have to ask who she was. The resemblance between mother and daughters was very strong.

"I was wondering where you two had gone," she said to the girls. "I should have known you'd be in here with the local hero."

"Is Dad okay?" Debbie asked.

"He's sleeping," she told them. She looked at me. "Are they bothering you?"

"Beautiful women never bother me, Mrs. Amici. Please come in."

"Call me Carol," she said, entering the room. "I suppose they've asked you all kinds of questions already?"

"No they haven't." I defended the sisters. "As a matter of fact they were just about to tell me a story about a good friend of theirs."

"And who might that be?"

"Their father," I said.

She looked at her daughters affectionately. "Mind if I listen in?" Carol Amici asked as she sat in a chair near mine. Her daughters found chairs, and we formed a circle.

"Who's first?" I asked.

Dominick Amici's women took turns telling me about his life, and their year-long battle to save it. Angelina Polcari Amici, Dominick's diminutive mother, had enjoyed good health and passed away in her sleep at the age of 104. Unfortunately, her youngest son, sixty-six-year-old Dominick, didn't inherit enough of her extraordinary genes. Two years after she died, Dom collapsed while playing golf. Extensive testing showed that Dominick had myeloid leukemia, a virulent form of blood cancer.

The family's first reaction was denial.

Dominick can't be sick.

191

Look at him.

He's six foot five inches tall and 250 pounds.

He's immortal.

More doctors and more tests confirmed the original diagnosis.

The family raged against the injustice of it all.

Why him?

Why us?

It's not fair!

Outrage was replaced by determination and Amici's Army attacked myeloid leukemia head on. They learned early in the battle that myeloid leukemia was a deadly enemy that showed no mercy and took no prisoners. In the orderly process of life, old cells died and new cells replaced them. Myeloid leukemia changed the order. Abnormal blood cells randomly appeared when they were not needed. They multiplied faster than normal cells and killed them. Inevitably the body's immune system crashed and the patient died.

"I remember with my mother's multiple myeloma," I said, "she got terrible tumors from all the bad cells collecting in her system."

"There are no tumors with myeloid leukemia," Carol told me. "But the results are the same. The cancer destroys everything."

"My mother died twenty years ago. There must be new treatments by now."

Carol sighed. "There are a lot of new methods. They just didn't work for Dominick."

They told me about their twelve-month ordeal with stem cell and umbilical cord blood cell transplants. They had taken Dominick to the Shands Hospital in Gainesville, Florida, which specializes in these transplants. Dominick's treatment started with massive doses of chemotherapy intended to kill the abnormal blood cells. These treatments also kill normal cells, and left Dominick extremely susceptible to infection. He was kept in isolation for months to prevent him from catching something. Carol spoke of the loneliness and frustration she and Dominick experienced during those months.

The doctors could not find a suitable stem cell donor for Dominick, and without a transplant the chemotherapy would actually hasten his death. Finally, they were able to locate umbilical cord blood cells that had enough of the compatible components to be effective for Dominick. They performed the transplant, put Dominick in isolation again, and waited for the results. The transplant failed. The doctors at Shands told the Amicis there was nothing more they could do for him. By this time Dominick was so weakened by the treatments that the doctors doubted he had enough strength to survive the ambulance ride back to Boca.

"That was three months ago," Lisa said, shaking her head. "He's still alive, and he's still fighting."

"Amazing," was all I could think of saying.

"He really believes he can still beat this thing," Carol said. "He takes short walks and exercises with his therapist. His mind and his will won't give up."

"He sounds like a special guy," I said. "I hope I get the chance to meet him."

Carol sighed again. "I hope so, too."

"Let's change the subject," Lisa said, pointing at me. "Tell us what happened to you. You're the biggest news in town."

"The biggest news in town is going to have to wait," Claudette Premice declared from the doorway. "Mrs. Amici, girls, Mr. Amici is awake and cranky. Mr. Perlmutter, you have nine phone messages, and I'm not taking another one." She marched into the room and dropped a stack of pink slips on my lap. "I activated your phone. Answer it yourself."

Carol and her daughters walked to the door. "You got off easy today," Lisa told me. "Next time."

"He's probably not going to be here for a next time," Claudette said. "He's being released soon. Oh, and Mr. Wonderful, you have a visitor outside. I told her you weren't seeing anyone, but she asked if I would let you know she was here."

"She's not a reporter, is she?"

"She doesn't look like a reporter," Claudette said. "Says her name's Alicia Fine."

"I know Alicia Fine," Carol Amici said. "From Boca Heights."

"That's where I met her," I explained.

"She's a very nice person," Carol noted.

"Well, do you want to see this very nice person from Boca Heights or should I send her away?" Claudette sounded impatient.

"Nurse Premice, are you jealous of all my lady visitors?"

"Don't flatter yourself, Eddie Perlmutter." She put her hands on her hips. "I don't care if you are a star. To me you're just another catheter."

"Now that hurts." I covered Mr. Johnson with both hands.

"Now, don't you make me do it again," she warned with a smirk.

"You have my word," I promised. "I'd like

to see Mrs. Fine if that's okay with you."

Yeah, bring her on, Mr. Johnson rallied.

Carol waved from the doorway. "See you soon," she said, and they all departed.

I heard Alicia Fine exchanging pleasantries with Carol Amici and her daughters outside my room. A moment later Alicia Fine was at my door.

Chapter 13

SHE'S SO FINE

Alicia Fine looked fantastic.

"Hi," she said. Her smile was tentative. "Is this a bad time?"

"No, not at all," I said. "Please come in."

I watched her walk toward me and I wished I had a pause button. She looked spectacular. Her light-brown hair was cut stylishly short, and it complemented an imperfectly beautiful face that still had its original nose and lips. Her figure was full and sensual, and Mr. Johnson stirred despite his catheter trauma. I adjusted my robe snugly over Mr. Johnson to keep him in his place.

Hey, Mr. Johnson protested, *pick on someone your own size.*

Behave yourself, I told him.

Mrs. Fine sat on a chair next to my bed. I smiled at her, hoping she didn't notice what was happening under my robe.

Hey, you don't tell me what to do, Johnson

protested, still trying to stand up. *I got a mind of my own.*

I know. But not now, please . . .

If not now, when? Johnson had the balls to quote Rabbi Hillel. *Look at her.*

I'm looking, I'm looking. I tried to avert my eyes, but Johnson wouldn't let me.

Look at those legs, look at those boobs.

I'm looking.

The thighs! Check out those thighs, man.

I looked.

I say we fuck her.

Stop talking like that.

That's how I talk. I'm a penis. Come on, introduce me!

I will not!

Are you ashamed of me?

I'm very proud of you, I told him. *But it's not the time or place.*

Sure it is!

Shit!

You're confusing me with the asshole that lives behind me.

Will you stop?

When I stop you might as well be dead.

"Are you all right?" Alicia Fine asked. "You seem lost in thought."

Damn, she wants to talk, Mr. Johnson said, and he withdrew into his shell.

I knew the little prick would be back

sooner or later. "I'm fine, Mrs. Fine," I said. "It's nice of you to come."

"I tried calling you on your cell phone. Mike gave me your number."

"He told me."

"Did you get my message?"

"I haven't checked my messages. I was a little busy."

"Obviously you were busy," she laughed. Her teeth were perfect. Mr. Johnson stirred a little but I crossed my legs and the catheter gave him a painful tug.

Watch it, he warned me. *I'm a little tied up here.*

"What was your message?" I said, ignoring Mr. Johnson.

"I wanted to thank you for coming to my rescue yesterday. It was a horrible situation for me."

"A horrible situation is living in a shack by the side of State Road 7," I said.

She tilted her head to the side. "Excuse me." She looked perplexed. "I don't understand."

"I'm sorry," I said. "I'm a little disoriented. Listen, you don't have to thank me, I was just doing my job."

"Well you did a good job," she told me. "Mike disqualified Mildred Feinberg like you said he should, and I was declared champion because I was winning when she defaulted."

"That's good thinking on Mike's part. Congratulations."

"He told me it was your idea."

"Mike talks too much."

"Well thank you for being there for me."

I'm right here for you too, hot stuff. Mr. Johnson was back.

I squeezed my legs together and crushed the pest between my thighs.

"My pleasure," I said softly, clearing my throat.

Mine, too. Mr. Johnson was muffled but still game as hell. I cut off his circulation with a hard squeeze.

Son of a bitch, he mumbled.

"I heard you quit your job at Boca Heights."

I nodded.

"You did nothing wrong."

"I don't belong there."

"I thought you fit in quite nicely." She smiled. "People liked you."

"People hardly noticed me."

"I noticed you," she said, looking directly at me.

"With all due respect, Mrs. Fine, you notice everyone. You're a very nice person."

"I noticed you in particular."

"That's because I'm so tall, dark, and handsome."

We laughed together. "Actually, it was your broken nose that first got my attention."

"I have a broken nose?" I felt my nose. "When did that happen?"

We laughed again. "It probably happened when you were a boxer in the Golden Gloves."

"How did you know about that?"

"It was in the paper. Everything about you was in the paper. You've had a very exciting life, and it seems like the excitement never stops."

"That's me, all right. Mr. Excitement," I joked. "I think trouble just follows me around."

"Or you look for trouble," she suggested with that great smile of hers.

We were actually flirting, and Mr. Johnson knew it, but to his credit he remained calm.

"I read you lost your wife."

I nodded. "I heard you lost your husband."

"I didn't lose him. He told me to get lost."

"How long were you married?"

"Thirty years. Two kids, one married. I have two grandchildren."

You're kidding me! Mr. Johnson was stunned. *I've been standing at attention and saluting a grandmother.*

"You don't look old enough to be a grandmother."

"I'm fifty-two years old," she said. "I was nineteen when I got married. I was a mother at twenty-one and again at twenty-two. My daughter is thirty, with a boy and a girl of her own. My son is still single."

"Well, you look great. How could your husband leave you?"

"He said I lost something after all those years."

"What?"

"My youth," she said. "He married a woman who looks just like I did twenty years ago."

"He married a thirty-two-year old?" I said more than asked. "He must be crazy. What will they talk about?" I paused. "Wait a minute. That's a stupid question."

"Actually, it's a very perceptive question," she said. "You're pretty smart for a cop."

I noticed we laughed easily. She insisted I call her Alicia.

Alicia Fine's visit lasted long into the afternoon. I ignored several phone calls while she was there and I think she was flattered.

We talked briefly about Patty because Alicia asked. "Do you still miss her after all

202

these years?"

I told her I did.

"Is that why you never remarried?" she asked.

I told her I hadn't found anyone I wanted to marry.

"It must be wonderful to love someone so much," she mused.

I assured her it was wonderful, but it was also painful.

"It's painful when a loved one leaves under any circumstances," she said.

I told her I thought the pain of rejection was worse than the pain of death. "Death is never personal. You're chosen at random. Rejection is when you're not chosen at all, and that's very personal."

Then I suggested we talk about something else.

She asked if I had dated many women since Patty died, and I told her I had. She asked about my relationships, and I suggested, once again, that we talk about something else. She asked if I would tell her about my career.

I talked about whatever came to mind. I talked about my boxing, my parents, my grandparents, my middle initial, my terrible temper, and my lifelong desire to be a cop. I told her about the West End and how it was destroyed by politicians. I told her how I killed Gino Montoya, even though he lived thirty years after I broke his heart. I talked about the North End and the people who lived there. I told her about the wiseguys in Boston's Mafia and how they became made men. I told her about the first time I was shot, on the first day of forced busing in South Boston in 1974.

She seemed fascinated by my description of the rioting of white-Irish residents of "Southie" when buses carrying black students arrived in front of South Boston High on September 12, 1974. "I saw this middle-aged guy in the crowd pull a gun out of his jacket pocket. He was showing it to a friend and pointing a finger at the students. He wasn't aiming the gun at anyone, and I decided I wasn't going to give him the chance. I rushed into the crowd and grabbed him. In the scuffle, the gun went off and I took a bullet in my left thigh."

She punctuated my description with an "Oh my God."

You ain't kidding, Mr. Johnson remembered. *A few inches to the right, and I would have had my head blown off. The twins, too.*

She wanted to know what happened to the man with the gun.

"Not much," I told her. "It was an accident, and he had a license for the gun."

"Why were they busing in Boston?" Alicia Fine asked suddenly with interest, and I got the urge to kiss her. It wasn't a sexual urge. It was a "thank you for being here, thank you for caring, thank you for being so goddamn luscious, thank you, thank you, thank you."

"Busing didn't start in Boston," I explained. "North Carolina was the first state to require busing, in 1970. In '71 the Supreme Court upheld North Carolina's decision, and busing became the new thing. It didn't come to South Boston until 1974."

"Why South Boston?"

"Southie was about as racially imbalanced as you could get," I explained. "The neighborhood was almost a hundred percent white and predominantly Irish. It was a very clannish, very tough neighborhood."

"Whose idea was it to go there?"

"U.S. District Court Judge W. Arthur Garrity."

"He couldn't have been too smart."

"Harvard Law School graduate, appointed by Lyndon Johnson."

"I don't care. It sounds like he made an awful stupid choice."

"He did," I agreed. "Garrity ordered seventeen thousand kids bused away from their neighborhood schools. It was crazy. At one point there were five hundred police supervising four hundred students at South Boston High. In 1974 Southie was like Selma, Alabama, in 1964."

She asked what happened.

"It took twenty-five years for the busing program to end."

"Why did it stop?"

"Because everyone could see it wasn't working," I said. "It was a big mistake. It never should have started."

"It seemed like a well-intentioned program," she said.

"Isn't there an old saying about good intentions?"

"Yes." She smiled. " 'The road to hell is paved with good intentions.' "

"Exactly." I returned her smile so she wouldn't feel embarrassed. "I'm in favor of equal rights and civil rights. I swore to uphold these laws and I did. But busing took away as many rights as it tried to protect. Busing forced white families in Southie to take their kids out of a clannish, neighborhood school and send them across the city to a place they weren't wanted and didn't want to be. Then a busload of black kids arrives in Southie to replace the white kids who just left under protest. What did they think was going to happen? Busing wasn't the answer."

"What was the answer?"

"I'm just a cop, Alicia," I said. "I didn't have an answer then and I don't have an answer now. I just knew something had to be done."

"What happened to Judge Garrity?"

"He died in 1999, about the same time busing died," I told her. "Dead or alive, though, the people of South Boston will never forgive him."

She asked me about the second time I was shot and the third time just yesterday. I told her it was time to talk about her. She said there was nothing much to tell, but I insisted. It was early afternoon, and the sky had gone dark with clouds. A hard rain began to fall, and heavy drops crashed and splashed against the window. I suddenly felt tired and fought to keep my eyes open. "Mind if I get into bed again?" I asked.

"I should be going," she volunteered. "You need your rest."

"No. Don't go."

When I was settled under the covers with her help, she sat next to me on the bed. She touched my face gently with the palm of her hand. "You should sleep."

I took her hand and held it. "Tell me a

story?" I asked.

"You're like a little boy, Eddie Perlmutter." She smiled at me. "Okay, here goes. Once upon a time in a land far, far away from Far Rockaway —"

"Where's Far Rockaway?"

"It doesn't matter. Just listen and relax."

As I drifted away on a hydrocodone cloud, she spoke of a Long Island with giant castles on cliffs high above the Atlantic Ocean. The castles were in honor of King Benjamin (Moore) of Paints, King Harry (Guggenheim) of Cash, King Marshall (Fields) of Stores, and other "majesties" of the time.

The mansions had names: Commodore Hill, Old Westerbury Gardens, Hempstead House, Falaise, Eagle's Nest, and Chelsea. The mythical Great Gatsby lived in the imaginary enclave of West Egg on this gold coast. Daisy Buchanan, Gatsby's lover, lived in West Egg. Gatsby was great because he had everything but he was murdered by a man who had nothing.

Otto Kahn, the man Will Rogers called "the King of New York," had everything except acceptance. Kahn was a German-Jewish investment banker at Kuhn Loeb in New York City at the turn of the twentieth century. A resident of Morristown, New

Jersey, Kahn was denied membership to the local exclusive golf club. Incensed by the anti-Semitism of his neighbors, Kahn moved to Cold Spring Harbor, Long Island, in 1914, where he built Oheka (derived from letters in his name), a 109,000-square-foot mansion. Only Vanderbilt's Biltmore was bigger.

Years later, more Jewish potentates moved to the Gold Coast. The Long Island towns of Great Neck, Sands Point, Oyster Bay, Old Westbury, and Huntington filled with Jewish kings and queens with their princes and princesses. Princess Alicia was born to King Herbie (Cohen) and Queen Esther on December 31, 1953. Alicia was their third child and their only girl. Her oldest brother, Stuart, would one day rule the kingdom of Cadillac throughout New York State. Alicia's other brother, Max, renounced his royalty and became a carpenter in Colorado Springs, Colorado. Alicia, of course, married a prince.

The Cohen house in Cold Spring Harbor had a name. It was called "the Cohen House" by residents and "that Big Fuckin' House" by tourists. The Cohen house could not compare to Oheka, but it was still an outstanding example of opulence.

Princess Alicia was the fairest in the land.

The people of the kingdom loved her because she was kind and thoughtful. Princess Alicia was "Queen of the Prom" her senior year in private high school. The "King of the Prom" was Aaron Fine, the equally beautiful, but not nearly as wealthy, descendant of lesser nobility. They were the perfect couple.

Princess Alicia and Prince Aaron were inseparable. They attended Yale University together. The princess was loyal only to her prince. Unfortunately, the prince was also loyal only to the prince. When they married, she gave herself to him totally. His commitment wasn't as total. They eloped during their sophomore year at Yale when she was only nineteen. She married the love of her life. He married for the love of her lifestyle.

King Herbie and Queen Esther held a glorious wedding for the couple, even though they had eloped. Alicia was pregnant a year later, and her degree at Yale was put on hold. Aaron went to Yale Law School where he made *Yale Law & Policy Review* and passed the bar on the first try. By the time they had two children, he had had two affairs. She was content. He was not. They remained married for many years, but they did not live happily ever after.

"Mr. Perlmutter," I heard my name. "Mr. Perlmutter, wake up."

I opened my eyes. The princess was gone. A nurse was standing above me.

"Mr. Perlmutter, your grandson is here," she said. I smiled at her.

How nice, I thought. Then I remembered I didn't have a grandson.

I sat up in bed and saw Tommy Bigelow. He looked like a wet schnauzer. His wiry hair was soaked and packed down on his head. His clothes hung from his frail body like he had been swimming in them. "Tommy, what are you doing here?"

"I came to take care of you, in case those two guys from last night came back," he said, and then he sneezed.

"How did you get here?" I asked.

"I walked."

"How far?"

"I don't know. I started around five o'clock."

I looked at the clock. It was eight-thirty at night. I had been sleeping for a few hours. "You walked for three and a half hours?"

He shrugged. "I guess."

"Does anyone know you're here?"

He shook his head, *no.* He looked like he was going to pass out. I asked the on-duty nurse to take his temperature. I called Officer Matt McGrady. Matt was relieved to hear that Tommy was with me. His foster parents had already reported him missing. The nurse interrupted to tell me the kid had a temperature of 101. Matt said he would call the foster parents and come right over. Just then the kid collapsed on the floor.

Matt McGrady and I convinced the hospital staff to admit Tommy Bigelow to the hospital that night. We signed an agreement that said we were totally responsible for him. Tommy was tucked safely into the empty bed in my room. He was suffering from dehydration and exhaustion. Tommy's foster home, I was told, was over seven miles away. I wondered what had possessed the kid to undertake such a hike in a rainstorm, in the dark.

They gave Tommy fluids intravenously and pills for his fever. Matt and I watched him. Matt wouldn't take his eyes off the kid.

"You like him, don't you?" I said to Matt.

Matt sighed. "Yeah, I like him a lot. But I'm concerned about him. The kid needs a father."

"What about you?" I wasn't joking.

"I've thought about it." Matt's answer didn't surprise me. "My whole family loves him. I love the kid, too. But I'm having trouble enough making ends meet now. I couldn't afford another mouth to feed."

"I understand," I said with a yawn.

They gave me another pain pill, and I was asleep before Matt McGrady left the room.

With Tommy there to protect me, the two you-pay-you-die guys did not return that night.

In the morning Tommy looked much better, and I felt much better. When they took the catheter out of Mr. Johnson he felt much better. We were examined and found fit to travel. We were given breakfast.

"Tommy, why did you walk here last night?" I asked.

He just shrugged and didn't look at me.

"You could have been hit by a car or something," I told him.

He shrugged again and he looked up at me. "I tried to call lots of times but no one answered," he explained. "So I got worried."

I remembered the constant ringing of the phone yesterday while I was under the spell of Alicia Fine. He was concerned, and now I was concerned.

"You know, Tommy," I said softly, "I'm not Barney Ross."

"You're my Barney Ross," Tommy said.

It was the second time in my life someone said that to me. The first time I felt honored

by my grandfather's exaltations. This time I
felt cornered by a young boy's expectations.

CHAPTER 14

ANOTHER DAY IN PARADISE

Paradise is where I am.

— VOLTAIRE

Mal Tanenbaum, Tommy's foster father, came to the hospital the next morning to take Tommy home. "I'm embarrassed," he said to me. "We didn't even know he was gone until late last night."

"You don't have to apologize to me," I told him. "It's not easy taking care of kids."

"Mr. Perlmutter" — Mal put his hand on Tommy's shoulder — "there are five hundred thousand kids in American foster care. My wife and I do our best. But sometimes a kid falls through the cracks."

"Not this kid," I said.

Tommy seemed to like Mal, but I didn't sense any love between them.

Shortly after they departed, Steve Coleman arrived to take me home. We looked into Dominick Amici's room on the way out, but he was sleeping. He didn't look

215

good. We stopped at the nurse's station, and I asked for Nurse Premice. She was gone for the day after her night shift.

Steve and I went directly to the Boca Heights pool area to relax. We ordered two sodas from the snack counter and sat in the shade of a table umbrella.

"My brother-in-law is pissed off you haven't returned his calls," Steve said.

I pulled several pink message slips from my shirt pocket. "Tell Togo I haven't returned anyone's call," I said. "I haven't even read my messages."

Steve's cell phone rang. "I can't take this call here, it's against club rules." He got up from the table. "I'll be back in a few minutes." I heard him answer the phone as he hurried from the forbidden zone.

I surveyed the pool area. It was pristine now, but I could imagine the bedlam caused by out-of-town, out-of-control grandchildren and overindulgent grandparents overwhelming the place during school vacation.

I watched a stout Boca Heights woman get out of the pool. She had been swimming laps. She wrapped a towel over her ample shoulders and patted herself down.

"Another day in paradise," she said to another stout lady on a lounge.

"Yes, another day in paradise," her friend agreed, looking up from her reading.

They smiled at each other, sharing a delicious secret.

Another day in paradise? I asked myself, still under the influence of painkillers. *Is it paradise for that Haitian worker, cutting foliage over there?*

The landscaper, wearing a wool stocking hat, was wielding a power tool that looked like something out of Stephen King's imagination.

Was it another day in paradise for the white bag boy loading oversized golf bags for oversized golfers onto standard-sized golf carts? Was the black short-order cook in the snack shack, sweating into the potato salad, in paradise? Maybe yes. Maybe no.

One person's paradise can be someone else's hell, I concluded.

Steve returned to the table, and I returned from the ozone. An hour later I was at my San Reno one-bedroom apartment. It was only noontime, and I was already exhausted. I closed all the window shades, flopped on the sofa, and began reading the twenty-eight phone messages.

I discarded Tommy Bigelow's ten messages. The *Palm Beach County News* had called me three times asking for an interview. A call from the grievance committee informed me that Mrs. Mildred Feinberg had withdrawn her complaint against me. There was a message from Chief of Police Frank Burke asking me to contact him to set up an appointment. Burke was acting chief because the regular chief had been suspended for corruption. Matt McGrady and Barry Anson each had left a couple of messages for me and Togo called three times.

I returned Acting Chief Burke's call first, as a professional courtesy. Burke greeted me with enthusiasm. He complimented my police work and said he wanted to meet at my earliest convenience. I said it was convenient now. Burke gave me directions to the Boca police station. It was on Second Avenue, a few miles south of the P.A.L. facility and the ecstasy lab.

The Boca Raton police station was a plain building directly across the street from a plain city hall, adjacent to an even plainer public library. I was expecting something more upscale.

The entrance to the building was modest, and the lobby looked like a high school foyer. A wall of honor with framed photos was the first thing I noticed.

There was an organizational chart displaying pictures of the command level, middle level, and officer level of the department. The mission statement was prominently displayed:

**TO ENHANCE THE QUALITY
OF LIFE IN THE CITY OF
BOCA RATON THROUGH
PROGRESSIVE POLICE SERVICE
IN PARTNERSHIP WITH THE
COMMUNITY**

I walked to the front counter and rang the bell. A civilian woman came to the desk and slid open the glass window.

"Can I help you?"

"I'm Eddie Perlmutter, here to see Chief Burke," I explained.

Her face lit up, and she turned to her fellow workers. "Hey, Eddie Perlmutter is here, the cop from Boston."

There were six workers in the office. One man stood up at his desk and began clapping his hands. Then all of them were standing and clapping. I smiled. What else could

219

I do? It was kind of embarrassing.

Acting Chief Frank Burke appeared while I was shaking hands with the staff.

"I figured you were causing all this commotion." Burke smiled and patted me on the back. "Welcome."

Burke was in his early forties. He had an athletic physique and wore his uniform well. His mustache was trimmed perfectly, his hair was cut short, and his smile was genuine. He looked like the hero, not me.

Burke gave me a complete tour of the station. We visited the computer room first.

"We couldn't function without computers nowadays," he said. "Every one of our one hundred and fifty police cars is equipped with a Panasonic computer."

"When I started on the force, computers were bigger than a police car."

"I don't know how you guys did it."

"Hunches."

We saw the evidence room. Burke referred to it as "the CSI lab." We took a tour of the police chief's office, the executive suites, conference rooms, meeting rooms, the internal affairs office, and the road patrol briefing room. In the detectives' area I was given a hero's reception by several of the detectives on duty. A friendly German shepherd approached and rubbed my crotch with his nose.

Get out of my face, you Nazi bastard, Mr. Johnson growled at the dog.

"He's sniffing for drugs," a young detective explained.

"I could use some drugs in that area." I got a pretty good laugh from the young guys with that one, but Mr. Johnson didn't think I was funny.

I only struck out once, he protested.

Twice, I reminded him.

How about all the times I stood up for you?

Can we talk about this later?

Sure. But no more penis jokes. Okay?

Okay.

Our last stop was the basement. There were six holding cells and Burke pointed to one. "We've had one suicide in this area in our history," Burke told me. "It was in that cell two years ago. A guy hung himself. It was our fault. He shouldn't have had his belt. He was only in for a DUI where no one got hurt. Nobody figured he was suicidal. We don't assume anything anymore. No shoelaces and no belts for prisoners, and regular inspections every twenty minutes or less."

I just nodded.

We entered the DUI room where I passed the test. The tour lasted about an hour and ended at Frank Burke's small, windowless office. Frank got us each a bottle of water and sat behind his desk. I sat facing him. "So what do you think of our little station?" he asked.

"Impressive," I said, "but isn't the holding area small for a city this size?"

"We don't hold anyone over eight hours unless absolutely necessary. We process paperwork and do probable-cause affidavits here, but we move the people out as fast as possible."

"Who holds the bad guys after eight hours?"

"The correctional facilities in Palm Beach," he told me. "Everyone arrested on criminal charges in Palm Beach County is supposed to be handled by the main detention center in Palm Beach. They fingerprint, photograph, and house the bad guys for as long as necessary. We can handle the photo and fingerprints here if the detention center is backed up. They have about nine hundred staff there and over three thousand beds. They book over fifty-five thousand people a year."

"Are a lot of those beds filled by Boca criminals?" I asked. "Boca doesn't strike me as a hotbed for crime."

"A hotbed, no," Burke concurred, "but

it's no paradise either."

"Funny you should say that," I commented. "Today I heard a woman at Boca Heights compare the place to paradise."

"I don't recall paradise having pimps and hookers," Burke said, and his raised eyebrows suggested that I should understand his comment.

"Are you saying there are hookers and pimps in Boca Heights?"

"Sorry, I assumed you read about it in the paper," Burke said.

"Read what?

"A guy named David Durant lived in the Shore Point community of Boca Heights and last year we busted him for operating an escort service from his house."

"What? Hookers with AARP cards?"

"No." Burke laughed. "The hookers weren't from Boca Heights. Durant lived there, but he did most of his business with Miami escorts."

"How did you catch him?"

"A disgruntled hooker turned him in."

"He's lucky she wasn't a disgruntled postal worker," I commented. "They shoot people when they're disgruntled. So, with no more pimps in paradise, what keeps you busy?"

"There are one hundred and ninety-eight

full-time police officers and one hundred and four civilians employed by this department, and there's plenty of crime to keep us all busy," Burke stated.

"What type of crime is big around here?"

"Cyber fraud," Burke said. "Boca has been described as the Capone Chicago of cyber fraud."

"You're not serious?"

"Yes, I am," Burke confirmed. "In 2004 a Boca resident named Scott Levine was indicted for the largest computer-fraud scheme in U.S. history."

"What did he do?"

"He stole detailed personal information on over a million people from a data aggregator named Axion. We worked with the FBI on that one."

"I had no idea."

"According to the Securities and Exchange Commission, Boca is the computer spam capital of the world. An SEC member was quoted last year as saying that Boca was the only coastal town in southern Florida that had more sharks on land than in the ocean."

"You could have fooled me," I admitted. "But white-collar crimes don't keep the street cop busy," I noted. "What are the street problems?"

"Auto burglary is big," he told me. "The old smash-and-grab routine. Smash a window, and grab what's on the seat."

"Takes about four seconds, right?"

"Right. And now we got the smash-and-grab-the-seat routine."

"Yeah, I heard about that back in Boston," I said. "I guess some of the seats are really valuable."

"Yeah, the Honda sport seats are a favorite around here. They're called performance jewels because they're kinda sleek and they're interchangeable with other Honda models like the Civic and the Acura. Those seats wholesale for about twenty-five hundred bucks."

"Snatching a seat sounds time consuming."

"It takes a real pro about twenty-five seconds to do the job," Burke said.

He told me about distraction crimes. "A guy posing as a contractor, or handyman, or maybe even a city worker, diverts a homeowner's attention while their partner robs the house. Usually they target the elderly."

"I was taught to respect my elders."

"Yeah, well most of the sons of bitches around here consider the elderly to be nothing more than easy marks," Burke said. "An old guy goes out to get his mail one morning, and two men stopped him, claiming they were there to fix his roof. While they were walking the property with the guy, two of their friends entered the house from the back and robbed it. The guy's wife was inside. They stole the rings right off her fingers and broke her arm."

"That's bad," I said.

"You must have had distraction crimes in Boston."

"Yeah, but not the same kind of stuff," I said. "In Boston the distraction was usually a bat across the side of your head or a gun in your face."

"We have plenty of that here too," Burke said.

Burke talked about robberies and rapes in the area. He told me how a seventy-five-year-old woman was run over in a parking lot trying to stop a car because one of the passengers had snatched her purse. Her body got stuck under the car and they dragged the poor woman a couple of hundred yards trying to get to I-95. She was the mother of four and grandmother of eight. The three kids in the car were minors from Riviera Beach with previous criminal records.

"Were they tried as minors?"

"Of course."

"Crazy." I sighed. "Could you have pursued them if they left the Boca city limits?"

"We can go into Delray, but after that we have to refer it to the sheriff's office."

"It sounds like Boca is logistically difficult for police."

"Correct. We have the north, south, and west districts to protect with sixteen cops per shift per district. Right now I have eighteen men sick, injured, or on vacation. We're shorthanded a lot. The criminals always seem to be at full strength."

"I know how you feel," I commiserated.

"Then we have the airport, inlets, shorelines, and trains to patrol."

"Sounds like a terrorist's paradise," I speculated.

"Another day in paradise," Burke said. "By the way" — he changed the subject — "that was terrific police work you did with those Russians."

"Thanks, Chief," I said.

"You're too good at police work to be retired, Eddie. We could use a guy like you around here."

"I'm too old to be a cop," I said.

"I was thinking of private detective work," Burke said. "All you need is a Class C detective's license in this state. You could get a license with no trouble. With your experience in law enforcement we could help you get a license in no time."

"I'm retired. Besides, you got plenty of good cops already."

"Yes we do," Burke agreed. "I'm proud of the caliber of men we have on the force. But we could always use a supercop." He leaned forward in his seat. "You're a natural, Eddie. It's in your DNA. Even after you were shot you had the presence of mind to think about an illegal entry."

"It probably would have been a legal entry anyway," I said.

"It would have been legal," he agreed. "But how the hell did you have the presence of mind to think about that with a bullet in your shoulder?"

"I lost a bust once because of an illegal entry," I said. "It must have been in my subconscious."

"You were almost unconscious," he said. "It's remarkable."

"I just reacted."

"You still have what it takes, Eddie."

"I also have a disability."

"Oh, yeah?" Burke smiled broadly. "Try telling that to the guy you set on fire or the guy you shot in the knee. What do you say we contact the Department of Agriculture and get you a license?"

"I don't want to be a farmer."

He laughed. "The Consumer Services Division of Licensing is in the Department of Agriculture and Consumer Services," he explained. "I can make some calls to Tallahassee today and probably cut through some red tape for you. Your credentials will make it easy."

"What's the rush?"

"I have two situations I think are perfect for you," he told me.

"Oh, really? Care to share them with me?"

"Let's get your license first and a gun permit. That's a Class G license. I'm a Sig Sauer man. What about you?"

"A Glock nine."

"Good gun," Burke said.

"Do you plan on having me shoot someone?"

"You already did."

"Speaking of shooting people" — I followed through — "what happened to Boris, Yuri, and Natasha?"

"Who?"

"My favorite Russians."

"Oh, those three," Frank Burke said. "We moved them right to Palm Beach. They were held over Sunday and arraigned Monday. They pleaded not guilty, of course."

"Of course. So they're in jail until the probable cause hearing?"

"They made bail."

"Bail?" My voice rose. "Three dope peddling, counterfeiting sons of bitches shoot me and get out on bail? Who was the judge?"

"Toulouse Rodriguez," Burke said. "She's very liberal."

"These guys are the ultimate flight risk," I said.

"They don't call her 'Turn 'Em Loose Toulouse' for nothing." Burke shrugged. "But she did set the bail at a million dollars apiece. They'll show up tomorrow for the probable cause hearing with that kind of money at risk."

"I don't believe this." I stood up and paced the room. "Let me guess, Chief. They paid the bail without a bail bondsman. Right?"

Burke removed a folder from the middle drawer of his desk. He spread the folder open on the desk. Upside-down, I saw the photos of the three Russian stooges clipped to the first page. Burke scanned some words under the photos by running his index finger across the typed sentences. He looked up at me and raised his eyebrows. "You're right," he confirmed. "That's just how it went down."

"And their lawyer paid the bail with three individual bank checks for a million bucks apiece, at around four-thirty that afternoon. Right?"

Burke scanned the folder for a second time. He scanned with his finger again and turned to the second page. He looked up at me slowly.

"How did you know that?" He was surprised.

"Because that's what I would do if I was a fuckin' counterfeiter," I said. "I'd pay the bail with fake bank checks late in the day so they couldn't be deposited until the next morning and then I'd walk out of jail and run like hell."

"You're saying those checks are no good and those three guys are long gone." Burke was having trouble accepting what I was telling him.

"Frank," I said, looking him directly into his eyes, "I'm willing to bet my pension that there will be nothing Russian in that courtroom tomorrow unless someone sneaks in a bottle of vodka."

The next morning, as I predicted, there was nothing Russian in the West Palm Beach courtroom. No Russian comrades, no Russian caviar, no Russian dressing, no Russian sable, no Russian cosmonauts, no

Russian army, no Russian front, no Russian Marxists, no Leninists or Stalinists, no Russian roulette, no Russian ballet, no Russian vodka, and no Russian defendants.

The CFO of the local branch of Bank of America appeared in front of the judge to certify that the three certified bank checks the defendants had submitted to the clerk's office were certifiably worthless.

"Best forgeries I ever saw," he said.

There was a lot of finger-pointing, so I decided to get out of there before someone pointed at me. Outside the courthouse I saw the reporter from the *Boca News* who had interviewed the Pugilist Professor at the P.A.L. gym. He shook my hand enthusiastically. "I'm Jerry Small," he said, smiling. "It's an honor to meet you. I read all about you in the newspaper."

"You must have written about me yourself. Every other reporter did."

"Naw." He blushed. "That's too big a story for me. I've only been on the job for a little over a year. My boss writes the important stories under his own byline. I get the local-interest stuff like the Pugilist Professor story. I gave him that name myself."

"Nice touch. So, how did that turn out?"

"Good, I think," Jerry said. "The kid's amazing. I'd like to write a story about his friend."

"Tommy Bigelow? What for?"

"That kid is stuck in the foster care system, and I think it's sad."

"So, why don't you write the story?" I asked.

"I tried. My boss turned it down."

"Why?"

"He said he didn't like the angle."

"I think you should write it anyway."

"Thanks. But you're not my boss."

The door to the courthouse burst open, and reporters, lawyers, defendants, and spectators made a noisy exit. Several people recognized me, and a few reporters approached, followed by curious onlookers.

One aggressive reporter worked his way to the front. "Jerry." He smiled broadly at the young reporter. "Introduce me to your friend."

"Arnie Bass, Eddie Perlmutter," Jerry said. "Arnie's my boss."

"Pleased to meet you, Eddie." The big smile remained.

I guessed he was in his mid-thirties.

"You're quite a story around here. How about an interview?"

"They already told my life story in the paper."

"Well, what do you think about the criminals you arrested being set free on bail?"

"Actually they were released on bail," I said. "They set themselves free."

"Well, don't you think Judge Rodriguez was a bit remiss in allowing bail in a case of this magnitude, and shouldn't the district attorney have been more insistent that no bail be set?"

I could smell an ambush, and I didn't like it. "No comment," I said. "I don't know the judge or the district attorney."

"Were the Boca police responsible in any way for this mess?" Arnie probed.

I noticed the other reporters were getting annoyed by Bass dominating my time.

"The Boca police were great. They saved my life."

Arnie Bass was disappointed. He was digging for dirt. "Certainly you must have something negative to say about these criminals jumping bail," he tried again.

I thought for a moment and looked over at Jerry Small. Why not? "I have plenty to say. But I've agreed to give my exclusive story to Jerry Small."

Everyone looked at Jerry Small, and Jerry Small looked stunned.

"Why Jerry Small?" Arnie was unhappy. "He's just a trainee."

"I liked the article he wrote about the

Pugilist Professor," I lied. "And I think his views on foster care in Florida are very interesting."

The other reporters circled Jerry.

"How long have you known Eddie Perlmutter?"

"Not long," Jerry stammered.

"How does Perlmutter feel about the judge?"

"No comment," Jerry said.

"What are your views on foster care, Jerry?"

"You'll have to read it in the paper."

"How did you get the exclusive?"

"Just lucky." Jerry Small looked at me.

I winked and walked away.

CHAPTER 15

A BLAST FROM THE PAST

Cold weather blew into Boca two weeks after the Russians blew out of Palm Beach. High winds, cold enough to freeze your lemons, roared through the area. Small people warnings were issued.

I awoke at dawn on a Sunday morning in late February. The sky was a gray sheet of slate. Palm tree fronds rapped urgently on my bedroom window, trying to get in the room and under the covers. Anxious to experience Florida's version of winter, I dressed and left my apartment. It was cold outside, but not the Boston kind of cold that turned my knuckles and knees into aching, rusty hinges.

I drove slowly past the Boca Heights Golf Course on Yamato. I saw wildly gyrating silhouettes of heather and palm trees. There were whitecaps in the manmade lakes. A radio announcer said the wind-chill factor was forty degrees. A Baptist minister told me I had a friend in Jesus. I turned off the radio. I had enough friends.

I drove east on Spanish River Road to Route A1A and pulled into an empty parking lot overlooking the public beach. I got out of the car, leaned into the wind, and walked toward the ocean. When I reached the low metal fence that separated the parking lot from the sand, I clutched the railing and enjoyed the spectacle. Red flags on sturdy poles stood at horizontal attention, warning even the hardiest Canadians to keep their crazy asses out of the water. The ocean was rocking and roiling. Waves were crashing on the beach, gouging gorges in the sand, and carrying the silt out to sea. My coat and hair became soggy from the sea spray, and I retreated to my car, smelling like wet wool.

I started the Mini and turned on the heat for the first time since I had been in Boca. I took off my wet coat and tossed it on the backseat. My shirt was damp, and I started to shiver. When the warm air from the heater touched my cheeks, I felt very tired and tilted my car seat as far back as it would go. I closed my eyes and dreamed.

I smelled flowers. I was in a king-sized bed under a down comforter. My head was resting on a feather pillow. I saw amber walls colored by sunlight that filtered through window curtains. Alicia Fine was asleep on the pillow next to me. She reminded me of the way Patty looked when she slept.

The comforter was at her waist, and I was treated to the sight of her naked breasts. I was tempted to touch her, but I didn't. Her eyes fluttered open, and she looked at me in surprise. She pulled the covers up to her neck.

"What are you doing here?" she demanded.

I didn't know what I was doing there.

"What are you doing here?" she repeated.

I felt like an idiot.

I heard a rapping at the door.

"It's the police," she said triumphantly. "They've come to take you away."

The tapping grew louder. I struggled to get out of the bed, but I was weighted down by the thousand-pound comforter. The mattress turned to quicksand. I was sinking slowly, suffocating.

"Are you okay in there?" A deep voice was calling to me.

I opened my eyes uncertainly.

Through the rain-splattered window of my car, I saw the face of a young man in a policeman's hat. He was tapping at the driver's side window of my Mini. I quickly rolled down the window and felt the rush of cold air on my face.

"I guess I dozed off, Officer," I said.

"No problem," the young man said politely. "I just wanted to make sure you were all right."

"Yeah, I'm fine."

"You look familiar," the cop observed.

"I've been in the papers a lot lately," I told him.

"That's it," he said. "You're the supercop from Boston, right?"

"I'm the cop from Boston," I said. "I don't know how super I am."

"Hey, you made a great bust," he said. "And thanks for saying such nice things about the Boca police."

"I owe you guys my life," I told him.

"I'm Rick Riley." He held out his hand.

"Eddie Perlmutter." I smiled.

We shook hands.

"Nice to meet you, Eddie," he said. "Take care. It's gonna be a rough winter day."

"You call this winter?"

With a little guidance from Chief Burke, I received my Class C private detective license and gun permit within two weeks. The day after I got my license, I received a morning phone call from Mr. Ely Samuels, who identified himself as the president of the Community Management Association for Boca Heights.

"The CMA at Boca Heights is looking to hire a private investigator to handle a couple of matters for us," he told me. "And we'd like to talk to you about the job."

"Did Frank Burke tell you to call me?" I asked.

"The police department doesn't get involved with private investigators," he said unconvincingly. "Let's just say I heard it through the grapevine."

The CMA office was in a small, secluded building off the community's main street. Samuels was a small, bald man who looked to be in his late sixties. He introduced himself as a retired lawyer from Chicago. He sat behind his desk and got right to the point.

"Based on your past reputation and the way you handled the Russian counterfeit operation," he began, "the CMA is interested in retaining your services for the purpose of investigating two matters at Boca Heights."

"I've been a Florida detective for twenty-four hours," I said. "Certainly you could find someone with more experience."

"Your reputation precedes you, Eddie," he

complimented me. "You've been in this line of work your whole life. We're comfortable offering you the assignments."

"What do you have in mind?" I took the bait.

The first matter was the murder of Robert Goldenblatt.

"Steve Coleman told me about the murder," I said. "As I recall, Goldenblatt was killed with a golf club."

"A Bazooka four iron to the head," Samuels confirmed. "It cracked his skull."

According to Samuels the prime suspect had become terminally ill and the police investigation had stalled.

"What do you want from me?"

"The community would like to retain your services," Samuels told me, "to conduct our own investigation."

"What do you expect to gain by that?" I asked.

"Closure." Samuels leaned forward in his seat. "There's a black cloud hanging over Boca Heights. We need to find out what happened to Robert Goldenblatt."

"You want me to pick up where the police left off?" I asked.

"Exactly." Samuels nodded. "We want some answers for the community and for the families involved."

"I understand." I nodded. "So, who is the suspect?"

"Dominick Amici."

"Tell me about the other matter," I said immediately.

Samuels told me that a neo-Nazi family named Buford moved into Boca Heights three months ago and within weeks began causing problems. During a minor dispute their eighteen-year-old son told one of the neighbors, "Hitler didn't kill enough of you Jews." When the offended Jewish neighbor complained to the boy's father, Forrest Buford replied curtly, "Mind your own business."

The neighborhood association wrote the Bufords a letter, demanding a formal apology. In response, the Buford family didn't respond. Randolph Buford, their son, responded by giving "the finger" to everyone he passed while racing through the neighborhood in a black PT Cruiser that looked like a Nazi staff car. He displayed a swastika tattoo on his right arm and wore one on a necklace around his neck. Forrest Buford played loud German military music in his backyard. Mrs. Buford never spoke to anyone in the neighborhood, and their fifteen-year-old daughter, Eva, was a female version of her brother.

The neighbors complained to the Community Management Association, and the CMA sent more impotent letters to the Bufords, which were also ignored by the family. Eventually, the neighborhood association contacted the police.

"The police said there was nothing they could do," Samuels explained. "Frank Burke said the Bufords weren't breaking any laws. He suggested we handle it internally."

"What do you know about the Bufords?" I asked.

"We did a little research. They're originally from Tobacco Junction, South Carolina, which is —"

"The home of Aryan Army," I finished his sentence. I knew all about those slimy, hateful bastards, though I never had the privilege of busting one.

Samuels nodded. "The Bufords are card-carrying members of Aryan Army, a spinoff of Aryan Nations."

"All these Aryan assholes hate Jews," I said. "What are the Bufords doing here?"

"I don't know," Samuels admitted. "But they're causing a lot of dissension among the members."

"People normally band together against a common enemy," I told him.

"Not here," Samuels said. "We're too busy

arguing with each other. I was hoping you could get us organized. Maybe come up with a strategy to pacify the Bufords."

"You can't pacify people like this," I told him emphatically.

"Maybe you can reason with them," Samuels tried.

"You can't reason with these hate-mongers either," I insisted. "I wouldn't waste my time on strategies like that and I don't want the case."

"Do you have any suggestions?" Samuels asked dejectedly.

"I'm the wrong guy to ask," I told Samuels. "I deal with things differently than you might like."

"Is there anything I can do to change your mind?" Samuels tried.

"Let me think about it," I said. "Maybe I'll come up with something."

"We really could use your help," Samuels said sincerely.

"I'll help you with the Goldenblatt case," I decided.

CHAPTER 16

BOCA SYMPHONY

I found religion again in Boca.

"OH MY GOD," I praised the Lord.

"OH MY GOD!" Alicia Fine prayed responsively.

Mr. Johnson and I had dreamed of lying next to Alicia since the moment we first saw her. This time we weren't dreaming. She was there in the flesh, and we were luxuriating in the afterglow of a passionate duet. It was a classic recital played by two passionate, slightly out-of-practice musicians who had never performed together before.

What we lacked in finesse, we made up for with enthusiasm. After a tentative start, we began matching each other note for note. Mr. Johnson gave Alicia a standing ovation, and she agreed to an encore.

After a fifteen-minute intermission, the conductor's baton was raised again and we began again. The grand finale was far more subdued than the overture. When the piece was finished, the two artists embraced.

"Bravo, Maestro."

"Brava, Diva."

Alicia's head rested on my right arm.

"Thank you, Jesus," I said.

"You're Jewish." She giggled. "Why are you thanking Jesus?"

"I'm thanking everyone," I confessed. "I can't believe I'm here with you."

Alicia had phoned me the same day I met with Ely Samuels. I hadn't talked to her since she visited me in the hospital almost three weeks before. I thought of her often and so did Mr. Johnson. But I didn't think I belonged in Alicia Fine's world. She was a prom queen and a Long Island princess. I was a gym rat and an ex-cop.

"How are you feeling?" she asked nervously over the phone. "I expected to hear from you."

"I'm sorry," I said. "I've been busy." I felt like a real loser.

"I understand," she said softly. "Are you feeling better?"

"Yeah, I'm okay," I said. My heart was racing. An awkward silence followed, and I used the opportunity to think of myself as the consummate schmuck.

"Well, all right then," she sounded embarrassed. "I guess I'll be seeing you around."

"Yeah, sure," I said unconvincingly.

We exchanged good-byes. My throat hurt from the pounding of my heart, and my head ached.

You asshole, I said to myself. *What's the matter with you?* I picked up the phone and punched in her number.

"Hi, this is Alicia." A recorded message greeted me. "I can't come to the phone right now, but leave a message and I'll get back to you as soon as I can."

"BEEP!"

Where the hell could she have gone in five seconds?

"Alicia Fine." I don't know why I used her last name. "This is Eddie Perlmutter." I was rushing the words. "Just wanted you to know that I really appreciated your visit in the hospital, and I'm sorry I fell asleep during your story . . . and thanks for calling." I hung up.

"Fuckin' imbecile." I hit redial and got the answering machine again.

"It's me again." I sounded like an idiot. "To tell you the truth, I think about you all the time. I think you're beautiful and nice and sexy and —" I heard a click at the other end of the line.

"Eddie?" Alicia said.

"Have you been listening all this time?"

247

"Yes," she admitted. "Thank you for saying such nice things."

"It's easy to say nice things about you."

"Would you like to see me again?"

"I would love to see you again," I said. "When?"

"Now."

"Now? I'm all dirty and sweaty. I just finished teaching a boxing class at the Police Athletic League."

"You can shower here," she said.

LET'S GO! Mr. Johnson cheered.

And that's how I became a player in the band.

CHAPTER 17

BOCA GRAFFITI

I received a phone call from Chief Burke on my cell phone at Alicia Fine's house a couple of days later.

"I've been calling your apartment all morning," he said.

"I'm not there," I told him.

"Care to tell me where you've been?"

"No."

"Do you know anything about the Buford house being vandalized early this morning?"

"I know I'm not surprised."

"Four windows were broken, and a Star of David was painted on the house."

"There was only one Jewish star?" I asked like I was annoyed.

"Where were you at three o'clock this morning?" Frank ignored my attempt at humor.

"Am I a suspect?"

"Maybe," Burke said.

"Why?"

"You've got a reputation for some pretty aggressive behavior during your career," Burke told me.

"I'm retired."

"That's what I heard," Burke said. "But shortly after Ely Samuels told you about the Bufords, the Buford house was vandalized."

"Thank you for recommending me to the CMA by the way," I said.

"I didn't recommend you," Burke said.

"Then how did you know I met with Ely Samuels?"

"I'd hate to think you were involved with this vandalism, Eddie." Frank ignored my question.

"Then don't think about it."

"Don't say I didn't warn you," Frank Burke said.

"Warn the Bufords," I advised him.

"Are you working on the Goldenblatt case?" Burke changed the subject.

"Now how would you know that?"

"Lucky guess."

"I have a meeting with Dominick Amici tonight at the hospital," I told him.

"Tough case," he said. "Let me know if I can help you with anything," Frank offered.

"How are you at breaking windows and painting?"

"Smart-ass," he said, and hung up.

Alicia sat next to me on her sofa. "Who was that?"

"The Boca chief of police," I told her.

"What did he want?"

"He wanted to know if I had anything to do with the Buford house being vandalized this morning."

"Do you? You left my house at two this morning."

"You were awake?" I was surprised.

"Yes."

"Why didn't you say anything?"

"I was afraid to ask why you were leaving," she said. "Now I know why you were leaving, and I'm still afraid."

"There's nothing for you to be afraid of," I assured her.

"I'm afraid of violence, Eddie," she said. "I hope you got it out of your system."

"Alicia, this is my system," I explained, "I attack whatever I find threatening."

"The Bufords didn't threaten you," Alicia said.

"Yes they did," I disagreed. "When someone says Hitler didn't kill enough Jews, that's a threat to all Jewish people."

"The Bufords aren't Hitler," she persisted.

"If Hitler were alive today" — I raised my voice — "people like the Bufords would be the first in line to put Jews in ovens. I'd just as soon bake them first."

She hugged herself. "You're frightening me, Eddie." She shivered.

"The Bufords should frighten you."

"I'm not sure I can condone your actions," she said.

I saw a red spot, and it surprised me. Alicia had pushed the wrong button. I got up from the sofa. "I'm not asking you to condone anything," I said as I headed for the door.

"Where are you going?" she asked.

"Home," I said, opening the door.

"Can't we talk about this?" she tried.

"No," I said, closing the door behind me.

There are some things I just can't talk about.

Dominick Amici was awake when I entered his hospital room at seven-thirty that evening. His skin was a sickly shade of yellow but there was a smile on his drawn face. Carol Amici was there, and she introduced us.

"Hey, supercop," he said in a North End voice. "How you doin'?"

His handshake was firm but boney. I sat by his right side. "You mind sittin' on my left side? I got a glass eye in the right."

"No problem," I said, moving instantly.

252

"Did you lose your eye to cancer?" I asked.

"No. To a BB gun when I was eleven years old. My older brother was fuckin' around with it," he explained.

"Sorry," I said.

"Forget about it," Dom said like a wiseguy, and he laughed. Then he coughed until he was short of breath. He drank some water through a straw then put on an oxygen mask. He gradually began breathing easier. He removed the mask when he spoke. "So, I understand you want to talk to me."

"Well, first I wanted to meet you. Your wife and daughters have told me so much about you."

"Sorry," he said, "but the guy they told you about ain't here no more."

"I heard you were a great entrepreneur," I said, trying to lighten the mood. "And you built a chain of photo film development stores that was the biggest on Long Island."

"Yeah," he smiled, "and I sold it to big city schmucks who ruined it."

"Timing is everything," I confirmed.

"Yeah." He nodded sadly. "Did they tell you about my potato chip company I started after I left the film business?"

"No, I didn't hear about that," I said as Carol laughed in the background.

Dom laughed, too. "My potato chip factory used to stink up the whole town with the smells from all the flavors I tried."

"Why potato chips?" I asked.

He thought for a moment. "Why not?"

I liked Dominick immediately and wished he wasn't sick. I wished the Bufords were sick instead.

"So, you took the Goldenblatt case," Dominick said bluntly.

"Yeah," I answered. "Why not?"

We shared a laugh.

"So let's get right down to the basics," I said like a cop. "Did you kill Robert Goldenblatt?"

"You got me, copper," Dom laughed. "I hit the little fucker on the head with a golf club after making sure everyone in his neighborhood knew I was there to kill him."

"Stop joking," Carol reprimanded her husband.

"It doesn't matter," Dom insisted. "I'm too sick to go on trial, and this whole case will die when I do."

"Why are you the prime suspect?" I asked.

"It's a long story."

"I have time."

"Can't you think of a better way to spend your time?" Dom asked.

"Not if I can prove you're innocent," I

told him.

"Who cares?" Dom sounded frustrated.

"I care," Carol interrupted. "And the girls care."

"How many years have you two been married?" I asked.

"We'll be married forty-one years next week," Carol said.

"I didn't get you a present," Dom told her.

Carol got up from her chair, walked to his bedside, took off his oxygen mask, and kissed his dry lips. "You're my present," she told him gently.

"I know," he whispered, and I saw a tear in his good eye.

"Now, Dominick, you tell Eddie Perlmutter what happened that night," Carol told him.

"You really want to hear all this?" Dom turned to me.

"Yes I do," I said.

"I already told the police the whole story."

"Tell me," I said. "I'm a good listener."

Chapter 18
CIRCUMSTANTIAL CIRCUMSTANCES

Dom gave me permission to tape-record his version of the Goldenblatt incident. He wheezed and coughed frequently, and it took over an hour. When he was finished, he fell asleep.

I looked at Carol. "What a story," I said.

She shook her head slowly. "I know," she said sadly. "What do you think? Can you help us?"

"I don't know," I admitted. "About the only thing I feel certain about is that your husband didn't kill Robert Goldenblatt. I just can't see him bashing in anyone's head with a golf club."

"I'm glad someone else feels that way," she said.

"The evidence against him is all circumstantial," I commented.

"Well, circumstantial evidence has a lot of people believing that Dom is a murderer." Carol was frustrated.

"A lot of people believe in God, too."

"I think that's a bad comparison," she said defensively. "We believe in God. We're very religious."

"I'm not talking about religion, Carol. I'm talking about circumstantial evidence. Someone once said that everything written in the Bible was based on circumstantial evidence."

"Thomas Paine said that," Carol said dismissively, and she didn't sound happy with Thomas Paine or me. "I find it offensive."

"I appreciate how you feel, Carol," I said sympathetically. I didn't want religion to become the issue. "Legally speaking, however, circumstantial evidence is not from a witness who saw or heard anything. Circumstantial evidence is a fact that is inferred from another fact. Do you know anyone who can testify that the Bible is totally accurate as written?"

"Of course not," Carol conceded. "But I believe the Bible."

"And some people believe Dom's guilty," I said.

She looked sad and I felt bad.

"I see your point," she conceded. "And without a trial these people will always believe that Dom is a murderer."

"I'm afraid so," I said honestly.

257

"Maybe he'll get well," she said, "and have his day in court."

I didn't respond. There was no need. Dom was not going to get well.

"I don't want him to be remembered like this," Carol said.

"Neither do I," I told her. "I'll do everything I can."

Carol kissed me on the cheek and said, "Thank you."

CHAPTER 19

THE BOCA BUILDER

Dominick felt that in order for me to understand the circumstances surrounding the death of Robert Goldenblatt, I needed to understand the development of Boca Heights. So he gave me a history lesson on Boca real estate development. When I drove back to my apartment and saw three familiar Arvida signs on the drive, the name finally meant something to me.

Arthur Vining Davis was born in 1867 in Sharon, Massachusetts, a small town south of Boston. Davis, a pioneer of the aluminum industry, founded Alcoa Aluminum in 1907. In 1958, when he was a mere ninety-one years old, Davis began looking for new frontiers. He chose South Florida real estate and founded Arvida Development Company — ARthur VIning DAvis, get it? — "to set aesthetic precedence for future commercial and residential development in Boca Raton." Davis died in 1962 at the age of ninety-five but his dream lived on.

In 1966, IBM bought 550 acres of land from Arvida on Yamato Road in Boca Raton for the construction of a massive manufacturing and marketing facility. In 1975, fifteen years before IBM developed their first personal computer, Arvida built the Arvida Financial Park of Commerce on Yamato Road. To accommodate IBM executives and wealthy residents, Arvida built a private golf course several miles west of Commerce Park and named it Boca Heights Golf Course. They built a second private course nearer to IBM and called it Broken Sound Golf Course.

In the mideighties demand for land and housing in Boca Raton boomed. Arvida took advantage of the opportunity and started building two new residential communities near their two golf courses. They named one community Boca Heights Country Club and the other was named Broken Sound Country Club.

Arvida built and sold the houses at both communities faster than planned. Eventually two thousand acres of the former farmland became the site of two gated communities with nearly three thousand houses and condos. The amenities at both clubs included two golf courses, more than twenty tennis courts, a clubhouse, a health club, a dining room, meeting rooms, and card rooms.

By the midnineties when all housing development in Boca Heights and Broken Sound was completed, IBM made the decision to move out of Boca Raton. Arvida had to be more aggressive in marketing their two new gated communities in order to compete with the fast-growing competition. A unique golf membership structure provided prospective home buyers at the two communities with an option. They could join one course for one fee or both courses for a higher fee. It seemed like a good idea at the time.

The people who bought homes at Boca Heights and joined both courses had a "Two Course membership." The homeowners who opted to belong to only one course were known as "One Course members" and they were all assigned to the same course. Broken Sound developed a similar system and used its own terminology for their membership categories. The golf amenities at the two communities were basically the same.

After the construction of all the home sites was complete, Boca Heights Country Club members were entitled to assume management of the club. Arvida, however, was not anxious to give up the profitable management of the club and this led to a lawsuit.

Accusations flew. Members accused Arvida of all sorts of things and Arvida denied everything. Arvida had a force of in-house, wannabe-great attorneys and Boca Heights had a cadre of usetabe-great attorneys. A long, drawn-out war was inevitable.

On October 16, 1995, a lawsuit against Arvida was filed.

I read the complaint. It was a class action suit, alleging that Arvida had engaged in various acts of misconduct. Arvida was charged with misconduct in the establishment, operation, management, and marketing of the golf course and recreational facilities, as well as the alleged improper failure to turn over the facilities to the homeowners on a timely basis.

In the complaint the lawyers were seeking forty-five million dollars and other unspecified compensatory damages, the right to seek punitive damages, treble damages, prejudgment interest, and attorneys' fees and costs. The whole nine yards.

The case dragged on for years and cost both sides millions of dollars. The result was an unsatisfying financial settlement on behalf of the community members in 2001. Arvida was out of the community with a profit to show for their efforts. The members won a Pyrrhic victory.

Arvida's departure had an impact similar to when the British left Jerusalem in 1948. The inhabitants went to war with each other. The One Course members and the Two Course members attacked each other with long lists of grievances.

According to Dominick, e-mails flew through the air like mortar shells. Both sides suffered casualties, and their books ran red with ink. Withering surcharges, referred to as assessments, incited neighbor to turn against neighbor. Civil behavior ended, and civil war began.

I realized I was only hearing one side of the story, so I talked to other people at the club. The conversations went something like this:

Eddie Perlmutter: What's your problem with the One Course members versus the Two Course members?
One Course Member #1: The Two Course members are screwing us.
E.P.: How?
OCM #1: We subsidize their course and can't play there.

E.P.: Do you have proof of this subsidy?
OCM #1: Proof? What are you, a fuckin' detective?

Eddie Perlmutter: The One Course members claim they subsidize the Two Course members.
Two Course Member #1: They're full of shit.
E.P.: That doesn't really answer the question.
TCM #1: Sure it does.
E.P.: Look, all I want is a simple answer. Is it true that One Course members subsidize the Two Course members, even though they can't play on the Two Course?
TCM #1: You got proof of that?
E.P.: No.
TCM #1: Then it's not true.
E.P.: Can you prove it's not true?
TCM #1: Proof? What are you, a fuckin' detective?

Eddie Perlmutter: Why don't you just take out a Two Course membership?
One Course Member #2: Why should I? I'm a homeowner at Boca Heights, and the members own the club. If I'm an owner of the club, and the Two

Course is part of the club, then I should be able to play there without having to pay an initiation fee.

E.P.: But what about the current Two Course members? They paid as much as forty thousand dollars extra to join the Two Course.

OCM #2: Something should be done about that.

E.P.: Like what?

OCM #2: I don't care as long as it doesn't cost me anything.

Eddie Perlmutter: Do you think the One Course members are getting screwed by not being able to play on the Two Course? They're property owners like you and feel they should be entitled to play on both courses.

Two Course Member #2: In other words, they want something for nothing. Fuck 'em.

E.P.: But they claim they're subsidizing the Two Course members with extra payments.

TCM #2: No one's ever proven that. But think about this, Eddie: The Two Course brings up the value of the One Course and the overall property at Boca Heights. A new home buyer has the option of playing on two courses at Boca Heights. It's an advantage. And another thing, most Two Course members play only on the Two Course, even though they pay to play on both courses. If the Two Course members played on the One Course on a regular basis that course would be overcrowded. So, everyone benefits from the setup here.

E.P.: The One Course members don't think so.

TCM #2: They're a bunch of assholes.

E.P.: That seems to be the answer to a lot of issues around here.

I was confused by the claims and counterclaims. When I suggested an audit of the Two Course books to determine if the One Course members were actually subsidizing a facility they couldn't use, I was either told "Mind your own business" or was given some explanation I didn't understand.

I was also drawn into the assessment wars. Arvida left Boca Heights with several inadequate amenities. The facilities had needed to be improved but no one could agree on what needed to be done.

"We don't need a Taj Mahal for a new clubhouse."

"Cheap bastard. I want the best things

money can buy, and I don't care what it costs."

"Who needs a new health club? I don't use the old one."

"You should, you fat shit."

"I want to keep the understated elegance of Boca Heights."

"By 'understated elegance' you mean you don't want to spend any money."

"Everyone on the board of directors is stupid."

"The membership voted for the board of directors."

"The membership is stupid."

"You're a member."

"Are you calling me stupid?"

"We don't need a six-million-dollar new front entrance."

"I never leave the place. Why should I pay for a new entrance or exit?"

There were fifteen hundred homes with four thousand opinions at Boca Heights.

Robert Goldenblatt had been a man with a lot of opinions, and he expressed them regularly. He was a former president of the club and an aggressive guy. He was in favor of minimum spending, and he wanted a merger of the two types of memberships with no extra cost to the One Course members. Goldenblatt was a big man and an intimidating physical presence. He usually got his way.

Dominick Amici was a vocal supporter of having the best of everything, and he thought a merger of the two memberships with no compensation for the Two Course members was grossly unfair. Dominick was as big physically as Goldenblatt. He usually got his way, too.

Amici and Goldenblatt argued regularly at meetings, and it was no secret that they had developed an unhealthy dislike for one another. They seldom spoke to each other, except to debate the issues, and they avoided each other otherwise.

Then "the e-mail" was sent by Robert Goldenblatt to the entire club membership after a particularly acrimonious meeting. Dominick didn't have a copy with him when he told me the story at the hospital, so he could only give me the basics of the year-old missive. It went something like this:

At the club meeting tonight, Mr. Dominick Amici was once again loud and obnoxious throughout the proceedings. Mr. Amici's thinking is so outdated it is prehistoric and of no value in today's world. He should leave the management of the club to people who are intelligent enough to understand the problems at Boca Heights and do something about them.

The members I talked to about "the e-mail" agreed that it was in terribly poor taste. ("But it was certainly no reason for Dominick to plant a four iron in Goldenblatt's forehead.")

When I asked why everyone seemed so sure Dominick had committed murder, the various answers I received boiled down to the following:

Robert Goldenblatt was killed the same night "the e-mail" was distributed to the membership. It was easy to understand why Dominick Amici would be so offended. Also, at a little after nine on the night of "the e-mail," Dominick's car was seen by Goldenblatt's next-door neighbor, screeching to a halt in front of Goldenblatt's house. It was a cloudy, windy night. Dominick ran toward the open garage shouting, "Goldenblatt, you asshole, I wanna talk to you." Goldenblatt pushed a button on the garage wall to close the overhead door, but Amici managed to get into the garage an instant before the door closed. Two more neighbors could hear the banging and screaming coming from inside the garage. The next-door neighbor who had been there from the beginning of the confrontation quickly told the arriving dog walkers what had transpired. They suddenly heard a loud bang, and then Dominick Amici appeared, running through the front gate. He had obviously exited through the back door of the garage that led to the courtyard behind the front gate. He looked panicked, and there was blood on his hands.

"That man is crazy," Dominick said to the bystanders as he got into his car and drove away. The garage door was still closed, so the onlookers entered cautiously through the front gate and opened the back door to the garage. Robert Goldenblatt was found lying dead in a pool of blood with the blade of his four iron embedded in his forehead. The police confirmed that the four iron had Dominick's fingerprints on it, but the blood on his hands was proven to be his own, not Goldenblatt's.

The circumstantial evidence was impressive. I had a lot of work to do.

I met Ely Samuels in front of Robert Goldenblatt's house in an area called Harbor Point. No harbor and no point. Expansive, expensive homes backed up to a large, man-made lake on the east side of the street. There were no homes on the west side. Goldenblatt's house was an interesting structure. As you faced the house, the garage was to the left below a balcony of a two-floor, two-bedroom guest house that was separate from the main house. The main house was behind a ten-foot-high wooden gate. We entered the courtyard, where I saw a small swimming pool and the man-made lake behind the house.

Samuels led me into the garage through the courtyard garage door. Across the three-car garage was a large overhead door to accommodate two full-sized cars. There was a separate small overhead door to accommodate a compact car. He pressed two buttons on the wall next to the door, and both overhead doors went up. We walked across the garage to the front of the house and looked back again. "So Amici pulls up there." Samuels pointed. "Goldenblatt is in the garage practicing golf with plastic golf balls."

"Why was he practicing in the garage? Why not in the driveway where there's more room?"

"Good question," Samuels said. "It was very windy that night and the plastic golf balls probably would have blown to Pompano."

"So why practice at all on a night like that?"

"Goldenblatt had developed the shanks."

"Is that like the shingles?" I asked.

"No. It's like death. It's when a golfer hits the ball sideways instead of straight."

"On purpose?"

"No, of course not."

"Then why does he do it?"

"He can't help it. There's something wrong with his swing," Samuels explained.

"So, Goldenblatt was trying to correct his swing by hitting plastic golf balls in his garage on a windy night?"

Samuels nodded.

I shrugged.

I surveyed the garage, trying to re-create what had happened that night. I pictured the struggle between the two men, which should have been even enough, considering that they were both enormous. Yet, Amici said he ran away from Goldenblatt. Was he running from the scene of the crime, or was he running from a maniac with a golf club?

Samuels exited through the open front of the garage while I waited by the heavy wood and metal back door. When Samuels was safely outside I pressed the buttons to close the overhead doors. I opened the back door and stepped into the courtyard, still holding the door handle. I turned to look back at the garage, then let go of the heavy door. A gusty breeze off the lake blew the door shut with surprising force. The door slammed loudly. It was a relatively mild day, but the breeze still had enough velocity to slam the door shut forcefully.

I walked past the pool to the back fence and looked out at the lake. The breeze was warm and steady off the water. I went to the back garage door and opened it again. When I released the handle the breeze off the lake slammed the door shut again.

I inspected the courtyard area. The Goldenblatt main house was one level, but high ceilings inside made it a tall structure. I guessed the peak of the roof at approximately twenty feet. Thanks to Boca's zero lot-line zoning, the house next door on the south side was only a few feet away from Goldenblatt's pool area. The house had two levels and was taller than Goldenblatt's house by several feet. The houses were separated by high palms and thick vegetation.

The breeze off the lake was squeezed between the two houses to the front of the Goldenblatt lot and the two-story, unattached guesthouse. The two buildings created a wind tunnel that funneled enough wind velocity from a mild breeze to generate a gust strong enough to slam a heavy door shut with authority.

I left the courtyard and joined Samuels in front of the Goldenblatt house.

"What took you so long?" he asked.

"I took a dip." The air was calm in front of the Goldenblatt house and it was several degrees warmer than the courtyard. "Actually, I was trying to remember the basic laws of physics that I didn't learn in high school."

"And what did you remember?"

"Nothing," I admitted.

"Got any theories?" he asked.

"Yeah, I think so."

"You're joking." He raised his eyebrows.

"My theory might be a joke," I conceded, "but I'm not joking."

"I'm listening," he told me.

"Don't strain yourself," I said, "because I'm not talking. I need to gather my thoughts into a cohesive bunch of bullshit."

We shook hands and got into our cars. I let Samuels leave first, and then I drove to the nearby neighborhood of Vintage Estates and the Buford house.

Young Buford was in front of the white stucco house scrubbing off the large, blue Star of David I had painted near the front door. Hope Blue Alien Spray Paint was a bitch to get off any surface unless you had an industrial solvent like ITW Daymon

Graffiti Remover and a wire brush. I didn't know what he was using but the Israeli blue paint drizzled down the side of the house discoloring the walls.

I stopped my car in front of the house and watched the little Nazi scrub. He was dressed entirely in black and had a buzz cut on the sides of his head and a thin, short dyed Mohawk running down the middle. He was a Goth. I had dealt with Goths in Boston years ago and recently at the Publix supermarket in the Regency Mall. I couldn't stand the morbid little motherfuckers. Randolph was squat, with a flat face and unremarkable features, except for a pair of vacant blue eyes that stared at me when he sensed my presence. I stared back, trying to tell him with a smirk that I was the artist who had decorated his walls. Just then Forrest Buford came out of the house carrying a bucket and a brush. He was a tall man with broad shoulders. His sandy-colored hair was close-cropped, and his thick neck supported a wide, flat, humorless face. Father and son both stared at me now.

I put the Mini in gear and drove slowly past the house. Their suspicious eyes followed me. I extended my left arm out the open driver's window and gave them a Nazi salute, and then, with a subtle twist of my wrist, I gave them the finger.

Chapter 20
A MATTER OF DEATH AND LIFE

I crashed on my rented living-room sofa and clicked on the television set with the remote control. I checked my watch. It was five-thirty in the afternoon of another sunny day in Boca. Today, however, was different from any prior sunny afternoon. Today was the last day of Dominick Amici's life. By now he was receiving a morphine drip at Hospice by the Sea to ease his departure. They say you can't die in your own dreams, but what if you die while you're dreaming?

The African Queen, starring Katharine Hepburn and Humphrey Bogart, was on television. I'd seen it before. Katharine Hepburn looked great. It would be a long time before she would start shaking from Parkinson's. I guess the best people can hope for is to get old before they get sick.

Dominick Amici was sixty-six years old when he was diagnosed with leukemia. He would be sixty-seven when he died. He would be thirty-seven years younger than his amazing mother was when she died.

Dominick had agreed to go to hospice that afternoon, only ten days after telling me the Robert Goldenblatt story. Dominick didn't want to go. He wanted to stay with his wife and family. He wanted to play golf and poker with his friends. He wanted to watch his grandchildren grow up. But when his priest, Father Tom, told Dominick it was okay for him to say good-bye to his family on earth and join his family in heaven, Dominick agreed. With his church's blessing, Dominick Amici was prepared to go to the afterlife he had been promised since the beginning of his life.

I was at the hospital when Dom made his decision to leave us, and I wanted to scream, "Stay here with us. There is no afterlife!"

But I didn't want to disrupt his peace of mind and the unquestioning faith of his family. And what did I know anyway? Maybe there was an afterlife, and Dominick could be a par golfer when he got there. Every time Dom talked about being a par golfer, his buddies would say, "Yeah, sure, Dom, in your next life." Maybe now Dom was only a heartbeat away from being a par golfer.

Whether there was an afterlife or not, though, I had unresolved concerns about *this* life.

My relationship with Alicia Fine was stalled. We had talked only once since the night I left her apartment, and our last discussion was awkward.

Alicia Fine's nature was to avoid confrontation. My nature was to confront.

"The Bufords never did anything to you," she reasoned.

"They won't get a chance."

"Violence doesn't solve anything."

"Aryan Army thinks that violence solves everything."

"So your answer is to be violent like them?"

"No, my answer is to be more violent than them."

Alicia and I didn't talk again after that phone call. There was nothing to talk about. We were from different worlds. In my world you had to fight back against creeps like the Bufords.

I dozed off watching Bogie and Hepburn bobbing in the water. Somewhere between asleep and awake I accepted that Dominick was going and Alicia was gone.

"You pay. You die," I heard from the bottom of a well.

I tried to open my eyes, but I felt as if there were weights on my lids.

"You pay. You die," I heard again.

I managed to get one eye open, and I saw the round faces of the men who had tried to kill me in the hospital. This time I wasn't drugged. I bolted upright on the sofa, and threw myself in the direction of the two men. There were no catheters or intravenous tubes to drag me down. There was, however, a coffee table. I caught both my shins on the sharp edge of the heavy table and toppled forward. I rolled onto my back and looked up. The two faces were still there, inside the television set. I was confused. I sat upright on the floor and looked at the television screen. The older man was smiling cheerfully at me, and I heard him say clearly, "You buy. You pay. You die. We pay. Right, Howard?"

"That's right, Dad!"

Printed words came on the screen:

LIVE RICH! DIE RICH! BARRY KAYE & ASSOCIATES.

It was an advertisement for a local insurance company.

"And now back to our movie."

"Schmuck!" I called myself when I realized that I had been attacked twice by a father-and-son life-insurance team.

"You buy (our insurance), you pay (the premium), you die (pass away), we pay (the death benefit)."

I decided not to tell anyone.

I pulled myself up from the floor and glanced at my watch. It was only eight p.m. and there was still plenty of time to play another round of Follow the Goth, the same game I had been playing all week.

I showered and dressed quickly in my black stakeout clothing. I stuffed my Glock in the waistband at the back of my pants and hid it under a Windbreaker. As I opened the door to my apartment, I had second thoughts and removed the gun from my pants and put it away. I knew if it was too convenient I would be tempted to shoot a Goth. Unarmed, I drove my Mini Cooper to the Boca Mall. I put on the radio to 91.5 CLASSY. It played great soft hits for all ages. "Mockingbird" by Nino Tempo and April Stevens was just ending and a commercial came through loud and clear.

"You buy, you pay. You die, we pay!"

CHAPTER 21

BOCA GOTHIC

Definition: Goth: "One who is rude, uncivilized, a barbarian, a rude ignorant person."

Origin: "East Germanic, Teutonic tribe that sacked Rome in the early fifth century."

I had been following Randolph Buford for a week and he was consistent. He would park on the south side of the mall, where he would meet four fellow night crawlers. There were two gangly white males and two fat, homely white females. They all had bad skin. For nonconformists the Goths looked remarkably alike. They wore baggy black clothes, cheap trinkets, streaked hair and tattoos, with jewelry in their noses, lips, eyebrows, and ears.

The Goths wandered aimlessly through the mall, poking fun at shoppers and occasionally bumping into some undersized, old person for laughs. The presence of the mall security kept these idiots subdued inside the mall. The trouble took place when

Randolph and his Goth friends were outside. In the remote areas of the parking lot, I observed them slashing car tires and bending radio antennas. Last night I watched as they carved swastikas on the sides of a new four-door, black Mercedes sedan. I saw a few red spots, but I didn't act. I wanted to bust these bastards for something more felonious than anti-Semitic key carvings. Maybe tonight would be my lucky night.

Out of the shadows of the parking lot lights, I saw the silhouettes of two chunky girls, two wispy teenage boys, and squat Randolph Buford. The five of them stopped at an old, rusty Buick and punctured all four tires. I wanted to beat the shit out of all five of them, but not over four rubber wheels. While they were doing their carvings in the fading gray of the car doors, I saw two figures slowly approaching. A young brown woman was aiding an older black woman who was using a walker. When the young woman saw what Randolph and his boys had done to her car, she walked ahead of the older woman and started screaming at the group. I couldn't make out her words, but I saw her waving her arms and shouting. Then all hell broke loose. Randolph punched the defiant woman in the face, knocking her to the ground. I saw the fat girls laugh and poke each other. One of the male Goths shoved the old lady to the ground and kicked away her walker. I was out of my car and running toward the mayhem as fast as I could. My right knee was angry with me, but I ignored the pain. I saw the third male kick at the old woman who tried to fend him off with upraised hands. She received a boot to her side.

"Bastard," she screamed, and moved her own frail leg in a feeble attempt to kick her attacker.

The Goth who had knocked the elderly woman down was drawing back his foot slowly, looking for a good place to kick the fragile old woman again. I got there while the Goth's foot was still drawn back. Using a soccer-style sweeping motion, I kicked the attacker's upraised foot out from under him and pushed him forward so that he crashed face-first on the pavement with a splattering sound. The fat girls stopped giggling. They gawked like witnesses to an auto accident. Randolph was too busy tearing at the younger woman's blouse and bra to pay much attention to the smashing-pumpkin sound his friend's face made.

The boy who had punctured the tires turned toward me with his knife in his hand.

I guessed the blade was about three-inches long. It was no kinjal, but it had enough length to puncture something more life-supporting than an old tire. The sight of the knife didn't stop me from moving forward. I was doing what I had been born and trained to do: Attack!

The boy crouched and pointed the knife toward me. I crouched and held my hands out to my sides, waiting for him to make the first move. We stared at each other. He looked familiar. The nose ring gave him away.

"You never shoulda left the cash register at Publix," I said to him.

With a quick slapping motion of my right hand, I grabbed the loop of the ring on the bottom of his nose and tore it from the flesh that separated his nostrils. That kid sure could scream. Both hands went to his bloody nose, and one of the lard-ass girls said, "Ewww, gross. Let's split."

"You son of a bitch," the injured Goth cursed. "I'll kill you."

He took his knife hand away from his gushing nose, just long enough for me to grab his wrist and pull it toward me. I ducked under his arm like I was doing the lady's part of a Lindy dance step. I was behind the bleeding checkout clerk as fast as a sixty-year-old gimp could perform a sophisticated karate move, and I twisted his arm as I moved. Eventually I got into a position where I could jam the knife he was still holding in his hand into his right butt cheek. Man, that Goth could howl. I let the kid fall to his knees, his hand still clutching the knife handle that protruded from his ass. I threw a right hand at the Goth's face but maneuvered my fist past the target and hit him with my right elbow instead. The kid fell forward, unconscious. I turned quickly and saw that I had Randolph's attention. He stood up, leaving the hysterical woman on the ground, and I expected him to charge me. Instead, the little Nazi seemed frozen in place.

"I know you," he managed to croak hoarsely.

"No, you don't," I said, approaching him cautiously. "You've seen me but you don't know me."

"You're the guy in the Mini Cooper from Boca Heights." He pointed at me.

"And you're an Aryan asshole from nowhere." I kicked him squarely in the balls.

All I heard was a grunt. Randolph dropped to his knees and fell forward. He tried to get up by rolling over on his back, but I jammed a foot onto his chest to hold him in place. "Stay," I commanded him like a bad dog.

He stopped moving.

"I know you, too," the brown-skinned woman said as she did her best to pull her blouse together. She was on her feet. Nurse Premice?

"Claudette?"

"Yeah, Claudette," she said in a shaky voice.

Claudette walked past me and went to the old woman who lay muttering on the ground. Claudette knelt next to her and said some words of comfort. The prone woman answered in a voice strong enough to indicate she would survive. Claudette helped the woman sit up. The old woman's face was bruised and bloodied. I wanted to kick all three guys in their six balls.

I heard the wail of a siren and saw two approaching police cars, followed by an ambulance. Claudette turned from the old woman. "I called 911 on my cell while you were busy," she explained. She stood up and faced me.

"Have you been following me, Claudette?" I said, trying to lighten the moment.

She laughed nervously. Then she started to cry. I walked to her and put my hands on her shoulders.

"Those bastards," she sniffled as she leaned into me. "Those evil little bastards." We stood still for a moment holding each other. She recovered quickly and pushed away from me. "Where are the two girls who were with them?" she asked.

"Who cares?" I asked. "More importantly, how's Queen?"

"You remembered her name," Claudette said. She seemed impressed. "She's tough. She'll be all right."

"Is dat da white boy you was telling me about?" Queen asked in a gravelly voice.

"Grandma!"

The police arrived and checked out the scene while the ambulance attendants looked after the injured. They tried to put Queen on a stretcher, but she refused.

"Dem boys need a stretcha a lot more den me," she said, looking scornfully at the fallen boys in black.

Randolph was struggling to sit up. The Publix boy with the knife in his butt was squirming and groaning. The kid lying face-first on the pavement was motionless except for his labored breathing.

One of the policemen approached me. "Eddie Perlmutter, right? I met you when you toured the police station with Frank Burke. I'm Danny Burns."

"Officer Burns." We shook hands.

"What happened here?" Burns asked.

"Ask her," I pointed to Claudette.

Claudette explained everything.

"She called me white trash," Randolph defended himself.

We all looked at him.

"So, you punched her in the face," I said.

"That's right," he confessed proudly.

"Randolph, you give white trash a bad name," I said.

"How do you know my name?" he asked.

"Lucky guess."

"You just happened to be in the area, Eddie?" Burns asked.

"Pure coincidence," I said.

"It's a good thing he was here," Claudette interjected. "That boy over there was tearing my clothes off like he was planning to rape me."

"That's a lie," Randolph protested. "I wouldn't rape no half-breed monkey like you!"

"Oh no?"

Claudette put her hands on her hips. Her ripped blouse opened, revealing a torn black bra and skin the color of coffee ice cream. Mr. Johnson took notice.

"Were you planning to try on my blouse?"

She covered herself up again and pointed

at another Goth.

"That one over there, the one lying on his broken, ugly face, was working on kicking my grandmother to death."

"What about that guy?" Burns pointed.

"The one with the knife in his ass?" I asked.

"Yeah, him."

"I disarmed him."

"You'll have to come to the station and make a statement," Officer Burns said.

"Of course," I assured him.

"You too, miss," he said to Claudette.

"Okay. But what about those fat white girls?"

"What girls?" Burns asked.

"There were two girls with these guys," I explained. "They ran off."

"How would you describe them?" Burns asked me.

"Two fat, homely white girls dressed in black," Queen said.

"Eddie?"

"I couldn't have said it better myself," I acknowledged. "I'm sure you'll find them. They don't blend in real well in Boca."

The three boys were taken away in the ambulance, but Queen refused to ride with them. I assured Officer Burns that we would meet them at the Second Avenue police station to make our statements.

"Thank you for helping us," Claudette Premice said.

"Yeah, tank you, Eddie Perlmuttah," Queen said to me. "You a good mahn. No wonder my granddaughta talk so nice about you."

"Grandma!" Claudette squirmed.

"You got to get a mahn like Eddie here, girl. You single, Perlmuttah, right?"

I nodded and smiled.

"So how about brown sugah over dere?"

"Grandma!" Claudette protested.

"Your granddaughter is beautiful," I told Queen.

Queen grinned, showing empty spaces between her front teeth.

By the time we had finished our statements at the police station, it was nearly midnight.

"I'll drive you two home, and you can have your car fixed tomorrow," I offered.

"We can take Ms. Premice home, Eddie," Burns said. "Queen is going to the hospital for observation."

"I am not," Queen disagreed.

"Oh yes you are, Grandma," Claudette told her. "That boy may have broken something. They gotta check you out."

Queen looked around. She could see that

she was getting no support.

"Okay, I'll go to the hospital so long as Eddie Perlmuttah dere take my granddaughta home," Queen insisted.

Claudette rolled her eyes.

"Okay with you?" Officer Burns asked me.

Mr. Johnson nudged me.

"My pleasure," I said.

"We'll get Queen to the hospital and check her in," Burns said. "We'll dust their car for prints, look for evidence, and have it towed to our garage. You can get it in the morning."

Mr. Johnson was wide awake.

CHAPTER 22

THE QUEEN AND I

Forrest Buford barged in the main entrance of the Boca police station just as we were preparing to leave. The large, angry Aryan demanded that his son be released immediately. Red spots started playing tag in front of my eyes the instant he entered the room. He was an intimidating presence, and he knew it. What he didn't know, however, was that I couldn't be intimidated.

Acting Chief Frank Burke arrived just as I was stepping in front of the Aryan asshole. Burke had been called at home due to the severity of the charges. Burke told Buford that Randolph wasn't going anywhere until the morning, when he would be transferred to the West Palm Beach prison for his arraignment.

"Bullshit," Forrest Buford roared.

"Keep talking like that and you can share a cell with him," Burke said calmly.

"Look, Chief Burke," Buford was mollified, "you and I have met before."

"Yes, we have, Mr. Buford," Burke said, glancing at me. "Your house was vandalized not too long ago."

"Then you know we're local home-owners," Buford tried. "And not a flight risk. We're solid citizens of Boca Raton."

"I know you're a solid citizen of Aryan Army," I interjected.

Forrest Buford looked at me like I was an annoying insect. I suppose from his perspective I was.

"I know who you are." He looked down at me. "You're that Jewish cop from Boston everyone thinks is so special."

"Me? No, I'm no one special at all," I feigned modesty before displaying spite. "I'm just a little Jew who kicked your son's ass while he was sexually assaulting that nice-looking lady over there."

Just for laughs I pointed to Queen.

"Yeh, dat's right," Queen said.

Even Claudette stopped scowling long enough to smile. I saw Burke smirk.

"That black trash?" Buford stammered.

I saw a black policeman in the outer office look up from his paperwork and frown.

"I'll have you know," I stated, "that this woman is a direct descendant of the king of Haiti."

"What king of Haiti?" Buford looked like he would explode, so I lit his fuse.

"Haiti only had one king, you dumb fuck," I said.

"Who you calling a dumb fuck?" Buford took a menacing step toward me.

I stepped toward him. Burke stepped between us.

"Mr. Buford," Burke said firmly, "stay calm please. Eddie, watch your mouth."

"You fuckin' Jews expect me to believe that my son tried to rape that old hag," Buford snapped.

"Mr. Buford." Burke raised his voice. "First of all, I'm not Jewish. I'm Irish Catholic."

"He hates Irish Catholics too, Frank," I interjected.

"And second of all" — Burke ignored me — "your son did not try to rape *that* woman." He pointed at Queen. "He's accused of assaulting *that* woman." He pointed to the lovely Claudette sitting quietly in the corner. "He punched her in the face and tried to tear her blouse off," Burke explained.

Buford gave Claudette a look of contempt.

"Jews, niggers, and Catholics." Buford had a hate snit. "You're all going to be sorry you ever met me," Buford snarled.

"I'm sorry already," I let him know.

Buford stomped toward the front door.

"Asshole," I said as he passed me.

He glared but didn't stop.

"I thought that went well," I said when Buford was gone.

"That man don't like nobody," Queen observed correctly. "How you think he feels about voodoo?"

"I'm sure he hates voodoo too, Queen," I said.

"Yeah, well, I make a little doll of him and stick a needle up his tight ass," she chuckled.

The black cop in the outer room laughed.

Queen departed with Officer Burns for the hospital. Claudette and I headed for Delray Beach in my Mini Cooper. It took about fifteen minutes on 95 North to get to Delray and another fifteen minutes driving east on Atlantic Avenue to reach the Haitian area known as Osceola Park. I followed Claudette's directions to a neighborhood of small private houses.

The streets were clean. The lawns were tiny. The houses were white. The people were black. The only white face I saw was my own in my rearview mirror and I didn't look that great.

I stopped the Mini in front of the house

she indicated. The one-level dwelling was no better and no worse than the other houses on the street.

"Would you like to come in?" she asked.

"No, that's okay," I said. "You must be exhausted."

"Actually I'm not," she told me. "Too much adrenaline. I'd like some company."

"You sure?"

"Positive."

The house seemed smaller inside. I looked at family photographs on the walls and tables. There were all black faces in the pictures except for one photo. There was a white man, very handsome, with blond, wavy hair standing next to a very attractive black woman. I picked up the picture from the table.

"Your parents?" I asked.

"Yes," she said, taking the picture from my hands and looking at it reflectively. "Do you know about Haiti, Eddie?" she asked.

"Not much," I said. "I know it's a poor country."

"It is a very poor country with a troubled past," she said.

"Is that why you came to America?"

"I had no choice," she said. "I had to leave Haiti."

"Why?"

"It's a long story."

I sat down on her sofa. "Tell it to me."

"It's been a long day," she said unconvincingly.

"You won't be able to sleep for a while anyway," I said. "You're too wound up. Talk to me."

She sat in a chair across from me. "Okay," she sighed. "Did you know that Columbus discovered Haiti the same year he discovered America?" she began.

"Hey, 1492 was a good year for him," I interjected. "I wonder if he played that number?"

She smiled. "There were a million Arrowak Indians in Haiti when Columbus arrived. In three hundred years the natives were wiped out by war and disease."

"In America we killed our Indians, too," I reminded her.

"Yes you did," she said. "That seemed to be the Europe an way in those days."

"Not all Europeans. A Dutch guy I knew from South Africa back in the seventies told me that the only difference between America and South Africa was that his ancestors didn't kill their Indians."

"Interesting perspective," she said.

"It's a self-serving point of view," I said.

"Well, anyway," she continued, "Columbus claimed the island for Spain and named it Hispaniola. The Indians were gradually replaced by black slaves brought to the island by Spain and France. Slave labor fueled the entire economy there for hundreds of years."

"Still sounds like America," I said.

"There does seem to be a pattern," she said "But, at the end of the eighteenth century things began to change on the island. The spirit of the 1789 French Revolution spread to Hispaniola and a voodoo priest named Hougman called for a civil war to free the island's slaves."

"How do you know all this?"

"My white father was a diplomat and a student of history," she explained. "My mother was educated. They wanted us to know our heritage."

I nodded my understanding.

"Black heroes like Toussaint Louverture, Jack Desallines, and Henri Christophe led the slaves to freedom by defeating the French army. The slaves won their emancipation in 1793."

"The French lose again," I said.

"They weren't done yet," she said. "Napoleon sent his brother-in-law, Charles LeClerc, and forty thousand men to Haiti to restore order."

"We're talking about *the* Napoleon?" I asked.

"Yes, that Napoleon," she confirmed.

"He was short like me," I said.

"I think he was shorter than you," she laughed. "But you both seem quite formidable."

"It's a short guy thing," I told her. "So what happened to LeClerc?"

"Louverture welcomed LeClerc to Haiti with open arms," she said. "And LeClerc rewarded the hospitality by having his host arrested and shipped off to Fort-de-Joux in the French Alps where he froze to death."

"What about LeClerc?"

"He remained on the island to restore order."

"So Louverture froze in the Alps while LeClerc baked in Haiti?"

"Exactly," she said. "A lot of French soldiers in Haiti got yellow fever and died. Most of the army was sick. By the time the second Haitian revolution took place the French were too weak to resist. It was a rout for the Haitians. France finally abandoned the island in 1803 and in 1804 Haiti became the first black republic in the western hemisphere."

"So why didn't everyone live happily ever after?" I asked.

"My father believed that the Haitian leaders were too corrupt and the Haitian people were too volatile," she said.

"All the leaders couldn't be corrupt," I said.

"Maybe not," she conceded. "But from 1843 to 1915 Haiti had twenty-two presidents and not one of them was impeached. They were overthrown or worse."

"What do you mean, *worse?*"

"In 1915 President Guillaume Sam was dismembered."

"You're joking," I said in disbelief, and for some reason I laughed.

"No, it's the truth." She covered her mouth with both hands to stifle a laugh.

"What are we laughing at?" I asked.

"The absurdity of it all, I guess," she said, sighing. "But it's true. After only five months in office Sam was implicated in the massacre of one hundred sixty-seven political prisoners. The citizens vowed revenge and came after him the next day."

"What do you mean they came *after him?*"

"A mob chased Sam from his home to the French legation where he tried to take refuge."

"Did the French protect him?"

"Not a chance," she said. "A group of prominent Haitian citizens, dressed in morning coats and bowler hats, dragged Sam from the house and threw him over a wrought-iron fence to a mob surrounding the embassy."

"Was he already dismembered when they threw him over? I mean did they throw him over piece by piece?"

"No, they threw the whole man over the fence," she told me. "The crowd on the other side dismembered him. Isn't that bizarre?"

"That's one word for it," I said. "Then what happened?"

She got up from the chair and walked to a bookcase. She retrieved a scrapbook. She sat with the book on her lap and thumbed through the pages until she found what she wanted. She removed an embossed newspaper article. "Here, read this. It's a copy from an old newspaper article written by a young American diplomat who was on the scene in 1915."

"Why did your family save this paper for so long?"

"Read it first and then I'll explain."

I held the article to the light and read the words written nearly ninety years ago. *"There was one terrific howl of fury. I could see that something or somebody was on the ground in the center of the crowd, just before the gates, and when a man disentangled himself from the crowd and rushed howling by me, with a severed hand from which the blood was dripping, the thumb which he had stuck in his mouth, I knew the assassination of the President was complete —"* I stopped reading. "Holy shit," I said. "I don't believe this."

"Finish reading," she insisted.

"Behind him came other men with the feet, the other hand, the head, and the other part of the body displayed on poles, each one followed by a mob of screaming men and women." I handed the paper back to her. "Lovely," I said. "And what's the significance of this particular article to you?"

"The man with the president's thumb in his mouth was my grandfather," she said solemnly.

"Get out of here!"

"It's true," she said.

"So, your grandfather was the president's right-hand man," I said.

To her credit, she smiled a little at my feeble attempt to take the edge off the story. "I prefer to think of him as a political dissident," she said.

"Are we talking about Queen's husband?" I asked

"Yes," she said. "His name was Charles DeValle."

"Do you take after him?" I asked.

"In some respects I do."

I sat on my hands.

"You're quite safe in that regard," she said, shaking her head like I was being silly.

"Good," I said, placing my hands on my lap. "Do you remember your grandfather?"

"Not much," she said. "Mostly I know what Queen told me. She said my grandfather was filled with hate."

"What did he hate?"

"He hated the white men who took his ancestor, Tamu Oliwande, from her home in Nigeria and brought her to Hispaniola in chains. He hated the white plantation owner Peter Boyer who impregnated Tamu when she was fifteen and disavowed the baby boy because the child was too black. He hated his ancestors for allowing thirty thousand whites to enslave five hundred thousand blacks. He hated his mixed blood because he felt like he did not belong in either the white or black world."

"That's a lot of hate to carry around," I said.

"Yes it is," she agreed. "My grandfather hated President Sam, too. So, when Sam was thrown over the fence my nineteen-year-old grandfather cut off his partially dismembered right hand and stuck the hand in his mouth by the thumb. He stopped deliberately in front of European witnesses and showed them the severed hand. He wanted the world to know that the citizens of Haiti would defend their independence with the same ferocity they used dismembering President Sam."

"America has never been afraid of thumb suckers," I told her proudly.

"Be serious," she said without enthusiasm. "My grandfather was a brave man."

"He was brave," I agreed. "But don't you think he was a little over the top?"

"Maybe he could have used more self-restraint," she said.

"Maybe he could have used some heavy-duty Ritalin," I said. "My grandfather was a very brave man too and fearless."

"Tell me about him."

"Another time," I said. "It's still your turn."

"Okay," she said as if she had a lot more to get off her chest. "A few days after Sam was dismembered, President Wilson sent U.S. Marines into Port-au-Prince to restore order. He said they would only be there temporarily."

"Were they temporary?

"No," she said. "They remained in Haiti for twenty years."

"Why am I not surprised?" I said, thinking of America's current foreign policy.

"Haiti was under the thumb of a foreign power again and this made my grandfather very angry," Claudette continued.

"Your grandfather had a thing with thumbs, didn't he?" I interrupted. "And are you trying to tell me he wasn't angry when he cut off Sam the Man's Hand?"

"Of course he was angry then." She was getting impatient with my attempts at humor. "But now he was angry with the United States."

"Can I interrupt for a second?"

"Sure."

"What did he do with the president's hand?"

"Eddie!" she exclaimed.

"It's a valid question," I defended myself.

"You're morbid."

"Maybe," I said. "But what do you do with a severed hand after you've sucked the thumb? Do you walk up to a stranger and ask if you can give him a hand?"

"I don't know what happened to Sam's hand." She reached across the short distance between us and lightly slapped my hands. "You're impossible," she said.

I grabbed her hands in mine and held them. When I didn't let them go immediately she looked into my eyes uncertainly. Then she looked down and pulled her hands free. She appeared flustered.

"I'm sorry," I said, not sure why I was sorry. "Please go on."

She told me that her grandfather hated foreign rule and resisted U.S. policies every step of the way. "Despite his protests against the puppet governments set up by America, each president elected during the time U.S. troops were in Haiti served a full term. The first president elected after the Americans departed in 1941, however, was overthrown in 1946. Demarsais Estime succeeded the deposed Elie Lescott but he was overthrown in 1950. The next president, Petey Magliore was overthrown in 1956."

"Not much job security," I said. "When did Queen come into the picture?"

"Charles and Queen met at a political rally against Eugene Roy shortly after he was elected in 1930. My grandfather would have been about thirty-four at the time. My grandmother was only eighteen."

"They didn't like President Roy either?"

"No, they thought Roy was corrupt, too," she said. "Queen was very political and very beautiful. My grandfather didn't have a chance. They were married six months after they met and Queen gave birth to a baby girl within a year."

"Your mother."

"My mother," she confirmed. "They named her Bridgette and in 1955 Bridgette married Allistar Clarke, a white diplomat from London."

"Your father," I confirmed.

"Yes," she said. "In 1956 a physician named Francois Duvalier was elected president of Haiti."

"Papa Doc," I remembered. "From what I've heard he should have been dismembered."

"You're right," Claudette said. "Papa Doc proved to be the most heartless president of all. He recruited a ferocious group of thugs to protect him and named them the Ton Ton Macoutes. To look mysterious and menacing they wore dark sunglasses even at night."

"Maybe they just wanted to look like Ray Charles," I tried.

"There was nothing funny about those men," she said quickly.

"I'm sorry," I said. "I shouldn't have said that."

"That's okay," she said. "From a distance things don't look as frightening as they do up close."

"Did you see much of those guys up close?"

"Too much," she told me. "I was born in 1960. I looked more white than black and my grandfather wasn't sure if he liked me or not at first. I became his favorite eventually." She smiled at the memory. "He was fifty-seven at the time and still a political activist. He voted for Duvalier in 1956 because he believed the soft-spoken doctor would improve health care and the standard of living. By the time everyone realized Papa Doc was the most dangerous man on the island it was too late to do anything but run away. Educated people deserted the island by the thousands in what we called the brain drain. In the end there was a shortage of doctors and professional people."

"Why didn't your grandfather leave?"

"He loved his country and vowed to continue to fight for change," Claudette said.

"Wasn't he afraid of the bad men in the dark sunglasses?"

"He wasn't afraid of anything," she said, and I thought of Hans Perlmutter again.

"What happened to him?"

"The Ton Ton Macoutes killed him," she said without emotion. "They shot him in the back of his head. He was set up by some friends who weren't as brave as he was."

"Bastards," was all I could think of to say.

"The Ton Ton Macoutes visited our house the next day," she went on. "I remember the skinny black man with gold teeth and black sunglasses talking into my father's face. He told my father that only his diplomatic status was keeping his family alive. He warned my father that our family would be constantly watched by Papa Doc."

"Why didn't you leave the country then?"

"My father thought he could change things," she said. "My mother wanted to stay and try to avenge her father's murder." Tears came to her eyes. "Papa Doc died in 1971, eight years after my grandfather was murdered. His stupid son, Jean Claude, who was called Baby Doc took over. He was not as violent as his father but he was not as smart, either. He was fat, dumb, and lazy. Our economy totally collapsed under his 'leadership.'"

"Did more people run away?"

"Yes. Even my father gave up. He ended his diplomatic career in 1980 and made plans to take us to America."

"Wise choice," I said.

"Yes, but it was too late," she told me sadly.

"What happened?"

"My father hired a private plane to take us off the island to Miami," she said.

"Informants told the Ton Ton Macoutes we were leaving the country and Baby Doc decided it was not in his best interests for a knowledgeable diplomat and his family to leave the island. His solution was to kill all of us."

"Scary guy," I said.

"Yes, a very scary guy," she said. "My grandmother and I were out of the house doing last-minute errands and we left my parents and my younger sister, Danielle, at home."

"Was that the sister who died of drugs?"

"Yes." Tears appeared in her eyes and I was sorry I asked. "When my grandmother and I returned home that day we found my mother and father dead on the floor by the front door. They had each been shot in the head."

"You don't have to tell me this," I said.

"I want you to know," she insisted.

"All right, but stop if it's too upsetting for you."

She cleared her throat and continued. "We heard my sister Danielle scream from the master bedroom." Claudette closed her eyes. "Queen picked up a large carving knife from the kitchen table and handed it to me. From a closet she took the machete my grandfather had used to cut off the right hand of the president in 1915. We moved quietly to the partially open bedroom door. We could see into the room. Two black men stood by the bed laughing while on the bed a third man was raping my sister."

"Are you sure you want to talk about this?"

She didn't acknowledge me at all and her eyes remained closed as if she was in a trance. "My grandmother pointed at the two men and then herself. Next she pointed at me and to the man raping Danielle. I understood. My grandmother moved quickly toward the first man and swung the machete at his neck. His head fell to the floor." Claudette squeezed her eyes tighter. I saw sweat on her face. She was reliving the moment.

"The second man turned in time to witness his own murder. He ducked but the machete cut off the top part of his head. The man raping my sister turned to see what was happening and I was there to stab him in the face, below his eye. I pulled out the blade and stabbed him in the top of his head." Her voice cracked. She sobbed. "There was blood everywhere."

"Claudette." I leaned forward and put my hands on her shoulders. Her eyes snapped open. "That's enough."

"We burned down the house, Eddie, with my parents and those horrible men inside."

I eased her from the chair and held her in my arms. She cried against my chest.

"We took the plane to America," she whispered. "But part of each of us died in Haiti."

"I understand." I stroked her hair. "You don't have to talk anymore."

Claudette put her arms around my waist and nuzzled against my chest. I heard her sniffle a few times. We didn't move. We just held each other.

"So, do you still think your grandfather was like mine?" she asked.

"Yes, definitely," I said. "They were both very brave men."

"Did your grandfather dismember a president?"

"No, but he did kill a bear with a knife when he was only fifteen years old."

"Sounds like he was fearless," she said.

"Like your grandfather," I said.

"And like you." She looked up at me.

"Why would you say that?"

"I watched you fighting those terrible young men," she said. "You were like a wild animal."

"I lose control sometimes," I said.

313

"You're not afraid of anything, are you, Eddie?"

"No," I answered her honestly.

Without warning she stepped back and ripped my shirt open like Buford had done to her blouse. Her nails scratched my chest and I felt like I was being seduced by a panther.

"I might be a little afraid of you," I admitted.

She looked at me intently. "You should be."

We didn't make love. We mated, fucked, grunted, pushed, bit, scratched, and panted. Sweat drenched our bodies, and we slid in and out of each other as if our parts had been custom-made for this purpose. Every position was perfect.

Claudette was on top of me, grinding away on Mr. Johnson, who didn't give an inch.

Bring it on, he challenged her. I was proud of him. After all, the big prick was sixty years old.

Claudette finally collapsed on the bed next to me. "I can't believe you're sixty years old," Claudette gasped, looking at Mr. Johnson still standing.

"I am, he's not," I told her, pointing to Mr. Johnson. "He's like Peter Pan. He never grew up."

"I think he grew up just fine," she said, and kissed Mr. Johnson on his bald head.

That's the way I like it, ah huh, ah huh, I heard him sing until he heaved a great sigh of relief, bowed to his partner, and retired for the night. *Till we meet again.*

Sex with Alicia Fine had been an elegant evening at the symphony. Sex with Claudette Premice had been a crazy night of hot jazz. I was beginning to love all kinds of music.

I gazed at the granddaughter of a Haitian revolutionary. She gazed back at me, the grandson of a Russian legend. We continued looking at each other until sleep finally closed our eyes.

CHAPTER 23

HEROES AND VILLAINS

The next morning, after a brief jazz session, Claudette Premice and I were at the auto center at Sears, waiting for four new tires to be installed on her old Buick. My cell phone rang.

"I heard you're a hero again," a familiar male voice said.

"Of course I am," I replied. "Who is this?"

"Your favorite news reporter."

"Geraldo?"

"Okay, your second favorite."

"How you doin', Jerry?" I asked the young reporter formerly of the *Boca News.* He was writing for the *Palm Beach County News* since I gave him my exclusive about the Russian gangsters. He had his own column now.

"I'm at the West Palm Beach county courthouse," Jerry told me.

"Good for you," I interrupted him. "But before we get into that, when are you going to do the article on the foster kids?"

"It starts tomorrow," he told me. "It's a four-part series in the local section, running four days in a row."

"Great. Were you careful with the wording about the trust fund?"

"What do you think?" he asked casually.

"Look, Jerry, we have to be very cautious, or we'll have every nut in south Florida trying to adopt Tommy Bigelow."

"I know," he said defensively. "And I was very clear. Tommy Bigelow has a seventy-five-thousand-dollar trust fund set up for his upbringing and education. The trust is tightly controlled by court-appointed trustees who have absolute authority over how the trust money can be spent. And, if Tommy should die, the trust is cancelled immediately."

"That should discourage fortune hunters, don't you think?"

"I would think so. But you said you only had one person in mind anyway."

"I'll be disappointed if it doesn't work out that way."

"Are you sure you want to take a risk with all that money?" Jerry asked.

"I'm taking the cash value out of an old insurance policy I had for my wife. Who knew she'd die first? She'd approve of what

I'm doing. Now what about the court-house?"

"A teenage kid named Randolph Buford was arraigned this morning for assault and attempted rape last night."

"Oh, that."

"You were listed as making a citizen's arrest. How did that happen?"

"Lucky," I said. "I assume the Nazi bastard pleaded not guilty and was released on bail."

"In Florida there's a standard bond," Jerry explained. "The judge released Buford on a twenty-thousand-dollar bond."

"That's too bad," I sighed. "The kid is a menace."

"Fortunately other people share your opinion," Jerry said.

"Who?"

"The DA's office."

"No shit," I said. "What did they do?"

"Barry Daniels, from the DA's office, rushed the information to the circuit court where Judge Avery Jacobs drew the case."

"I assume Buford's affiliation with Aryan Army was read into the record."

"Correct."

"To Jewish judge Jacobs by Jewish district attorney Daniels."

"Correct again," Jerry said.

"Bail denied," I said, already aware of the negative consequences.

"Close to correct," Jerry said. "Jewish judge Jacobs, with attorney Daniels urging him on, immediately decided that Randolph Buford was a danger to society and a flight risk. He set a circuit bond at two hundred and fifty thousand."

"Buford's father went ballistic, I bet."

"Nuclear is a better word," Jerry noted. "They had to restrain him from going after the judge."

"Now what?"

"A representative of Aryan Army attended the arraignment," Jerry reported. "Outside the courthouse the lawyer referred to Aryan Army as the Brotherhood, another name for these lunatics, same as Aryan Nation. He declared that the Brotherhood was going to hire a big-time defense attorney, probably a Jew, and request a change of venue. They claim that it's impossible for a member of their organization to get a fair trial in South Florida."

"There's a twisted logic in what he says."

"The logic stops there, I'm afraid." Small sighed. "Aryan Army announced they plan to demonstrate in Palm Beach. There's a great propaganda opportunity here for the Aryan Brotherhood. They got Jews and blacks conspiring against good old white supremacists. It's a natural. The circuit grand jury is scheduled to convene in a week. Harland Desmond, president of Aryan Army, has promised that the Brotherhood will be there en masse."

"Will there be a formal function at Mar Lago to welcome the Nazis?" I asked.

Jerry laughed. "The rich and the super-rich aren't too thrilled about the prospect of having a few hundred skinheads running around their neighborhood."

"Why not? I think skinheads can be cute in their own way, like baby alligators," I said. I disconnected from Jerry Small and told Claudette the story. We spent the next hour talking about Nazis, and finally her car was ready.

"Will I see you again?" she asked tentatively.

"I was counting on it," I told her.

"I wasn't sure." She shrugged. "Last night was kind of weird. I didn't know if it was a one-time thing for you."

"I'm not that kind of guy," I said.

She laughed.

"I'll call you this afternoon at the hospital," I promised.

She seemed pleased.

I showered at my apartment and was getting dressed when the cell phone rang. A friend of Carol Amici was calling to tell me that Dom had passed away at six o'clock that morning. I felt guilty. When Dom died, I was having great sex with a beautiful woman who bit my neck, scratched my back, and kissed every inch of my body in an unbelievably contradictory combination of violence and tenderness. By the time I wrote down all the details of the memorial service, I no longer felt guilty. I felt lucky to be alive.

Dom's memorial service was held the next night at the St. Francis Funeral Chapel in Boca. The service was scheduled to start at seven. I got there early to get a good seat, but the hall was already filled.

I waited in a long line to view Dom's body. I was startled to see how little remained of him. I expressed my condolences to the family. Carol was composed and calm. Her daughters hugged me and introduced me to their families. I forgot everyone's name in a minute.

I stood in the back of the room as the ceremony began. The priest made some remarks about how there was only one God and Dominick was with him in heaven. "If Dominick Amici didn't make it into heaven," Father Tom said, "then we all have a problem."

A friend of Dominick's from Boca Heights made a few remarks. He tried to lighten the mood with anecdotes. "Dominick suffered from the Stockholm syndrome," the man said. "He had so many Jewish friends he thought he was Jewish, except for the religion and circumcision part."

Even I laughed.

"Does anyone here know why Italians hate Jehovah's Witnesses?" the man asked.

Most of the mourners knew the answer. *"Because Italians don't like any witnesses,"* they said in unison. It was one of Dominick's favorite jokes, and it was a "feel good" moment.

When Dom's friend finished I looked at the crowd. I saw a lot of smiling faces and watery eyes. I also noticed a small, middle-aged man standing by the exit with his arms folded across his chest. He was scowling, red-faced, and fidgety. A friend of Dominick's from New Jersey was at the podium preparing to make a few remarks. I got up from my seat as quietly as I could and said, "Excuse me," all the way down the narrow row, doing my best not to step on anyone's toes. Unfortunately, I stepped on a Boca Babe's pink-painted big toe. "Asshole," she muttered and spoiled that "old-time religion" feeling for me. When I was free of the aisle, I headed directly toward the disgruntled mourner who seemed to sense I was coming for him. As I approached, he unfolded his arms, stepped away from the exit door and shouted, "DOMINICK AMICI IS A MURDERER! HE MURDERED MY FATHER, AND HE SHOULD BURN IN HELL!"

Statements like that are not regarded lightly by devout Catholics, who take burning in hell literally. Personally, I prefer the seventy-two-virgin Muslim afterlife idea, but it's not a multiple-choice kind of thing.

Everyone had turned toward Robert Goldenblatt's son, who stood defiantly in the back of the room. Before anyone could say, "Kick that squirrel in his nuts," I twisted his arm behind his back in a perfect "policeman's come-along" and pushed him to the door.

"You're breaking my arm," the man protested.

I knew I wasn't breaking anything and I kept his arm where it was until we were out in the street.

"You're breaking my arm," he repeated, weaker this time.

"No I'm not," I said, and let him go.

He rubbed his shoulder and glared at me.

"He killed my father," Robert Goldenblatt's son told me.

"I heard you the first time," I said. "And I'm sorry about your father." I held a hand out to him.

He looked tentatively at my extended hand.

"I'm Eddie Perlmutter," I told him.

He slowly put his hand out and took mine. His handshake was halfhearted. "I know who you are," he told me. "I'm David Goldenblatt, Robert Goldenblatt's oldest son."

"I understand how you must feel, David. But this is a hell of a place to present your case."

"There won't be a case," he said with frustration. "That's the problem. With Amici dead there won't be anything. My father's death will never be explained, and there will never be closure for my family."

"I'm investigating your father's death right now," I told him.

"I heard something about that," he said. "Why?"

"Boca Heights wants closure, too," I said.

"I know Amici killed my father," David Goldenblatt said. "Case closed."

"What if I told you I thought Amici was innocent?" I asked.

"I'd say you were crazy," David said. "If

Dominick Amici didn't kill my father, then who did?"

"I'm not prepared to say just yet," I said. "But when my investigation is complete you'll hear from me."

"There's no other explanation for what happened," David Goldenblatt said, but he wasn't angry anymore.

"Yes there is," I disagreed, "and I'm going to try to prove it. All I want you to do is promise me you won't bother the Amicis anymore."

"I wasn't planning to," he said sadly. "I just wanted to get this off my chest."

"Will you apologize to the Amici family if you're wrong?"

"I'm not wrong."

"That's not an answer."

"If I'm wrong I'll apologize," David Goldenblatt conceded.

"You're not such a bad guy," I told him.

"Neither was my father," he told me.

I suggested that David leave the area before the rest of the mourners exited. He agreed.

"You'll be hearing from me," I promised.

The mourners filed out of the funeral home a few minutes later. Everyone was talking about David Goldenblatt's outburst.

"That son of a bitch," Debbie Aiello, one

of Dom's daughters said to me, her eyes red from crying. "How could he do something like that?"

I put a hand on her shoulder. "He lost his father, too," I reminded her, "and his father's death hasn't been resolved. He's very angry."

Carol Amici came up to me with her daughter Lisa. "Thank you for getting that man out of the room," she said. "That was awful."

"Yes it was," I agreed. "But he really believes Dominick killed his father."

"I know." Carol fought against her tears. "It's a shame, Eddie," she went on. "Dominick was such a good person. For him to be remembered like this is a crime."

"I used to be in crime prevention," I said, hugging her. "I'll see what I can do."

CHAPTER 24
A BOCA FAREWELL

The next morning I was front-page news in the *Palm Beach County News* again thanks to Jerry Small. Claudette and I read his article under the covers of my bed, where we had spent another night in a lively jazz session.

Jerry Small's article was entitled "Oh What a Knight" and was laced with so many superlatives about me that even I was impressed with myself. Jerry referred to me as "Sir Eddie the Boca Knight."

Claudette had her head on my chest as I read aloud about "Eddie Perlmutter's heroic rescue of two damsels in distress."

She gave Mr. Johnson a healthy squeeze. "My hero," she said with an exaggerated sigh.

"Careful," I warned her. "He'll get a swelled head."

"I hope so," she laughed.

Jerry's article reviewed my career in

Boston and noted my accomplishments since I moved to Boca. He mentioned that I had become a licensed private detective in Florida and was working on cases for Boca Heights in cooperation with the Boca police. The article also confirmed that hundreds, maybe thousands of members of Aryan Army were planning to invade Palm Beach the following week.

Aryan Army had received a parade permit to march in the Palm Beach streets in protest of Randolph Buford's arrest. The license was granted for the day the Palm Beach grand jury convened to hear the Buford case. Labeling the entire matter a "Jewish-Black conspiracy," Aryan Army's lawyers were not only demanding a change of venue but a public apology.

Jerry Small identified me as the only witness. I'm sure Jerry meant well, but I felt as if he had painted a bull's-eye on my back for the sharpshooters of Aryan Army.

I flipped to the local section of the paper and found the first installment of the four-part foster-care series I requested. It featured a bright, young kid named Tommy Bigelow as a perfect candidate for adoption.

Claudette went to work at the hospital, and I went to Dominick's funeral at Saint Joan of Arc Catholic church on Palmetto. It was a modern building with high ceilings. Muted sunlight filtered through the stained-glass windows and gave the church a mellow, Godly glow. It was a beautiful day even though Dom was dead. Rain would have been more appropriate.

There were over a hundred people in the church, and I figured ninety-nine percent were Jewish. Maybe six Catholics were in attendance, not counting the family, the priest, the altar boy, and the deacon.

I knew I was getting curious looks. My celebrity status was growing with each bullet and crime I stopped. I smiled at familiar faces and was surprised to see Alicia Fine in the row in front of me. She turned to face me, and the first thing I did was picture her naked. Mr. Johnson stirred. What schmucks the two of us can be.

She smiled.

I nodded.

Mr. Johnson stretched a little. *What's up?* he asked.

She whispered, "I want to talk to you."

I nodded again.

The music of "Ave Maria" filled the room as the pallbearers wheeled Dom's casket down the center aisle. "Ave Maria" is a masterpiece, and it always made me wish I believed in God. The organist paused at the end of "Ave Maria" then plunged into "Amazing Grace." I lost control and blew my nose into my hand.

Why the hell did I do that? I thought.

The grossed-out woman to my right passed me a tissue. I wiped my hand and my face clean, and I thanked the woman without looking at her. By the second chorus of "Amazing Grace," I had raised my right arm in the air and lowered my head while I sang. I had seen this done at a Baptist ceremony one time. When I first saw this levitating routine I thought it looked like fun. It was like hailing a cab while trying not to be recognized. I glanced around the church and noticed that I was the only person playing "hail a cab." I immediately put my arm down. Apparently, the raised-arm rapture was strictly a Baptist thing, not a universal Christian thing. The woman next to me with the tissues looked at me out of the corner of her eye like I was a complete imbecile. "Wrong pew," I said with a shrug, and kept right on singing.

When the priest invited Dominick's friends and family to come forward and receive communion, the Jews in attendance froze like deer in headlights. Carol and the immediate family approached the priest with their hands folded in front of them.

They were followed by six of Dom's Catholic friends. The entire communion was over in about seven minutes.

"That was the shortest communion in history," Father Tom joked.

The congregation laughed, and the service ended on a positive note. No one was happy that Dom had died, but everyone there was happy that he had lived.

CHAPTER 25

ANIMATED IN BOCA

I spent the week following Dom's funeral working with two independent forensic experts. We set up shop in my apartment.

Peter Barry was a six foot four, 165-pound computer geek with a master's degree in computer science from the University of Miami. His specialty was forensic computer animation. Peter taught me that there were two types of three-dimensional graphic animation. One was descriptive animation, which was based strictly on the testimony of a witness. The other was scientific forensic animation, where all objects must obey the laws of physics and conform to facts determined by a forensic expert. Our lead forensic expert was a transplanted Bostonian named Doug Santos, a sixty-seven-year-old gentleman with a doctorate in physics from M.I.T. He had worked on complicated forensic cases with the South Florida police since his retirement from

M.I.T. five years ago. Our common goal was to develop an irrefutable forensic animation, narrated in Dominick's own words, that would prove Dom did not kill Robert Goldenblatt.

We started with a re-creation, using police evidence and professional diagrams of the scene. Santos sat next to Barry providing the facts and figures while Barry's fingers flew across the keyboard compiling the data. I was totally useless except for playing the Amici audiotape when needed.

We worked long hours and I didn't quit until late at night. I wouldn't even break to answer the phone. After the second night on the job, I collapsed on my bed and played my telephone messages. I had a message from Togo, one from Claudette, and one from Alicia, who asked that I call her regardless of what time I got home. I decided not to call. Recent conversations with Alicia had been stressful, and I just didn't have the energy. I got undressed, crawled into bed, and thought about the last time I had seen Alicia. It was outside the church after Dominick's funeral.

She looked great that day. Perfect. I wanted to tell her how spectacular she was, but I just said, "Hi."

"I read about you and the Buford boy in

the paper this morning," she said. "You did a very courageous thing. Congratulations."

I wanted to tell her that I loved her body and that I thought her face was a work of art. I also thought of confessing to her that I wasn't so wonderful and that I'd had consensual sex with the intended rape victim. Instead, I just said, "Thanks."

"I was hoping you'd call me last week," she said.

"I wasn't sure you wanted to talk to me. You weren't too happy with me the last time we were together."

"I was surprised by your behavior," she said.

"You mean none of your other friends would have trashed a Nazi's house?"

"None of my friends would resort to vandalism as a solution for anything," she said.

"You need new friends."

"You need self-control."

"That's what Dr. Kessler said about me," I told her. "He was the Boston police department shrink who tried to analyze why I had such a bad temper and a death wish. He determined I had intermittent explosive disorder."

"What's that?"

"It means I'm a hothead."

"Eddie, be serious."

"I am being serious," I said. "Under certain circumstances my head actually gets hot, and I see red spots and get pretty crazy."

"That's dangerous," she said.

"It's not like it happens all the time. I really have to be provoked."

"Like when a woman is being attacked."

"Exactly." I nodded.

"Did you have this disorder when you vandalized the Buford house?"

"No," I told her. "I was orderly and totally under control."

"Then why would you do such a thing?"

I wanted to tell Alicia Fine that people like the Bufords would just as soon rape and kill her (not necessarily in that order) as reject her invitation to Passover dinner. I wanted her to understand that the criminals and bullies of the world found it infinitely easier to confiscate prosperity than earn it.

But I didn't tell her anything that day. I just shrugged and said, "That's the way I am."

I fell asleep in my bed and dreamed I was at a Nazi rally in 1939 Germany.

"You can get further with a kind word and a gun, than with a kind word alone," Hitler screamed.

The assembled imbeciles screamed right back at him, "*Sieg Heil,* big guy."

"Success is the sole judge of right and wrong. The victor will never be asked if he told the truth," Adolf promised the cretins.

"*Auf Wiedersehen,* Jews," the multitude of *Mistkerls* (shitheads) roared.

"The only thing money won't buy is poverty," the little corporal told them.

"We didn't know that," the geniuses exclaimed.

"Yes, we are barbarians. We want to be barbarians. It is an honorable title." Hitler was on a Kaiser roll.

"*Kussen sie meinen esel* [kiss my ass], Allies!" the fanatics cheered.

"Gimme a B!" the mustachioed former paperhanger screamed in my dream.

"B!" the assembled multitude of *Arschlochs* (assholes) gave the big A a big B.

"Gimme an A!" Adolf did a cartwheel across the stage in his lederhosen.

"Here's your fuckin' A!" the united uneducated responded.

"Gimme an R!" Schiklgruber screamed.

"R!" cheered those who would get rich killing Jews and taking their stuff.

Eventually the word *barbarians* was spelled. The home crowd did their version of "the wave" accompanied by a resounding

"Sieg Heil" that would soon be heard throughout Europe.

I woke in a cold sweat and trudged to the bathroom. I had been doing a lot of night trudging to the bathroom since I turned sixty. As I stood waiting at the toilet I thought about my dreams. I had been doing a lot of standing and waiting at the toilet lately, too.

I concluded that in Alicia Fine's rosy world the Hitler B-A-R cheer would have spelled the word *Bar mitzvah* and everyone would have danced the hora afterward.

I shuffled back to bed hoping my dream would not pick up where it left off. It didn't. I had a different dream.

I was standing inside the security gate of Boca Heights on Yamato Road. A horde of Aryans clamored to gain entrance. The Buford family was trying to open the gate from the inside. All the residents of Boca Heights had deserted the community and gone on a cruise on a large Carnival ship. I was the last line of defense when the Aryans broke down the flimsy gate and swarmed over Boca Heights like locusts. I waved my grandfather's kinjal over my head and went down fighting.

Before the Aryans could kill me I fell out of bed and landed on my ass.

By our fourth day on the job, Doug Santos and Peter Barry had made tremendous progress. Their computer-generated model was starting to flicker and move.

"I wish I knew what you guys are doing," I said, feeling useless.

Doug Santos patted me on the back. "I'll give you a crash course, Eddie. Peter and I are creating a computer simulation."

"Is that the same as a computer animation?" I asked.

"No," Peter interjected. "A computer animation is computer-generated images where each frame is altered slightly to give the impression of movement. A simulation is much more complicated. It involves the input of a lot of sophisticated rules of physics and mathematics. A computer simulation is a re-creation of the real thing, accompanied by expert testimony supporting the visuals."

"So, the animation is a version of the story, and the simulation is the story supported by facts."

"Established facts," Doug emphasized. "We're taking Dominick's words and determining scientifically whether or not his story is true."

"Will the finished version give us something definitive?"

"I think it will." Peter Barry smiled proudly. "If we put in the proper facts, we should get a scenario that shows exactly what happened."

"Is my theory feasible?" I asked.

"Yes, it's feasible. We'll know for sure tomorrow."

"When will the simulation be complete?"

"The next day, I hope," Peter Barry sighed.

"I really appreciate everything you two are doing," I thanked them. "The court of public opinion has no judge and jury, but maybe we can salvage a man's legacy."

"That's why we're here." Doug spoke for both of them.

We were all on the same page.

I spoke to Togo that night and brought him up to date.

"You need any help?" he asked.

I assured him I didn't need help.

"I can't believe it," Togo laughed. "You're all over the news more than when you was in Boston. It's amazing."

We both laughed.

"Everyone here is proud of you," he said.

"Thanks. That means a lot to me."

"How's your arthritis?"

"I'm like a new man most days," I told him.

"That's good," Togo said. "And your love life?"

"I'm like an old man most nights," I joked.

"You seeing anyone?"

"Actually, I'm seeing two women," I bragged.

"They aren't Jewish are they?"

"One of them is."

"Take the other one," Togo advised.

"Why? You have a Jewish wife."

"She busts my stones," he laughed.

I called Alicia and got her answering machine. I left a short message saying I would call again.

I saw Claudette once during the week. I rushed to get her into bed, where I promptly fell asleep. She waited until the next morning to get even.

I was at home on the fifth day of the project when I got a call from Jerry Small of the *Palm Beach County News.*

"Nice job on the foster care articles, Jerry," I complimented him. "I read all four."

"A lot of people read them," he said.

"Did you get any calls?"

"Over a hundred," he said. "But most

importantly I got the call you were hoping for."

"Matt called?"

"Yup!"

"When?"

"After the second article."

"That was two days ago. Why didn't you tell me?"

"I wanted to let things progress a little."

"I assume they have," I said.

"Absolutely. In fact, I'll let Matt tell you himself," Jerry surprised me.

"Hi, Eddie." Matt McGrady was on the line. "I guess you were testing me, huh?"

"Not really," I said. "I didn't want to put you on the spot, Matt. So, I just asked Jerry to put the information in the paper, and I hoped for the best. Besides it was a good story, and it might help other foster kids."

"It was a good story," Matt agreed. "My wife and I went to see Tommy and told him we wanted to adopt him."

"He must have been thrilled."

"He was," Matt told me. "He wanted to know if you could be his uncle."

"He told the people at the hospital I was his grandfather," I reminded him.

"Now you have a choice," Matt said.

"Tell him I'll be his best friend," I decided.

"Good choice," Matt said. "About the

money, Eddie," Matt continued. "My wife and I feel funny taking your money."

"I didn't give you any money," I said. "It's for Tommy."

"Well, I'm just a little uncomfortable."

"Don't be," I assured him. "It's my pleasure. Is your wife happy?"

"She's been hugging that kid all day," Matt said. "She can't stop crying, she's so happy. We both feel guilty that we let money stop us from doing this before."

"Hey, you had your own family to consider," I defended him. "You have nothing to feel guilty about."

"Thank you, Eddie."

"Thank you, Matt."

We ended the call.

I thought I was your best friend, Mr. Johnson said when I was off the phone.

You're my closest and oldest friend, I assured him.

That works, Mr. Johnson said.

By the end of the day we had our first computer simulation of Robert Goldenblatt's death.

CHAPTER 26

BOCA JUSTICE

There were at least three hundred people in the Boca Heights clubhouse dining room awaiting the start of the Dominick Amici/ Robert Goldenblatt presentation. The room was set up with rows of chairs like a movie theater instead of the normal restaurant layout. There was a large projection screen at the front of the room. Doug Santos and Peter Barry were making their final preparations. It was a Sunday night, a week after Randolph Buford's arraignment, and only three days before his grand jury appearance. The meeting had been announced by e-mail and signs posted at the entrance of each Boca Heights neighborhood.

At exactly six p.m. I tapped the microphone, and the audience grew quiet.

"Thank you all for coming," I began. "Tonight we will be showing a computer simulation of what we have concluded happened to Robert Goldenblatt last year. A computer simulation is a reproduction of an event based entirely on scientific input using all the relevant laws of physics, spatial measurements, and physical conditions." I expected to be interrupted at this point. Every speaker was interrupted at a Boca Heights meeting. I was pleasantly surprised when the audience remained silent. "A computer simulation is not based on witness testimony or recall. It is based entirely on available facts. We are satisfied that our results are accurate."

"What if *we're* not satisfied?" The interruption truce was over. I recognized Seymour Tanzer's voice. Seymour was a retired lawyer from Scarsdale, New York. He loved to interrupt meetings with legal points of procedure. He was called "the Professor" by those too polite to call him "the Asshole." Most people called him "the Asshole."

"Mr. Tanzer," I said patiently, "there is absolutely nothing I can do if you're not satisfied. You can accept or reject the presentation. We are not taking any questions."

"What do you mean you're not taking any questions?" Another ego was heard. "What is this, a dictatorship?"

Bing. A red spot. I knew I didn't have the patience for this kind of forum. "Try to think of it as a documentary," I said. "This is not a community meeting where your opinions are invited."

"You can't tell us what to do," Seymour informed me. "If we want to ask questions or give an opinion we will."

RED! RED! RED!

I put down the microphone and left the podium. This was not for me. I motioned to Doug Santos to take over. Peter dimmed the lights. A split-screen picture of Dominick Amici and Robert Goldenblatt appeared. Both large, healthy-looking dead men appeared on the screen. The squabbling in the room stopped. Death has a way of changing people's perspective of what is important and what is not.

"Ladies and gentlemen, my name is Dr. Doug Santos. I'm a physicist and a former professor of physics at M.I.T." Doug's voice was authoritative. "I have produced hundreds of computer simulations used in complicated court cases throughout this country. My work has never been challenged. I was asked to work with Eddie Perlmutter to reconstruct events on the night of March 15, 2004, in order to bring clarity and hopefully closure to the unfortunate events that led to the death of Robert Goldenblatt."

Doug pointed to Peter Barry, who stood up. "Peter Barry is an expert on computer simulation. Peter used Eddie's forensic input and my scientific information to create the simulation you will see. I stand one hundred percent behind this re-creation." Doug moved to one of the computers and tapped commands. The screen changed to a three-dimensional simulation of Robert Goldenblatt's garage. Doug tapped until he had shown every angle of the garage. He tapped the Pause button.

"Ladies and gentlemen," Doug said, sounding like a docent, "you have just taken a virtual tour of the late Robert Goldenblatt's garage as it looked the night of his death. Every measurement is precise from every angle." He took a deep breath. "Now we'll bring animation to this simulation," he went on. "Animation is a series of images altered frame by frame to give the appearance of motion. The human mind can't absorb more than ten images per second. At ten to sixteen frames per second the animation flickers like an old-time movie. When the speed is over sixteen frames per second the motion becomes smoother. Professional motion pictures are shown at twenty-four frames per second and television is thirty. Our animation is shown at thirty frames per second so it is very clear. Now I'm going to ask Detective Eddie Perlmutter to take the mike again," Doug said.

I returned to the podium and shook his hand. "You would make a great lion tamer," I whispered in his ear. "Before Dominick Amici passed away," I began, "he allowed me to record his story. These are his words."

I worked a few buttons and knobs, and Dom's face filled the screen. The room remained quiet. "Is it on?" The voice of Dominick Amici filled the room. "It is? Okay. Well, my name is Dominick Amici, and I'm probably dead by now."

Everyone was paying attention.

Dominick started coughing. "Eddie, give me that mask, will ya?" The crowd listened to Dominick breathe in some oxygen. All the while his smiling photo remained on the screen. "Sorry," Dominick managed. "Anyway, this is not a deathbed confession because I have nothing to confess. I didn't kill anyone. But I am on my deathbed, so I have no reason to lie." More coughs. "Robert Goldenblatt and I were never great friends, but we weren't enemies either. When the members took over the Boca Heights club a few years ago, Robert and I started to disagree on a lot of stuff. We fought over assessments, club policy, and new facilities. You name it, and we fought about it. This went on for three years. I didn't think it was any big deal. People disagree all the time. Then, at one meeting, Goldenblatt and I got into a real heated argument. We're both big guys and I guess we're confrontational. Anyway, he started yelling at me, so I yelled at him. Before you know it the meeting was out of control, and everyone went home pissed off." More coughing. More oxygen. "I didn't think nothin' of it, but the next night I get a phone call from a friend of mine telling me that Goldenblatt sent an e-mail to the entire membership attacking me personally. I got online and read it. Goldenblatt wrote that I was stupid and my ideas were prehistoric or something like that. I mean what the fuck? Oops. Sorry. Wanna start again? No? Okay. So I'm really teed off at Goldenblatt. He's attacking me personally. My wife is gonna hear about this. My daughters live here. I got grandkids. I'm embarrassed and I'm pissed off." Coughing followed. "So I get in my car and drive to Goldenblatt's house to confront him man to man. He only lives around the corner." *Cough. Cough.* "I get to his house and pull up to the curb. His two cars were in his circular driveway so I can't park there. His overhead garage door is open, and I see he's in the garage hitting plastic golf balls into a net. I get out of the car and call his name."

I pushed some computer control buttons and Dominick's face disappears from the screen, replaced by the computer simulation of the front of the house with a view of the garage. In coordination with Dominick's words, a computer-generated three-dimensional car pulled up to the front of the house. Dominick's voice went on. "I yell, 'Hey Goldenblatt, I wanna talk to you.'"

An animated three-dimensional man exited the car and moved toward the garage.

"Would you look at that," a voice said from the audience.

"Unbelievable," was heard from another corner of the room.

Dominick continued talking, and the simulation kept pace. "Goldenblatt sees me coming." The figure in the garage simulating Goldenblatt looked up and moved toward the back of the garage. Two people walking a dog appeared in the bottom lower corner of the screen, and another person approached from the left. "Goldenblatt pushes a button to close his garage door." Dominick's voice was shaky, and he gagged a couple of times. The poor bastard was dying. "I moved quicker," Dom continued the narration. "I ducked under the door when it was about halfway down." On the screen the Amici figure had entered the garage; the overhead door finished closing. The simulation paused. We saw the front of the house, the cars, and the three witnesses. "So it's me and Goldenblatt alone in the garage." The scene changed to inside of the garage. Goldenblatt was at the back of the garage by the exit door, and Dominick was walking toward him. Goldenblatt is holding a golf club. "I yell at Goldenblatt to put down the golf club." All this action was being displayed on the screen in perfect coordination with Dominick's words. "Well, the son of a bitch comes at me. I grab the club and cut my hand on a sharp edge." The animation was awesome. "We swing around, so we're now in opposite positions. He's still holding the club, and now I'm out of breath and dizzy. I musta been sick already and didn't know it. So I reach for the back door next to me, open it, and take one step into the courtyard. I tell Goldenblatt to calm down again but this time Goldenblatt comes at me with the fuckin' club over his head like an axe. I'm yelling, 'Stop, stop, stop,' and he's yelling crazy stuff like, 'Fuck you' and 'Get away from me.' When he got close to me, I saw him stumble, but I wasn't going to wait around to make sure he was all right. I let go of the door and ran like hell. All I heard was a loud bang when the door swung shut." The computer showed the door slamming shut and Dominick running around to the front.

"I got in my car and drove away," Dom said. "I was really rattled. I got home, collapsed in my armchair, and tried to tell Carol what happened. I had blood on my hands from a cut but I don't know how I cut myself. The next thing I know the police are at the door." The animation had stopped with Dominick getting into his car and driving away. Now his picture was back on the screen. "I don't know what happened after I left that garage," Dominick said, "but Robert Goldenblatt was alive and running after me with a golf club the last time I saw him." *Cough, cough, cough.* "And that's my story."

The screen went dark and Doug came forward again. "Thanks, Eddie." He patted me on the shoulder and took the mike. "So, ladies and gentlemen," Doug addressed the audience, "Dominick Amici, from his deathbed, denies murdering Robert Goldenblatt." Doug walked away from the podium and moved closer to the audience. "But there is no denying the fact that an eight-ounce golf club cracked Robert Goldenblatt's skull and caused his death. The question is: Did Dominick Amici deliver that death blow?"

The audience sat in rapt silence awaiting an answer. Instead they got another question.

"Did any man deliver that blow?" Doug asked.

The audience started buzzing like a swarm of angry bees.

"What kind of a stupid question is that?" Seymour Tanzer asked loudly.

"Yeah, what kind of stupid question is that?" another man shouted.

More buzzing followed accompanied by a smattering of derisive laughter.

"Actually," Doug spoke into the microphone and held up his hand for silence. "This is not a stupid question at all."

The buzzing stopped.

"Scientifically," Doug emphasized the word, "it is virtually impossible for any human being to deliver a blow that could crack a man's skull and enter his brain using an eight-ounce, rounded-edge golf club."

"Dominick was a big man," Seymour heckled. "He was six foot five and about two hundred and fifty pounds at the time."

The buzz was back. Doug was unfazed.

"They were both big men. But that's irrelevant. I don't care how big Dom was," Doug said. "Medical pathology studies prove that it would take approximately four hundred pounds of force to cause the damage done to Goldenblatt's skull. That means the club would have had to be traveling at one hundred and fifty miles per hour."

"Impossible. No one can swing a golf club that fast," Mikey Tees spoke up from the back of the room. "Not even Tiger Woods."

"That is correct," Doug agreed. "The average professional golfer can achieve club-head speed in the one-hundred-miles-an-hour range," he told the group. "Tiger Woods has been timed at one hundred twenty-five miles an hour."

"Amazing," an anonymous admirer said.

"It is amazing," Doug concurred. "But it's not fast enough to crack a skull and penetrate a brain. And Tiger was timed using a conventional golf swing with a long driver. Goldenblatt died from a downward chopping blow of a four iron."

"So who bashed in Robert Goldenblatt's skull?" a man asked. "God?"

That got a few laughs.

"Yes," Doug said. "Robert Goldenblatt was killed by an act of God."

There was no stopping the nonbelievers in the audience.

"This is bullshit!"

"What are you, nuts?"

"This is ridiculous."

"Let me finish, please," Doug asked for quiet.

The noise died down when the back of Goldenblatt's house appeared on the screen. Doug had a laser pointer. "This is Goldenblatt's courtyard in back of the house." The red laser line traced the area. "As you can see, there is a narrow space between the two houses." Doug pointed. "This effectively creates a wind tunnel so that even on a relatively calm day there's a breeze off the lake that accelerates through this narrow area. The night Goldenblatt died, the weather bureau confirms that there were wind gusts over forty miles an hour. Coming off the lake and into this wind tunnel, the speed would be greatly increased." Doug pointed to an even narrower area where the back door to the garage was located. "Dominick says he was standing by this door the last time he saw Robert Goldenblatt." The simulation showed a three-dimensional figure at the open door. "This door leading to the garage was solid wood with a metal fire plate, and weighed approximately twenty-five pounds. I verified these specifications myself. Now, according to Dominick, a strong wind blew the door-knob out of his hand, Dom ran, and he heard the door slam shut." The animation showed the action. "So what happened on the other side of that slamming door?" Doug asked. He tapped some keys on the computer, and the three-dimensional animation of the inside of the garage appeared again. There was a man's figure simulating Goldenblatt holding a golf club out in front of him at eye level. The figure was running toward the open door where the Dominick simulation stood. The Goldenblatt simulation stumbled forward, head first. The Dom simulation flees. The door slams shut on the heel of the golf club, driving the toe of the club into the top front of Goldenblatt's forehead. The tremendous force generated by the door drove the toe of the club into Robert Goldenblatt's skull. Goldenblatt's head and body flew backward. He fell to the garage floor approximately five feet from the point of impact. Goldenblatt's body lay motionless on the floor with the golf club implanted in his forehead.

"Based on the laws of physics, the forty-miles-an-hour wind slammed the twenty-five-pound door shut with the force of approximately one ton of kinetic energy. That amount of residual energy is more than enough to crush Goldenblatt's skull, penetrate his brain, and throw his body five feet to where he was found." Doug paused and took a deep breath. "Ladies and gentlemen," he said, "based on these facts, we contend there was no murder the night Robert Goldenblatt died. There was a terrible accident. An act of God." Doug turned from the audience and handed me the microphone.

The lights went on. There was an eerie silence in the room. I started talking before anyone in the audience had the chance. "At this moment there is only one question you should be asking yourself," I told them. "And that question is, 'Could this have happened?' Could Robert Goldenblatt have been killed by a freak accident caused by high winds, a heavy metal-reinforced door, a golf club, and being in the wrong place at the wrong time? It definitely could have happened that way. Does anyone here remember how Tom Mix, the cowboy movie star died?"

"A car accident," someone volunteered.

"Actually he died avoiding a car accident," I said. "He swerved to avoid going over a washed-out bridge, and a suitcase in the backseat of his car slid forward, hit him on the back of the head, and killed him. It was all a matter of bad luck, like getting hit by lightning or a falling object or an airplane landing on a highway or an errant golf ball or getting strangled by a necktie caught in a rising garage door. All these things have happened. So, could Robert Goldenblatt have been killed by a heavy door slamming shut and driving a golf club into his head? Of course it could have happened that way. And that creates reasonable doubt as to whether or not Dominick Amici killed Robert Goldenblatt. A reasonable doubt is all it takes to find a person not guilty."

"Are we just supposed to accept this?" a random voice called out.

"You can draw any conclusion you want," I answered. "But wait. Is there a lawyer in the house?"

Maybe fifty hands went up.

"I should have known," I joked. "Okay, lawyers, if you think we've established reasonable doubt as to whether or not Dominick Amici killed Robert Goldenblatt, please put down your hand." There wasn't a hand left in the air. "The defense rests," I said. I put the microphone down and left the podium.

Before I could make an exit, I was confronted by retired lawyer and current pain in the ass Seymour Tanzer.

"Eddie, a minute, please." Seymour put his hand on my arm to slow me down.

"Seymour, I saw your hand go down," I scolded him with a smile. "No more questions."

Carol Amici came up to me on the other side of Seymour. "Thank you, Eddie," she said.

I turned away from Seymour, who, to his credit, didn't protest. I hugged Carol, and then I was hugging her daughters, Lisa and Debbie, who were also thanking me. "We did the best we could," I said.

"You did great, Eddie," Carol spoke for all of them. "Maybe now Dom can rest in peace."

I felt good until I saw David Goldenblatt walk directly to Carol Amici. I held my breath.

"I'm sorry about my behavior the other night," he said sincerely to Carol. "And I'm sorry for your loss."

I breathed a sigh of relief.

"I'm sorry about your father," Carol said graciously.

David Goldenblatt nodded to Dominick Amici's daughters, who returned the nod. He turned to me. "Good presentation, Eddie," he said, and shook my hand.

"Thank you."

"Eddie," a voice said impatiently.

"Are you still here, Seymour?" I turned to the retired lawyer. "I'm a little busy right now."

"That's okay, Eddie." Carol Amici kissed me again. "We're going home. I'm exhausted. This has been very stressful for us. Thank you again."

When the Amici family departed, several people took their places around me. I got the feeling I was being hemmed in, and I was uncomfortable. "I told you I'm not going to answer questions about the presentation," I said to Seymour.

"I don't want to ask about the presentation," Seymour surprised me. "You got my vote for reasonable doubt, like you said. I want to ask about something else."

"Okay, Seymour," I said. "What do you want to ask?"

"I want to ask you about Aryan Army."

CHAPTER 27

ARYANS AWAY

"What do you want to know about Aryan Army, Seymour?" I asked the retired lawyer.

"Are they as bad as Jerry Small says?" Seymour asked.

"They're pretty bad," I told him.

Jerry Small had written articles about Aryan Army in the *Palm Beach County News,* and he didn't paint a pretty picture.

"We don't know as much about Aryan Army as we do about Aryan Nations," I said to the group. "We know that Aryan Nations isn't as strong as it was in the seventies and eighties, but they can still be dangerous to your health."

Jerry wrote that Aryan Nations was founded in the 1940s by Wesley Swift and was originally known as the Church of Jesus Christ Christians. The organization believed that America would be God's final battleground where Jews would be annihilated.

After Swift died, Pastor Robert Butler assumed leadership in the midseventies and changed the hate group's name to Aryan Nations. Butler formed allegiances with the Ku Klux Klan, the American Nazi Party, the Worldwide Church of the Creator, the National Alliance, and the Silent Brotherhood. Butler also founded the Worldwide Aryan Congress in 1982. Unfortunately for Aryan Nations (aka the Brotherhood), a disaffected freak named Robert Mathews broke away from the Nation and put together a group of crazies called the Order. They staged a series of bank robberies in the early eighties. In 1984 Mathews was killed during a shootout with federal agents, and twenty-four of his followers went to jail. The Order was officially out of order. In 2001 Aryan Nations lost a lawsuit filed by a woman and her son, who were attacked and seriously injured by some of the organization's members.

The legal decision bankrupted Aryan Nations, and they lost their beloved Hayden Lake compound. They relocated to Pennsylvania but they were a fractured faction. Some disgruntled members originally from the southeast formed Aryan Army and moved their headquarters to Tobacco Junction, South Carolina. They were a wounded nest of snakes, but they could still bite you in the ass if provoked, and I guess Palm Beach County provoked them. First, a little Jew from South Florida (that would be me) apprehended one of their members. Secondly, two black women accused him of assault. If that wasn't offensive enough, a Jewish district attorney was going to prosecute their soldier and a Jewish judge had set an exorbitant bail. Aryan Army was pissed and they were going to rise again.

Jerry Small's articles in the *Palm Beach County News* were inciting people.

The Anti-Defamation League claimed defamation.

The United Jewish Appeal appealed.

The Jewish Federation made it a federal case.

The Jewish Defense League was defensive.

Jews for Jesus were confused.

The case became national news. In front of a South Carolina federal courthouse, Amos Bellamy, a cross-eyed tractor mechanic from Tarelton, spoke for another splinter group, the boisterous Silent Brotherhood. "We must secure the existence of our people and a future for white children," Bellamy quoted David Lane of the Order. Then he took off his NASCAR baseball cap and held it over his heart. "God bless America," he said to the camera.

It was reported that as many as five hundred anti-Semitic, antiblack, anti-Catholic, antieverything fanatics would appear in front of the Palm Beach courthouse in three days, demanding that the "fuckin' Jew judge FREE RANDOLPH BUFORD."

"Can we stop them from coming here?" Seymour asked.

"Some of them are already here from what I heard," I told them. "They were already spotted in Boca."

"How do we know for sure it was Aryan Army?" Seymour asked.

"Skinheads in a battered old car flying a Third Reich flag from the antenna tend to stand out in Boca."

"Can we stop them from marching?"

"We could kill them," I said.

"Murder aside" — Seymour looked at me uncertainly — "what are our options? Who knows where an event like that can lead?"

"It can lead to anarchy," I said bluntly. "That's what Aryan Army wants. They want their own country without us in it."

A worried-looking septuagenarian woman asked, "Is all this happening just because of the attack on those two Haitian women?" She sounded as if the attack had nothing to do with us.

"No, it's not just because two women were

attacked," I said. "It's because Aryan Army is a hate group and one of their members has to defend himself against just about everyone they hate. Black victims and Jewish authority aren't exactly what Aryan Army has in mind for the perfect society."

"The judge should have recused himself," Seymour said.

"The judge said he could be totally objective about the case regardless of his religion," I said.

"What about you, Eddie?" another man spoke up. "Without you there's no case."

"That's probably true," I agreed. "Are you suggesting I don't testify?"

"Maybe," the man replied. "It would save us a lot of trouble if we just appeased these bastards, so they'll go home."

"You can't appease these people," I said. "They're neo-Nazis. They think Hitler was right."

"I heard that the Anti-Defamation League is sending a representative," someone said hopefully.

"The Anti-Defamation League won't stop Aryan Army," I said. "Maybe the Jewish Defense League could slow them down but not the ADL."

"The JDL is too violent," one of the Jews protested.

"With Aryan Army you can't be too violent. Violence is all they understand and respect," I explained. "I know them. I've dealt with them in the past."

"Eddie," Seymour said. "This isn't Boston in the seventies or Germany in 1939."

"It doesn't matter," I said. "The rules are basically the same."

"We have laws to protect us," someone added.

"Yeah, and it was the law that gave the Aryans a permit to march in the streets of Palm Beach and tell the world about a Jewish–black conspiracy. I think it's going to be very ugly."

"Oh I don't think it will be so bad," a heavily made-up grandmother said with a wave of her hand. "I heard they're bringing two teenage-girl singers with them to perform during the protest. How bad could it be if they're planning on entertaining people with little-girl singers?"

I laughed. "Those cute, blond teenager singers would be Lyn and Loren Grace," I said. "They're sisters who sing under the name of Aryan Angels."

"That's right. Are they any good?"

"They've been on national television," I said.

"Really? What do they sing?"

365

"Anti-Semitic songs. Antiblack songs. Anti-Catholic songs."

"Seriously?"

"Seriously," I said. "One of them wears the number eighty-eight on her clothes."

"Why?"

"She's copying another couple of Aryan girl singers. H is the eighth letter in the alphabet. Double eight is for two H's, which stand for 'Heil Hitler,'" I explained. "They're very creative kids."

"Oh dear," one woman said, holding a frail hand to her wrinkled neck. "This is a nightmare."

"Now you're getting it," I congratulated her.

"I don't want these people marching in my backyard," Seymour chimed in again. "I don't want to hear them, and I don't want to see them. What can we do?"

"You could go on a cruise," I said facetiously, remembering my dream about everyone going on a cruise while Aryan Army attacked Boca Heights.

When I heard, "Hey, that's not a bad idea," from someone in the crowd I didn't know whether to laugh or cry.

"What do you think it would cost?" another member asked.

"We can look into it as a group and maybe

get a good rate."

"We could make this a Boca Heights event," one woman said. She sounded excited about the idea. "We could make it a theme cruise like Aryans Away. We could have a costume party."

I just shook my head.

"Eddie" — Seymour looked at me seriously — "how long do you figure these hate groups will be in Palm Beach County?" All eyes were on me now, hoping to get an idea of how long the cruise should be.

"They'll stay as long as it takes to get what they want," I told them.

"What do they want?" someone protested.

"First and foremost," I said, "they'd like us to die."

"That's not an answer," I heard.

"It's the only answer I have," I said.

"I read in the paper that the president of Aryan Army will be in Boca soon," someone said nervously.

"Yeah, Harland Desmond," I replied. "I heard he's here already."

"Can you talk to him? Try to reason with him."

"My grandfather taught me that you can't reason with a bear," I said.

"The man is hardly a bear," Seymour pointed out.

"Close enough."

"Certainly you could say something to him," Seymour tried.

"Yeah. I could tell him to get out of town," I said.

"Do you think he'd listen to you?"

"Only if I threatened to kill him."

The drive from the clubhouse to my apartment was a blur of headlights. I remembered reading once that man was the only creature on earth with a brain big enough to contemplate his own existence. So, I asked myself, "When there are Aryans at the gate threatening to huff and puff and blow the house down, can people with big brains really believe it's a good time to plan a costume party?" What were they thinking?

"There are Aryans at the gate."

"Tell them to go away."

"There are Aryans rioting at the gate."

"Tell them to keep it down."

"There are Aryans breaking down the gate."

"Call the manager."

"The Aryans have broken down the gate."

"Another goddamn assessment."

"There are Aryans pounding on the door of our house."

"Maybe they'll go away."

"There are Aryans chopping down our door."

"Pack the cruisewear."

"There are Aryans taking all our property."
"Who knew?"

My grandfather knew there was always someone trying to take someone else's stuff. There was always hate, and Aryan Army had hate oozing out of every pore. The people in Boca Heights only hated waiting in line, small dinner portions, bad restaurant tables, and poor service. The gentle people of Boca Heights were only qualified to fight with their children and each other. They were no match for professional haters like Aryan Army.

Who would defend the gates of Boca Heights, Boca West, Boca Teeca, Boca Grove, Boca Vista, Boca Woods, Boca Green, Boca Lago, Boca Marina, Boca Chase, Boca Highlands, Boca Falls, Boca Isles North, Boca Isles South, Boca Pointe, Boca Country Club, Delaire, Bocaire, Stonebridge, Saint Andrews, the Colonnade, Les Jardine, Woodfield, the Woodfield Hunt Club, the Oaks, the Sanctuary, Mizner Country Club, and Ponte Vecchio? Who had the courage? Who had no fear of the consequences? Who would live free or die like the residents of New Hampshire? Who would defend the defenseless?

"I'll do it," I announced as I got out of my car. "I'll carry the load for everyone."

"Why, thank you, Eddie," gray-haired, seventy-eight-year-old, twice-widowed Eleanor Silberstein said, and she handed me two heavy bags of groceries from Publix.

I went to bed still thinking about the Aryans Away cruise. At 4 a.m. my phone rang. I've never received a phone call with good news between the hours of 2 a.m. and 5 a.m. and this call was no exception.

"Eddie, did I wake you?" Frank Burke sounded agitated.

"No, Frank," I mumbled. "I was sitting here fully dressed waiting for your call."

"Sorry to bother you but —"

"You have some bad news," I interrupted him as I sat up and put on the lamp next to my bed.

"I'm afraid so," Frank confirmed. "The Jewish section of Memories Park was vandalized tonight. I'm told it's a mess."

"Let me guess," I said, rubbing my eyes with my free hand. "Some asshole painted swastikas there."

"Among other things," Frank said. "The papers have the story already. I thought I'd give you the courtesy of telling you myself."

"Those bastards don't waste any time do they? Anything I can do there now?"

"Not really," he said. "We're securing the area and leaving a guard. You can drop by in the morning."

"It is the morning," I said.

"It's more like the middle of the night," Frank remarked. "I'm sorry, Eddie."

"I know you are, Frank," I said, and hung up the phone.

Aryan Army had declared war on Boca and the invasion had begun.

I was at Memories at nine the next morning. Claudette Premice and Queen were already there. The police had taped off the area as a crime scene and one officer was still on duty.

"What are you two doing here?" I asked Claudette.

"Bad news travels fast," Claudette said. "We got a call this morning from neighbors of ours who are gardeners here. We wanted to see for ourselves," Claudette said.

"I'm glad you're here," I said, kissing her on the cheek.

"How 'bout me, Vanilla Ice?" Queen said.

"I'm glad you're here, too, Queen," I said, and gave her a peck as well.

I saw Jackson Lehman, one of the owners of Memories, who had shown me around the park during my first visit to Boca several months ago. Jackson was a nice guy who wanted to change the way people looked at death. He wanted Memories to be a celebration of life not a place of death. Unfortunately, there was no cause for celebration that morning.

The requisite swastikas were on the walls of the large mausoleum that already held hundreds of Jewish souls in the short time it had been opened. "DEATH TO JEWS" was painted in black over the Star of David at the front door. "FUCK THE JEWS" was scrawled prominently on all four walls. Across the road that divided the park was the Christian mausoleum, spotless and conspicuous by its pristine appearance and untouched walls. The message was clear.

Individual Jewish family crypts had been damaged and painted. Glass was broken. Doors were smashed. Paint was everywhere. Jackson Lehman had tears in his eyes.

"Look what these bastards did, Eddie," he said. "They destroy everything that's good. Won't it ever stop?"

"No, it has to be stopped."

While we surveyed the damage, a caravan of cars began arriving. Soon there were at least fifty people walking somberly around the grounds. Despite the swelling crowd, Memories remained quiet as a tomb and silent as a cemetery. It was the sound of Boca mourning.

I looked at the swastikas and blasphemy on the walls and thought of when I sprayed painted the Buford house. The two physical acts were similar but the motivations were entirely different. I was sending the Buford's a personal message that night. I was telling them there was someone out there in the darkness of South Florida who was just as barbaric as they were and not afraid to play without rules. I was sending a one-time message directly to them that their uncivilized behavior would be met with uncivilized behavior. I thought that *"Live and let live or prepare for war"* was a fair warning that left room for choices.

The message these animals left at the cemetery was different. Their message was, *"We hate you because of who you are and we have no respect for your living or for your dead."*

I noticed three black squirrels hopping around the wreckage. They darted, dashed, stopped and started, flitted, scurried, scrambled, scampered, and fidgeted. They never seemed comfortable with where they were or where they were going. I remember thinking that people who hate for a living must have squirrels running around in their heads. What else could explain their behavior?

The policeman on duty departed after telling Jackson the crime lab would be there soon. The park was left to the mourners. I was studying some rather large, deep footprints when Jackson Lehman put his arm on my shoulder. "Will you look at this," he said, shaking his head. "What balls."

I turned to see an Aryan Army version of *Goldilocks and the Three Bears* approaching. Apparently the good-looking members of Aryan Army who bathe regularly couldn't make it today. *Hello, red spots,* I thought as I watched four Halloween characters approach. If I were a black cat I would have raised my back and hissed.

The bears were *bully big,* an incongruous mix of muscle, bulk, fat, and swagger. They had huge shaved heads, thick tattooed arms, and round, bulging bellies indicating that intimidation was their strongest weapon. The three bears looked dirty. Goldilocks looked vile. Her blond, straggly hair was from a peroxide bottle. Her haggard face and rheumy eyes were from a liquor bottle. Her skinny, tattooed arms looked disgusting. Her pinched features tried to argue that she wasn't as old as she looked but her cigarette wrinkles made her actual age irrelevant. When you look like shit, age doesn't matter. Goldilocks was trash and the bears were her garbagemen.

"What are they doing here?" Jackson muttered to me.

"Gloating," I told him.

"Do you think they're the ones who trashed this place?" he asked me.

"Yes," I said to Jackson. "But they're betting we can't prove it. They're here to intimidate us."

"It's working." Jackson motioned with his head at the Memories mourners. They looked like deer caught in the headlights but instead of being paralyzed by the oncoming lights they were petrified by the approaching darkness.

I watched the foul foursome walk toward the crime scene and I could feel the fear emanating from the crowd mingling in Memories. To his credit, Jackson Lehman did not seem intimidated.

"I'm Jackson Lehman, the owner here," he said to them in a clear voice. "Can I help you?"

"Looks like you're the one who could use some help, motherfucker," Goldilocks said as she lit a cigarette with a silver Zippo lighter. She snapped the lighter lid shut by hitting it against her thigh and stuffed it in the front pocket of her jeans.

Every move and every word was well choreographed to make the most fearsome first impression possible. I wasn't impressed. Bravado is the first sign of bullshit.

"Yeah, looks like you had some trouble here," one of the bears said. "Now who would do such a nasty thing to a nice Jew cemetery?" His insinuation was obvious and meant to intimidate. The crowd was silently cowering.

"Yeah, what a shame," another grizzly said. "Who would do such a terrible thing to nice heeb property?"

"You would, Yogi," I said, stepping forward and stopping their advance.

"And just what might *you* be, mother-fucker?" Goldilocks blew smoke in my direction and looked me up and down disdainfully.

"I might be afraid of you but I'm not," I turned to the frightful woman.

"How about I kick your ass?" the biggest bear said, stepping forward.

"With your Xelement Fearless Flames," I said, indicating his black boots with the fire painted on the toe.

"That's right," he said, smiling. "They'd make a nice imprint on your scrawny ass."

"Like the imprints you left all over the

ground here last night," I said. "I'd say they're size fourteens, custom-made. I'd also say you weigh about two hundred and sixty pounds based on the deep footprints you left."

The four of them blinked in unison.

"Your friends over there left some excellent size-thirteen sneaker prints, too," I pointed out. "And I'm sure I'll find some dainty little boot prints made by your mother."

"Kiss my ass, motherfucker," she said to me.

"Thanks for the offer," I said. "But I'll pass."

"You can't prove those are our footprints." The booted bear put his hands on his hips and stood tall.

"You have me confused with the police," I said. "I don't have to prove anything. I know you did it and I'm gonna make sure you never do it again."

"Who do you think you are, motherfucker?" The blonde seemed to have a limited vocabulary.

"Eddie Perlmutter," I said, shifting my glare to her and closing my fists.

I saw the recognition in her eyes. The three bears looked at each other.

"The Boca Knight," she laughed. "You?"

"Little old me," I said.

"We've been wanting to meet you." She smiled meanly and the four of them started to separate from each other. They were experienced street fighters and would come at me from four different angles. I knew I could get two of them but I didn't have a chance against all four. I targeted the woman. She would be the easiest. Then I'd move for the biggest bear. I stood motionless wondering why the hell I wasn't the least bit frightened and why everyone else in the area was terrified. I took a deep breath and waited.

Claudette Premice stepped in front of me, looked me in the eyes, and winked. Then she turned to face Goldilocks. "You gotta get through me to get to him," she said.

The hideous woman snorted a laugh. "You shittin' me, motherfucker? What are you anyway, white or nigger?"

"I don't care what I am as long as I'm not you, you ugly bastard."

Claudette amazed me. I had made love to her enough to know she could beat up on most men but I had never seen her in action outside the hospital or the bedroom. I was impressed but I still didn't like our odds.

Jackson Lehman suddenly stepped in

front of me and stood next to Claudette. "You'll have to go through me, too," Jackson said.

Goldilocks and the three bears were confused. This was turning into a confrontation. They still looked like easy winners but the mood had changed. Someone else moved in front of me. It was Seymour Tanzer, the pain-in-the-ass retired attorney from Boca Heights. He didn't say a word. He just took his place next to Jackson. A frail female octogenarian bent by osteoporosis and aided by her similarly hunched husband moved next to Seymour. People began moving silently in front of me, one after the other, until I was behind a wall of people. No one was talking. No one was threatening. It was completely silent in the cemetery. I was impressed.

"What is this," Goldilocks snorted again, "the march of the living dead motherfuckers?"

No one answered her. The crime lab police car pulled into the lot and broke the silence.

"Okay, Boca Knight," Goldilocks said, motioning to her thugs, "we'll settle this another time."

After they had driven away my human shield turned to me. I saw relief, fear, and pride on their faces.

I picked out Seymour Tanzer, the lawyer. "Seymour," I said, "I didn't know you had it in you."

"I don't have it in me anymore," Seymour said. "I just shit my pants."

People laughed to relieve the pressure they all were feeling.

"Does anyone have any more questions about Aryan Army?" I asked them.

No one said a word.

CHAPTER 28

BOCA BOMBARDMENT

Buses and RVs carrying members of Aryan Army began arriving in Florida on the Monday preceding the Wednesday grand jury hearings. The Army had rented acreage near Yeehaw Junction, several miles east of Interstate 95, about an hour north of Palm Beach. Members of the Nation pitched tents and started partying. Campfires blazed, loudspeakers blared, and a couple of crosses burned. The Klan was with Aryan Army.

The county sheriff's office had a large contingent of deputies watching the revelry, but there was no one to arrest. It was like a college football pep rally the night before a big game. There was a bonfire. People cheered for inane speeches. Lyn and Loren Grace sang hate songs to an adoring crowd ("Shit, ain't they cute.").

Harland Desmond, president of Aryan Army, appeared on CNN at nine o'clock

Monday night. He was interviewed by a stylish female reporter in front of an enthusiastic group of neo-Nazi supporters. The pretty brunette reporter had to shout into her handheld microphone to be heard. "I'm here with Harland Desmond, the president of Aryan Army. Mr. Desmond, you seem to have quite a turnout here for your cause." She moved the microphone toward Desmond.

"There are more people coming," Desmond answered with enthusiasm. "You're witnessing democracy in action and the unity of the Church of Jesus Christ Christians."

I watched the Desmond interview alone in my apartment. I didn't want to be with anyone else for fear of an attack of IED. Harland Desmond was a short man with a thin face. He wore a Hitler-style mustache over his meager upper lip, and his thinning hair was parted and combed like his beloved Adolf's. I noticed crooked teeth when he smiled. Harland Desmond looked like an opossum.

A chant of "free Randolph Buford, free Randolph Buford" erupted behind Desmond and the reporter. Desmond's smile broadened and he raised a clenched fist to acknowledge the chant. "That's what we're here for," he shouted over his shoulder to his stooges.

"Mr. Desmond, how many members of Aryan Army are here tonight?" she asked.

"Hundreds," Desmond threw out a figure that no one could verify based on the picture on the TV screen. "Maybe thousands," he announced with no fear of contradiction. "White Christian America is here in search of justice," he raved on. The crowd roared.

"What does Aryan Army hope to accomplish here?" the reporter asked.

"We intend to get Randolph Buford released on bail and have his case moved to an area where he can get a fair trial," Desmond announced. The crowd roared their approval. I saw skinheads in the background giving the number-one sign with their index fingers.

"And where do you think Randolph Buford would receive a fair trial?" the reporter asked.

"Almost anywhere but here," Desmond laughed.

"And why do you say that, Mr. Desmond?"

"Several reasons, darlin'," Desmond said, holding his right hand up in a fist. "First of all" — he counted the pinky finger of his right hand with the index finger of his left hand — "the case against Randolph Buford is all hearsay. You understand hearsay, girl?"

"Yes, I understand the principle of hearsay, Mr. Desmond," the reporter answered patiently.

"Well, we got a whole lot of hearsay going on here-'bouts from a bunch of here-re-tics."

The crowd roared its approval again, and I heard the familiar redneck battle cry, "Now that's what I'm talking about!"

"I hear ya brother," Desmond shouted, looking over his shoulder again at the group. He turned back to the camera and resumed counting off on his fingers. "The guy who made the citizen's arrest of Randolph Buford is a Jew with a history of violence. He put two of those boys in the hospital." A second finger went up. "The women who claim they were attacked were black." Three fingers up. "The judge is another Jew." The fourth finger was raised. "And the prosecutor is a Jew." His thumb went last. "This is all a setup."

"The man who made the arrest is a highly decorated, retired police officer," CNN's reporter reminded him.

"You mean the Boca Knight?" Desmond laughed, quoting the title Jerry Small had given me. "Yeah, I read that nonsense by that Jew writer about that Jew cop. Comparing a Jew to a knight is a sacrilege. Real knights were brave Crusaders for Christ."

"Isn't that hearsay?" the reporter challenged Desmond.

"That's a fact." Desmond looked skeptically at the reporter. "And I'll tell you what else, little girl. If I was that phony Boca Knight, Eddie Perlmutter, I'd be watchin' my back right now."

"Are you threatening Mr. Perlmutter, Mr. Desmond?" The reporter jumped on his statement.

"I ain't threatening nobody," Desmond said quickly. "But there are a lot of members of the Army here who might be a lot less tolerant than me."

"Are you saying that members of the Army might try to harm Mr. Perlmutter?"

"I don't know nothin' about that, sweetie," Desmond chuckled. "But think about it. He's the only witness them black ladies got. He's all by hisself. He got no support. No backup. Somethin' were to happen to him . . ." Desmond let his voice trail off.

"There are a lot of people in this area who believe Mr. Perlmutter is a hero for rescuing those women and for standing up to Aryan Army, despite all the pressure from your group," the reporter said. "Maybe some of those people will support him."

"Who? The niggers? The Jews? The rich in Palm Beach?" Desmond's laugh was dismissive. "The Jews won't do nothin' to upset their apple cart. They're too fat and happy. The Jews will hide like they always do. The niggers? Those Haitians are too stupid and lazy to organize. The rich in Palm Beach? Don't make me laugh. They'll just get on their private jets and leave town Wednesday when we march. Sir Eddie the Boca Knight is going to stand alone, sweetheart."

"Then how do you explain the confrontation at a Boca Raton cemetery the other day when fifty people rallied to support Eddie Perlmutter at the recently vandalized Jewish cemetery?"

"That was no confrontation," Desmond scoffed. "Four of our people went to see the damage that had been reported on the news and about forty Jews and Mr. Boca Knight ran them off. My people weren't looking for any trouble."

"That's not the story I heard," the reporter said.

"Depends on who you talk to, little girl." Desmond smiled. "Anyway, Aryan Army is now prepared to march and face any trouble that comes our way. Ain't no one gonna stand up to us. Eddie Perlmutter is on his own."

"He doesn't seem concerned," the reporter said. "Can I ask you one more question, Mr. Desmond?"

"Sure, honey." Desmond was feeling good about his presentation. "Ask away."

"Why did the Buford family move from an Aryan enclave in South Carolina to a Jewish community in Boca Raton? There are more Jews in Palm Beach County than anywhere else, except New York City and Israel."

Desmond blinked.

"And there are more black Haitians in Delray Beach than anywhere outside of Port-au-Prince, Haiti," the reporter persisted. "Why did the Bufords chose to settle here?" Desmond was flummoxed.

"Well, I . . ." he tried.

"Isn't it true that Aryan Army believes that white Christians cannot peacefully coexist with Jews and blacks?" the reporter interrupted. "It's in your bible. Why would the Bufords move here?"

"I don't know," Desmond spoke softly. "You'd have to ask them."

"You don't know?" She turned to the camera. "Well I don't, either. But didn't Al

Qaeda set up sleeper cells in America before they attacked the World Trade Center? In our permissive democracy it's easy to infiltrate and assimilate to attack from within. Is it possible that Aryan Army has taken a page from the Al Qaeda training manual and moved members into the enemy camp?"

"Wait a damn minute," Harland Desmond shouted from off-camera. "Who said anything about terrorists?"

"Of course, this is just hearsay." The reporter smiled.

"Hold on there, girl!" Desmond remained off-camera.

"This is Miriam Goldberg," she interrupted him, "reporting live from Yeehaw Junction, Florida, with Harland Desmond, president of Aryan Army."

I was standing in my living room staring at the screen as Miriam Goldberg signed off. I went to the bureau where I kept my grandfather's kinjal safely in its sheath. I removed the blade. "Grandpa," I said out loud, hefting the weapon, "I've just seen my bear."

CHAPTER 29

ARYANS AT THE GATES

I switched off the television and sat on the sofa. I was still holding the kinjal. I thought about the interview. The verbal bomb about terrorists Miriam Goldberg dropped on Harland Desmond would hover over Aryan Army's rally like a mushroom cloud. I was proud of her. I decided to get some air. I tucked the sheathed kinjal in my waistband and went out.

I walked two flights down to the parking lot. I looked at a starry Boca sky, took in a deep breath of fresh air, and thought about what Harland Desmond had said during his interview with Miriam Goldberg.

"If I was that phony Boca Knight, Eddie Perlmutter, I'd be watchin' my back right now."

I wasn't worried. I knew how to watch my back.

While I was busy looking at the sky and complimenting myself on how well I watched my back, I wasn't watching my back. During my reverie someone sneaked up behind me and hit me on the back of the head with a hard object. I could feel my scalp split, and blood spurt. I went down on my knees then fell forward on my face. Instinctively I rolled away from the source of the blow and tried to focus my eyes. I saw a boot with Fearless Flames on the toe approaching my face. I turned my head as the instep of the boot met my mouth. My head movement probably saved my front teeth. My lips exploded, and there was blood in my nose and eyes.

"Hey, Boca Knight," a familiar voice said. "Harland told you to watch your back." He delivered a kick to my stomach. I curled in a ball, protecting my head with my arms. More kicks followed from boots and sneakers and it became apparent that these guys weren't there to warn me; they were there to kill me.

"Get him up," a second voice said impatiently, "and throw him in the car." I knew immediately that they intended to take me on a one-way ride to Yeehaw Junction where my murder was going to be the feature event of the Aryan Army rally. They were laughing and joking with each other as they beat on me, and I recalled my grandfather's advice about surprise and arrogance.

I was yanked from my fetal position to my hands and knees. I saw three pairs of legs around me. I was aware of the exact position of the kinjal in my waistband. Now it was my turn to laugh and I did.

"What the fuck you laughin' about?" one of them growled.

Another kick to my stomach made me grunt and suck in a breath. I instinctively put my right hand on my mid-section and gripped the kinjal's handle. I removed the dagger from my waistband. "*Surprise,* you *arrogant* assholes."

With a minimum of movement, the razor-sharp blade sliced across the nearest Achilles tendon I could find in a sneaker. The loudest scream I ever heard filled the night air and a second horrific scream followed as I cut the next guy off at the sneaker top. Both victims were on the ground writhing in pain. I was still on all fours. The third attacker, the one in the Fearless Flames, couldn't see what I had done to his friends, but he knew it wasn't good.

"Son of a bitch!" he managed as he jumped away from me.

I tumbled away from him and struggled to my feet. I lost my balance immediately. I staggered backward, tumbling over low hedges. I landed on my back and rolled down an embankment. "Get up, Eddie," my mind told me, but my body wouldn't comply.

The two cutups were still screaming. I heard a car engine start.

"No, no, don't move me," someone screamed.

"I gotta get you out of here," someone else answered.

A car door closed with a thud.

"Oh my God," a third voice wailed a moment later.

"I gotta move you."

Another car door slammed, the engine roared, tires squealed, and they were gone.

I dragged myself out of the shrubbery and into the parking lot. I reached for a car-door handle and pulled myself up to a leaning position against the car. I took inventory of the things I had.

I had all my teeth.

I had a concussion.

I had a headache.

I had blurred vision.

I had two bloody, split lips.

I had a broken nose, again.

I had at least two broken ribs.

I had no pain in my hands or my knees, which I thought was bizarre.

I had to have some help.

"Help," I called weakly to a passing shadow.

"Why, thank you, Eddie," my neighbor, Eleanor Silberstein said, and she handed me two bags of groceries from Publix.

"Call the police," I told her.

"Don't be silly," she giggled. "You can handle those little bags yourself."

At the hospital, the emergency room doctor told me I had two broken ribs, a concussion, and a broken nose. I passed out.

The next morning my hospital room was filled with police, and the nursing staff was getting nervous. Acting Police Chief Frank Burke arrived and immediately took control. He emptied the room and posted guards outside the door with instructions not to let anyone enter without his permission.

"Do you know who attacked you?" Burke asked, looking down at me.

I nodded.

"Who?"

"Mrs. Silberstein."

"Eddie, c'mon," Burke said impatiently.

"I didn't see a thing," I told him. "I was hit from behind. All I saw were boots, sneakers, and legs."

Burke held up a plastic bag containing the bloody kinjal. "What's this?" he asked.

"My letter opener," I told him.

"We found it in the bushes near where you collapsed. You must have dropped it."

"Did I drop the shopping bags, too?" I asked.

"The eggs broke," he confirmed.

"Damn."

"It's a big letter opener," Burke observed.

"Actually it's a Russian sword. My grandfather killed a bear with it."

"Who did you kill with it?"

"No one," I said. "But two guys won't be running the Boston marathon this year. While they were kicking the shit out of me, I cut their Achilles tendons."

Burke grimaced at the thought. "Why were you carrying the knife?"

"Would you believe it was a coincidence?"

"No."

"Well it was," I said seriously.

"You think these guys were from Aryan Army?"

"The Combined Jewish Philanthropies, more likely," I said. "I didn't give a pledge this year."

"Eddie, give me a serious answer, will ya?"

"You want a serious answer, ask a serious question. Of course they were from Aryan Army. They even mentioned Desmond's name. They were the same clowns that visited the cemetery minus their girlfriend."

"I wonder why she wasn't there," Frank thought out loud.

"Aerobics class," I said.

Burke laughed. "We'll get some people out to their rally right away and see if we can find two guys with a limp."

"Don't bother," I told him. "They're long gone by now. Desmond wouldn't keep them around."

A uniformed policeman entered the room and whispered something to Burke.

"You want to talk to a reporter from CNN named Miriam Goldberg?" Frank asked. "She's outside the door."

I thought about her great interview with Desmond. "Yeah, I'll talk to her," I decided.

"You sure you're up to it?" Burke asked.

"I'll be fine," I assured him, although my head was killing me.

Miriam Goldberg was tall, pretty, and very professional-looking in a dark business suit. She shook my hand firmly.

"Sir Eddie." She smiled warmly.

"Princess Miriam." I returned her smile. "Say hello to King Frank, a good friend of mine."

They exchanged greetings.

"I loved your interview with Harland Desmond," I told her.

"That man is so obnoxious," she said. "I couldn't resist taking a shot at him."

"That was more like a mortar round than a shot. Do you think there's any merit to the sleeper-cell theory?" I asked her.

"Why not?" she responded. "Why else would those bastards have moved here?"

"You make a good point," I said, wincing from a sharp pain in my side.

"Are you all right?" she asked sympathetically.

"I've been better," I admitted.

"You feel up to giving me an interview?" she asked.

"Not really," I said with a dismissive wave of my hand.

"C'mon, Sir Eddie," Miriam prodded me. "Let the public know how you feel."

"I feel like shit."

"And you look like shit."

"Thank you," I laughed, even though my side hurt. "And you want me to go on national television looking like shit."

"Yes," she said seriously. "I want the public to see what those animals did to you."

"It's no big deal," I said. "I've been hurt worse than this."

"That not the point, Eddie," she said. "If you want to strike a blow against Aryan Army you have to let people know how they operate."

"Okay, let's do it," I decided impulsively. She had pushed the right button.

Do what? Mr. Johnson raised his head a little. I couldn't believe he was even paying attention.

Miriam Goldberg had a camera crew waiting out in the hall, and it took about twenty minutes to get their equipment ready for a live session in my room. Miriam started the session with a review of my background. She explained the Aryan Army–Randolph Buford–Harland Desmond situation briefly and reminded the audience about her interview with Desmond from the previous night. She talked about the confrontation at the desecrated cemetery. Then she gave a summary of the injuries I sustained, making it sound as if I was lucky to be alive. Maybe I was lucky.

When she had finished her summation she turned to me. "So, Eddie Perlmutter," she said, her voice sympathetic, "how do you feel?"

"How do I look?"

"Not good."

"That's how I feel."

"Do you know who attacked you?" she asked, already knowing the answer.

The cameraman was doing a close-up of

my bruised face.

"No I don't," I admitted. "They came at me from behind. I didn't see anyone's face."

"Do you have any idea who it could have been?" she pressed.

"If I had to guess I'd say it was the three fools from Aryan Army who showed up at the cemetery the other day with the Wicked Witch of the North," I told her.

"Why do you say that?"

"If you saw her you'd know why," I said.

"No, I mean why do you say it was the same three men?"

"One of them was wearing a pair of Fearless Flame boots and the other two were wearing sneakers," I told her. "The same as the three stooges at the cemetery. Then, one of them told me I should have been watching my back," I said. "And that was what your friend Harland Desmond advised me to do, if you remember."

"I remember." She nodded her head. "But Harland Desmond is no friend of mine."

"He'd be the first person to tell you that," I agreed with her.

"Tell us what happened," she led me into my story.

I told her about the attack, the kinjal, and the severed Achilles tendons.

"That sounds horrible," she said.

"It would have been more horrible if I'd let them keep kicking me," I told her.

"Will they walk again?" she wanted to know.

"I don't know and I don't care," I said honestly. "I do know they won't be kicking anyone in the head anytime soon."

"And what about your injuries?" she asked. "How long do you anticipate your condition will delay the Buford hearings?"

"I don't expect any delay," I told her.

"Well the grand jury is scheduled to convene tomorrow," she said. "You're in no condition to testify."

"I'll be at that hearing," I insisted. "And I'll testify."

"You have a severe concussion and two broken ribs," Miriam said with concern.

"If I don't testify," I explained, "Randolph Buford's grand jury appearance will be postponed and the judge will have to release the little turd on bail. That would be a victory for Aryan Army, and that's just not going to happen."

"Does Randolph Buford's indictment mean that much to you?" she asked.

"Randolph Buford doesn't mean anything to me," I told her honestly.

"So, why is it so important to be at that hearing?"

"Someone has to stand up to these hateful bastards," I said. "They attacked me to stop me from testifying. They would have preferred to stop me permanently but if I don't testify tomorrow they get the next best thing."

"Aren't you concerned about another attack?" she asked. "They already tried to kill you once."

"I'm concerned," I told her honestly. "But I'm not afraid."

"You're not afraid of dying?"

"I don't want to die, of course," I stated the obvious. "But I won't live in fear, either."

"A newspaper reporter called you a Boca Knight," Miriam referred to Jerry Small's article about me. "What did he mean by that?"

"I don't know. Ask him," I said.

"I'm interested in your thoughts."

"I never thought about it," I told her.

"Would you think about it now, please?" she prodded. "We all know what Aryan Army represents. What does it mean to be a Boca Knight?"

I thought about what it meant to be a Boca Knight by remembering how I had always tried to live my life.

"I would say," I began thoughtfully, "a Boca Knight is a person willing to fight and die to defend everyone's right to live as they choose, in peace."

"So, a Boca Knight fights for human rights." She tried to turn my explanation into a good media sound bite.

" 'Boca Knights for Human Rights' does have a nice ring to it," I said, helping Miriam along.

"Thanks. I think so, too." She smiled in appreciation. "And where do Boca Knights come from, Eddie?"

"A Boca Knight is a state of mind, not a place," I told her.

"Do you think we have enough Boca Knights in Palm Beach County to stand up to Aryan Army?" she asked.

"I have no way of knowing that," I admitted. "Although I met some unlikely Boca Knights the other day at the cemetery."

"Harland Desmond said that it will be a different story tomorrow," Miriam told me. "He said Aryan Army will be in full force tomorrow and you'll receive no support. What if you're the only Boca Knight in town tomorrow?" Miriam asked.

"Then I'll stand alone," I said.

Miriam Goldberg turned to the camera. "Well there you have it. Eddie Perlmutter, the Boca Knight, is prepared to stand alone against Aryan Army if necessary," she said dramatically. "And we'll be there to cover this story live from the Palm Beach courthouse tomorrow morning. Join us. This is Miriam Goldberg wishing all you Boca Knights out there a good day."

The red light on the camera went off.

"Nice touch," I told Miriam.

"I try."

CHAPTER 30

BOCA KNIGHTS

From the police helicopter hovering a thousand feet above the ground, I saw what looked like an army of ants marching north on A1A. I could also see the northbound lanes of I-95 blocked with traffic. It was only seven o'clock Wednesday morning, the day Randolph Buford was scheduled to appear before the grand jury at the Palm Beach circuit courthouse.

Frank Burke had roused me from a peaceful sleep in my holding cell at the Boca Raton police station only an hour earlier. I had been moved by ambulance to the police station from the hospital Tuesday morning, shortly after my interview with Miriam Goldberg. The incarceration was my idea. I figured I was still an Aryan Army target, and I didn't want to put hospital personnel, patients, or visitors in harm's way. A hospital bed was squeezed into the cell, and I was hooked up to all the tubes I needed. Jerry

Small wrote that I had been taken into protective custody as a star witness.

"What's up?" I sat up in bed when the chief woke me. Immediately, I was dizzy and put my head back on the pillow.

"Nothing good, I'm sorry to say," Burke told me. "I just got a call from the Palm Beach chief, who said that traffic is backed up for miles off I-95 and hundreds of people are walking on A1A."

"Aryan Army?" I asked feeling nauseous.

"I guess. Some of their buses were spotted in the traffic surrounded by cheering marchers." Frank shook his head slowly. "You're scheduled to appear before the grand jury at about nine-thirty. We've got to get you there on time."

"I'll be ready in ten minutes," I assured him.

"We're going by helicopter," Burke told me. "I've already made arrangements with the department."

"Do we really need a chopper?"

"From the way the Palm Beach chief described the situation," Burke said, "it's a zoo out there. Nothing is moving."

"I really didn't think Desmond would get this much support," I confessed.

"Neither did I, but he did," Burke said. "Maybe your interview with Miriam Goldberg incited a lot of bigots. You were pretty expressive."

"Bigots are always incited," I said. "I just raised the level."

"Well you got me excited, Eddie," Burke said. "I wanted to be a Boca Knight after listening to you."

"You're a Boca Knight already, Frank," I praised him.

"Why thank you, Sir Eddie." He tossed me a bulletproof vest.

"You think I need this?"

"Wear it. There must be a lot of nuts out there today."

"There are a lot of nuts out there every day."

I was transported by wheelchair to a police cruiser and traveled with a police escort to the Boca airport. I was lifted onto the helicopter, still in my wheelchair, and Frank Burke boarded with me. He was wearing his bulletproof vest.

The helicopter started its descent into Palm Beach. I saw that the front lawn of the Palm Beach circuit courthouse had been cordoned off by police officers holding riot shields. From the air it looked as if thousands of people were below me. I closed my eyes. I had experienced the ugly sight of angry crowds before, and I knew that a mob's negative vibrations could drain a person's energy. My battery was already low and I had to conserve what little power I had.

I hid in the darkness behind my eyelids trying to conserve my strength. Unfortunately, I could still see with my mind's eye.

I saw a flickering black-and-white 1941 vintage news-reel image of marching fanatics on parade. I envisioned the endless supply of mindless morons goose-stepping behind barbarian leaders like Attila, Hitler, Hussein, Mussolini, Stalin, Amin, Mao, and bin Laden. I heard them chanting. "Death to Jews. Death to Serbs. Death to Americans. Death to pigs. Death to intellectuals. Death to anarchists. Death to Kurds. Death to everyone except us . . . in God's name, of course!"

The helicopter touched down but I remained behind closed eyes. I felt my wheelchair being lifted from the helicopter and placed on the ground. I heard a loud roar and knew it was time for me to face my bear. Ready or not, motherfucker, here comes Eddie Perlmutter. I struggled out of the wheelchair, stood up, squared my shoulders, opened my eyes, and looked at a massive man standing in front of me. He was not at all who I expected.

"Bruno Muscles?"

"Hey, Coach Eddie." Bruno Muscles smiled at me and gave me a North End hug that hurt my broken ribs. He patted my back. I smelled garlic.

"How you doin'?" Muscles rumbled. He lightened his grip, so he could look at me.

"Muscles, what are you doin' here?"

"We're all here," I heard a familiar voice.

"Togo!" I looked past Muscles to see my old friend standing there. More hugs. More pats. More *How you doin'?*s all around. Petey "Pants" was there. Tommy "Rats" was there. Reggie "The Doctor" Infante was there. Mikey Tees was there.

"How you *doin'*?"

"How *you* doin'?"

"*How* you doin'?"

"Hey Eddie, you remember Sal the Mumza," Togo said.

"Sure I remember Sal." I shook Sal's hand.

"I brought Anthony 'Nuts' too," Togo said. "He tole me you arrested him twice but he liked you anyway. Same with 'Fingers' over there."

"Fingers, you staying out of trouble?" I asked.

"I am but you ain't," Fingers, a small-time numbers runner, said.

407

I looked around at more familiar faces from the old neighborhood. "What's going on here," I asked.

Bruno Muscles put a hand on my shoulder and touched his forehead to mine. "We seen you on television, Eddie," he said. I loved the smell of garlic in the morning. "And your North End buddies wasn't gonna let you fight these fuckin' Aryan assholes by yourself. Togo chartered a plane so we could be with you. Let them Nazis try somethin' now."

Togo, the boys, and I formed a circle, and we put our arms on each other's shoulders. I bit my lower lip and kept my head down.

"Thanks, guys," I said.

"Hey, we're Boca Knights, too," Togo said, opening his jacket and showing me his tee shirt that had the words *BOCA KNIGHTS — How You Doin'* printed on the front. "There's a lot of Boca Knights here today, Eddie."

"Yeah?" I asked, still staring at his tee shirt.

"Look around you." Togo stepped aside and moved his arm in a grand, sweeping motion. My eyes followed his gesture, and for the first time I saw individual faces instead of a blur of humanity. I was stunned. There were as many black faces as white in the crowd. I blinked several times as if I had just walked out of a darkened theater in the middle of a sunny afternoon.

What the hell was Tommy Bigelow doing there with Matt McGrady?

Was that Barry Anson next to them?

Wasn't that Carol Amici and her daughters smiling at me? The grandchildren too?

Was that Seymour Tanzer, that pain in the ass?

Was that Mrs. Frost and Mrs. First behind Seymour?

Was that Mrs. Mildred Feinberg? Smiling? Waving to me? Noooo!

Was that the lady and her daughter from the shack on State Road 7? Yes it was.

Steve Coleman pointed at me. "You're the man," he shouted, and his wife, Barbara, waved enthusiastically.

It seemed like every golfer from Boca Heights was there.

Jackson, from Memories, was there wearing a Boca Knights baseball cap. Where the hell did he get that?

I turned slowly in a circle and saw nothing but smiling, happy black and white faces.

I saw a little girl, sitting on a man's shoulders, holding up a hand-painted sign that read: BOCA KNIGHTS —WE CARE!

Next to her a woman was holding a sign:

BOCA KNIGHTS — LOVE LIFE.

There were signs everywhere.

BOCA KNIGHTS — LIVE AND LET LIVE!!

BOCA KNIGHTS — RESPECT LIFE!

BOCA KNIGHTS — FOR PEACE!

BOCA KNIGHTS — EQUAL RIGHTS!

I was overwhelmed.

Sylvia Goldman, the bagel thief, was there. I don't how she got there but I didn't bother to ask. I just gave her a big hug.

Shankman, the lawyer from Philly, was there handing out business cards.

Louie Lipshitz and Dr. Goober were there. The doctor looked a little lost.

Barry Kaye from the "You die, *we* pay" commercial was there, too, with his son, Howard. They were both carrying signs.

BOCA KNIGHTS — GOD BLESS AMERICA

There were signs for women's rights, gay rights, immigrant rights, animal rights, the right to go left. But most of all it was a rally for everyone's right to live in peace.

The scene reminded me of the antiwar demonstrations years ago. The words *Make Love, Not War* had been replaced by *Boca Knights — Human Rights* but the message was the same: *Live the life you choose in peace.*

I saw Queen Premice walking toward me. Bruno Muscles moved in her path. "Where do you think you're goin', mammy?" he challenged her.

Queen made a fist and shook it at Muscles. "Mammy? Get out of my way you goddamn telephone pole," she growled at him.

I put a hand on the big man's shoulder. "She's my friend, Muscles," I told him.

He looked at me, then he looked at Queen. He looked back and forth again. "Yeah?" He was working it out in his mind. "You sure?"

"I'm sure," I assured him. "Her name's Queen."

"I don't see no crown." Muscles looked her up and down.

"How 'bout I crown you, you big dumb Eye-talian son of a bitch?" Queen was in his face.

"How you know I'm Italian?"

"You smell like a garlic garden, you big dummy," Queen said.

"Muscles, she's my friend," I interceded.

"If you say so," Muscles said, and before I could stop him, he had Queen in a bear hug. "Any friend of Coach Eddie is a friend of mine," he said, and kissed Queen on the cheek.

"Aw hell," Queen protested and wiped

411

her face.

Claudette Premice appeared in front of me. "Look what you did, Eddie," she said to me. "They're all here because of you."

"Why?" I still didn't understand. "What did I do?"

"You reminded everyone that they can be Boca Knights." She hugged me like a lover and a friend. "Sometimes people forget."

"Is the entire Delray Haitian community here?" I looked around at all the black faces.

"I did my best," she laughed. "They started marching yesterday afternoon. Hey, even Donald Trump is here."

"You're kidding."

"No, I'm not. There are all kinds of people here." Claudette was very excited.

I looked around in wonder. "Where are all the Aryans?"

"They couldn't make it today," she laughed.

"Why not?"

"All the roads are blocked with people," she explained. "The Aryan Army's chartered buses couldn't get through. They're stuck in traffic somewhere on I-95, I think."

"What about Harland Desmond?" I asked over the crowd noise.

"Last I heard," Claudette Premice shouted into my ear, "he disappeared into a crowd of demonstrating Haitians when he got off his bus north of the city and tried to wade through them."

"Disappeared?" I said loudly. "People don't just disappear."

"In Haiti they do," she said seriously. "Remember President Guillaume Sam?"

"Don't tell me about it," I said and covered my ears with my hands.

Claudette laughed.

Chief Burke tugged my sleeve. "We gotta go inside," he urged me.

"Okay," I nodded and turned to Claudette. "I have to go."

"Wave to your fans," she said as she kissed my cheek.

I turned and waved. The electric, eclectic, unarmed army of Boca Knights stood arm in arm, reveling in their differences and their human commonality, holding back the hounds of hatred together, for one glorious day. It was a reunion of strangers.

"It's unbelievable," I said, awed by the magnitude of the moment.

"We made a difference today, Eddie," Claudette said. "Maybe we even changed the world a little."

"We won the day," I told her. "But the world is still a dangerous place with dangerous people."

"That's why we need Boca Knights."

I saw Steve Coleman being interviewed by Miriam Goldberg.

"Why are all these people here so excited about Eddie Perlmutter and his Boca Knights?" Miriam asked Steve.

"Are you kidding me? Eddie's a hero," Steve shouted over the crowd noise. "He's like . . . he's like . . . a Social Security Superman."

"I like that," Miriam Goldberg laughed. She never should have encouraged him.

"He's a senior citizen Spider-Man."

"Cute," Miriam said with less enthusiasm.

"He's Harry Potter with arthritis," Steve raved on.

"This is Miriam Goldberg . . ."

"He's a Baby Boomer Batman."

"Reporting live from Palm Beach for CNN."

I walked past Steve and smiled. He winked at me.

Suddenly I heard a single voice cry out above the crowd noise, "WE ARE!"

And I heard another voice respond, "BOCA KNIGHTS!"

The second time around there were more voices. "WE ARE!"

The response came from many voices. "BOCA KNIGHTS!"

All together now . . . "WE ARE!"
I can't hear you. "BOCA KNIGHTS!"
They wouldn't stop.
I started up the courthouse stairs.
"WE ARE!"
"BOCA KNIGHTS!"
What you say?
"WE ARE!"
"BOCA KNIGHTS!"
At the top of the stairs I came face to face with Alicia Fine. She was wearing a "Boca Knights — Live and Let Live" tee shirt that made her look delicious. I saw her glance uncertainly at Claudette Premice walking behind me. We smiled at each other.

She's my choice, Mr. Johnson said.

Life is all about choices, I observed without committing myself.

Remember, we're in this together, Eddie.

You have a mind of your own, Mr. Johnson.

Hey, he said cheerfully. *I'm a penis. Of course I have a mind of my own.*

You'd think after sixty years I'd be able to make choices without you.

You're not old enough yet.

He was right, of course.

Two helicopters landed on the grass across the street from the court house. I couldn't see clearly but it looked as if Barbra Streisand and Oprah Winfrey were getting out of the first chopper.

"Is that who I think it is?" I asked Burke.

"Could be." He shrugged. "And there's Steve Abrams, the mayor of Boca."

From the second helicopter I thought I saw more celebrities.

"What are all these famous people doing here?"

"Looks like everyone wants to be a Boca Knight today," Burke observed, patting me on the back. "You should be proud of yourself, Eddie."

I *was* proud of myself. I was sixty years old and slowing down but I could still bring an opponent to his knees and a crowd to its feet. I had lived my entire life meeting violence with violence but I had won this battle with words instead of weapons. I had never been afraid of standing alone, but banding together with these Boca Knights today made me feel more powerful than I had ever felt before.

The last cheer I heard from the assembled multitude as I entered the courthouse made me smile and I raised my fist in salute.

"HUMAN RIGHTS."

"BOCA KNIGHTS."

Now that's what I'm talking about!

All things seemed possible.

ABOUT THE AUTHOR

Steven M. Forman was born and raised in the Boston area. After graduating from the University of Massachusetts, Amherst, he founded a one-man business and built it into a multimillion-dollar, highly successful worldwide enterprise.

Boca Knights is his first novel in his second career. He's working on the sequel, *Boca Mournings.*

He divides his time between the Boston area and Boca Raton, Florida, with his wife, Barbara.

On weekends he can be found at the soccer fields or gymnasiums of Boca watching his grandchildren Taylor and Bradley Cooper play.